Also by Jeremy Duns

Free Agent

SONG OF
TREASON

JEREMY DUNS

SIMON &
SCHUSTER

London · New York · Sydney · Toronto

A CBS COMPANY

First published in Great Britain in 2010 by Simon & Schuster UK Ltd
This paperback edition published by Simon & Schuster UK Ltd, 2011
A CBS COMPANY

1 3 5 7 9 10 8 6 4 2

Simon & Schuster UK Ltd
1st Floor
222 Gray's Inn Road
London
WC1X 8HB

www.simonandschuster.co.uk

Simon & Schuster Australia
Sydney

A CIP catalogue record for this book is available
from the British Library.

ISBN: 978-1-84739-452-1

Printed in the UK by CPI Cox & Wyman, Reading, Berkshire RG1 8EX

For my parents

Preventive Direct Action in Free Countries

Purpose: Only in cases of critical necessity, to resort to direct action to prevent vital installations, other material, or personnel from being (1) sabotaged or liquidated or (2) captured intact by Kremlin agents or agencies.

Policy Planning Staff Memorandum,
Washington, 4 May 1948

I

Thursday, 1 May 1969, St Paul's Cathedral, London

'Sir Colin Templeton was the most courageous, patriotic and decent public servant I have had the privilege of knowing. During his long career, culminating in seven years as head of the organization many of us gathered here today are honoured to serve, he faced this country's enemies unflinchingly.'

I paused, and as my words echoed around the magnificent building, I glanced up from the lectern and was overcome for a moment by the memory of the last time I'd seen the man I'd come to think of simply as 'Chief'. The way he had nodded at me when he had seen that my glass needed refilling: no smile, no words, just a tiny nod of the head. I relived, in a flash, the shuffling walk he had taken across the room, the sharp clinking as he had lifted the bottle from the cabinet, the shuffle back to pour me out a measure. Then the widening of his eyes as I had raised the gun and squeezed the trigger . . .

He hadn't flinched in the face of *this* enemy – I hadn't given him the time.

I gazed out at the line of stern faces in the front pew, bathed in the white glow from the windows high above. John Farraday was seated in the centre, dapper and bored. He was acting Chief now, but had already announced that in a couple of weeks he would return to the Foreign and Commonwealth Office, whence he had come. He was flanked by William Osborne, owlish in spectacles and tweeds. Once Farraday had gone he would take over, at which point I would be appointed Deputy Chief.

I'd got away with it: I was in the clear. A couple of months ago, this might have filled me with a sense of achievement, even triumph. But in the last few weeks I had been stripped of everything I'd ever held dear, left a trail of blood in my wake, and was now being blackmailed into continuing to serve a cause I no longer believed in. The triumph tasted of ashes, and all that was left was the realization that I had made a monu-mental error, and that it could never be reversed.

I glanced along the rest of the front row, which was filled out with Section heads and politicians, including the Foreign and Home Secretaries. Behind them, the congregation stretched into the distance, two solid blocks of Service officers, former army colleagues and family members, parted by the checked marble aisle. Several Redcaps hovered discreetly by the entrance, turning tourists away.

It was an unorthodox memorial service. The reading from Ecclesiastes, 'Jerusalem' and 'Dear Lord and Father of Mankind' were all standard fare, but the eulogy was being given by the murderer of the deceased, while the men who had plotted the fall of the government a short while ago were brazenly sitting next to Cabinet ministers. And around us all spun Wren's conception, as it had for centuries, cloaking us in false majesty.

I had washed down a Benzedrine tablet before leaving the flat in the hope it would stave off the remnants of my fever, but while it had succeeded in dulling the pain and heightening my senses – I could make out the grain of Osborne's tortoise-shell spectacle frames – it also seemed to have filled me with a feeling of recklessness. As I read from my hastily prepared address, I fought a rising urge to blurt out the truth to the congregation. I remembered hearing about Maclean's drinking in Cairo, and how he had eventually cracked and started telling colleagues he was working for Uncle Joe. Nobody had believed him, of course, and on hearing the story I'd blithely asked myself what could have brought him to such a state. But now, with the enormity of my sins bearing down on me, I wondered if this was where my crack-up was going to begin. It was an oddly tempting idea, like the thought of jumping in front of a train as it came into the platform. It would be a story to fill the Service's basement bar for years to come: the man who had confessed to murdering Chief in his eulogy at St Paul's. Perhaps they could get Bateman to make it into a cartoon.

I reminded myself that I was feeling the effects of the Benzedrine. I took in the Corinthian columns, the Whispering Gallery, and higher still the frescos stretching across the interior of the dome, then forced myself back to my address.

'But for some,' I said, raising my voice to counter my loss of nerve, 'Sir Colin was much more than the man charged with securing this country against foreign threats. He was a friend, a husband and a father.'

Christ, what had I been thinking when I wrote this? Other memories sprang into my mind: his delight at catching a large trout that summer in Ireland, after he had insisted on using his ancient 'lucky' bait; the way Joan had looked at him when we'd returned to the cottage with the tail of the fish poking out of the basket, knowing he'd want it for supper that night. And Vanessa, of course . . .

I stopped myself going any further down that track. I realized that my hands were gripping the sides of the lectern, and that they were coated in sweat. My voice had frozen in my throat. I couldn't do this – it was monstrous. My only sop was that it hadn't been my idea. 'You knew him best,' Dawes had said when the arrangements had been discussed. 'Nobody else was as close.'

I looked down at the rest of the address. It ran through Templeton's career, from military service to Cambridge to intelligence in Germany and beyond: his friendship with my father in Cairo, then Istanbul, Prague, London. His body in the Thames, thrown there by Sasha and me in the dead of night . . . Not the last bit.

I looked up again and was surprised to see Farraday standing by the lectern. He was fiddling frantically with his tie, whispering urgently.

'What is it?' I asked. He mounted the steps.

'You're making a scene,' he hissed, pushing past me. 'Return to your seat, or I'll—'

But I never found out what he'd do, because at that moment he fell to the ground, and blood started gushing from the centre of his shirt. The cathedral was filled with screaming, but my mind was now totally lucid. I looked up. The shot had come from somewhere in the Whispering Gallery – and it had been meant for me.

I started running down the aisle.

II

I reached the spiral staircase and began climbing it several steps at a time, the soles of my shoes clanging against the steps. From somewhere far above me, there was a further clatter of noise — was the shooter coming down? I plunged my hand into my trouser pocket and wrapped my fist around my car keys, the only weapon I had with me. How the hell had he brought a rifle into St Paul's? I kept climbing. The noises were fading, and my dizziness was increasing. Some long-buried memory told me there were 259 of the things, but I resisted the urge to count them and pushed upwards, upwards, trying not to think about what had just happened, regulating my breathing and concentrating on the task at hand: get to the top; find the sniper.

I reached the Whispering Gallery, but there was nobody there, not even a Redcap. I glanced down and saw that several of them were heading for the staircase, against the flow of the crowd. I looked around frantically. Had the sniper gone back down another way? Would he shoot again? And then I regis-

tered movement in my peripheral vision. It had come from
the far end of the gallery: a slim figure, bearded and dressed
in black. He had a case strapped to his back, no doubt containing
the dismantled rifle. He was heading towards a doorway that
led to the next flight of stairs.

I resisted the temptation to stop for breath and ran after
him, willing my feet to move faster, using my arms to hoist
myself along the narrow iron banister and ignoring the rising
heat in my chest, until finally I came out of the staircase and
felt the freshness of the morning air on my face. I was at the
base of the dome now, the Stone Gallery. My trousers flut-
tered in and out as the wind whipped against them, and I could
feel my cheeks beginning to do the same. Voices echoed in my
ears, and they were getting louder: the Redcaps would be here
soon. I realized I had to get to him before they did – who knew
what he might say if he was taken into custody? If he told
anyone I had been his target it wouldn't take long for them
to start speculating why, and having just cleared my name
that was the last thing I wanted.

I reached out for a moulding on the wall, and began edging
my way around the gallery as quickly as I could. Without
meaning to, I caught a glimpse of the Thames far below, a glittering snake swaying in the mid-morning sunshine. I forced
my eyes away and continued my journey around the platform.

The dome of the cathedral had been covered in scaffolding
for years – structural damage from the war – but all of it had
been taken down a few months ago. Or most of it had: as I
turned the corner, I saw that there was a ladder lying on the

ground, and what looked like a small pile of workmen's tools. Was this what the sniper had come up here for, something hidden in this mess?

Finally, I saw him. He had climbed onto the balustrade, seemingly oblivious to the wind and the height. He was sitting astride a climbing rope, which he had tied around the balustrade, and was now busy looping it around one of his thighs. He glanced up at me, then went back to his task, bringing the rope across his midriff and over one shoulder. I was just a few yards away, and pushed myself to get closer. If he was going to do what I thought . . . He brought the rope around one of his wrists, and took hold of it with both hands, one above and one below. He pushed himself back and started to fall.

It was now or never.

I surged forward and jumped blindly. He'd gone further than I'd thought, so that for a few moments I thought I'd mistimed it, but then came the crump of contact as I smacked into his back. I immediately clasped my arms around his torso, gripping as hard as I could and hoping to Christ that the rope was tethered tightly enough and could take the load of two men. The sniper started shaking his shoulders in an attempt to dislodge me, and as the ground approached two conflicting urges were passing through my brain – the physical one, saying 'let go, you madman' and the other one, saying 'if you let go you will die, if you let go you will die . . .'

I managed to hold on and we landed with a crash, the two of us a heap of limbs and bones. My whole body felt numb from the jolt of the impact, but I seemed to be uninjured. I was still trying to regain my bearings when I saw that the sniper had already let go of the rope and was off and running. It took me a few seconds to get to my feet and begin pursuit.

And he was fast, bloody fast, spurting down the narrow road, weaving his way around dustbins and lamp-posts. There was no traffic about, and he rushed across the pavement and darted down a grass-patched alley. I hurtled into it after him, my breathing coming heavily, half my brain still catching up from the fall. There was a thickening burr of noise, but it wasn't until I made it to the corner of Cannon Street that I saw the crush of people. Two massive placards bobbed above the crowd, reading 'PEACE AND SOCIALISM' and 'ALL OUT MAY DAY – SMASH THE WHITE PAPER'. The latter slogan was also being chanted by members of the column, the words echoing off the buildings.

Of course. The May Day march. It had turned violent last year, when it had been about Powell and immigration. This time Wilson and Castle seemed to be the villains, their crime being to propose trade union legislation. I caught the tinny strain of a loudhailer from somewhere in the direction of Lincoln's Inn Fields, and then there was the wail of a police siren seemingly very close by, and a clump of the column began moving off at a faster pace. The group behind were momentarily caught off guard, and I squeezed past a man in a checked shirt and jeans and squinted up Ludgate Hill, searching for a glimpse of the sniper. A sea of heads stretched into the distance. I looked for any unusual movement within it, for anyone running. Nothing. I turned and saw police and security staff massing around the entrance of the cathedral. Some of the Redcaps had seen me and were heading in my direction. I ducked back into the crowd and checked down Cannon Street again. Still nothing. Where the hell had he gone?

Then I saw him: a dark figure running up Ludgate Hill to Farringdon Street. Was he heading for the station? I pushed forward and began chasing him, calling out as I did in the hope that someone might stop him, but my throat wasn't working properly, and neither were my legs, and by the time I'd reached the end of the street he had already vanished. If he got on the Tube and I wasn't there with him, that would be it.

The drumming in my head and throbbing in my chest were telling me to stop to take some rest, but I forced myself to keep going and even made up enough ground to see him heading into the station entrance. I reached it less than thirty seconds later, and raced into the booking hall. He'd vanished again. And now I had to make a decision: under- or overground? The Underground seemed the better bet, as trains left much more frequently. There was a queue at the ticket office, but a quick glance told me my man wasn't in it. I couldn't see any inspectors and I guessed he had jumped over the barrier, so I did the same, pushing past people to try to catch sight of him.

As if by telepathy, he looked back at me the moment I spotted him. He was already on the footbridge, and I made my way towards him, keeping my eyes fixed on the rifle casing on his back. Behind him, a field of grey sky spread across the glass roof.

I reached the bridge and saw that he had ducked to the right, heading for the eastbound platform. I followed, shouting: 'Police! Stop that man!' This time the tactic worked. People stopped and turned to see who I meant, and the sniper slowed to avoid the attention. But he was confused, and an old lady with a bag of shopping bumped into him. There was a group of people coming across the bridge, and I noticed that they were carrying banners: reinforcements for the march, I guessed, or perhaps they'd had enough and were going home, but there was a crush and we were both finding it hard to get through. If only I could get a few steps closer to him . . .

A train started rumbling into one of the platforms below, and I looked down. It was the eastbound. I called out 'Police!' louder, pushing my way through until I reached the staircase, but it was like swimming in mud. The train grated to a halt and as I reached the foot of the stairs the doors juddered open and a crowd of people moved forward and into it. I couldn't see the sniper, but I had to gamble that he would get on board. My feet hammered down the platform and made it through the doors as they were closing.

I took a second to recover my breath again, my chest heaving, and then looked around. I saw him at once. He was in the next compartment, just a few yards away from me. He was standing there quite casually, partly obscured by a woman reading a paperback. I pushed the doors apart and stepped into the compartment. He looked up, and a smile broke out across his face, almost a leer. His right hand was thrust into his jacket pocket, and I could make out the outline of what looked like the barrel of a pistol. Just inches away, a man wearing a fisherman's sweater, canvas trousers and boots was seated next to a young boy, perhaps eleven or twelve years old, who was dressed almost identically in miniature. The boy's head was directly in the line of fire. The sniper raised his eyebrows at me and I nodded to show that I understood: not a step nearer.

This was my first chance to examine the sniper at close quarters. He was a youngish man, in his mid to late twenties, wearing a black suit with a dog collar – so that was how he had managed to get into the cathedral. He was of average height, but well built: unsurprisingly, considering the acrobatics he'd just pulled off. He had a wolfish look about him: a long handsome face, olive skin, thick shoulder-length hair, greasy with pomade or something similar, and a wild beard. The Christ-meets-Guevara look. No doubt it went down well with female revolutionaries, but he looked fake to me, like a fashion photograph. Despite the fixed smile he was sweating profusely, and I didn't think it was entirely due to physical exertion – every couple of seconds the muscles in his jaw twitched. Was he injured somewhere? Got it: his jacket was torn just below the left shoulder, a sliver of half-dried blood just visible against the dark fabric. Probably where the rope had burned him – I wondered how his hands felt.

I looked around the carriage, and saw that most of the passengers were clutching banners or sheets daubed with slogans. They weren't the students and flower children you typically saw on protests, but labourers and factory hands. A man in a boiler suit and boots caught my glance, and stared at my suit with open aggression.

'Been on the march, 'ave you?'

I shook my head, and looked intently at the sniper.

"Ark at 'im!' the man announced to the carriage. ''Is Lordship 'ere don't want nothing to do with the likes of us.'

'I've been at a funeral,' I said coldly. The man went quiet and started looking at the toothpaste advertisements.

The sniper smiled softly to himself. If he were to show his gun, panic would ensue and it would probably be to his disadvantage: the train would be stopped, transport police would board. But he knew I would try to avoid him taking that route, so as long as he kept his threat discreet he had the upper hand. Perhaps I could pull the emergency cord – that would flush the bastard out. I thought better of it. The gun could end up going off. On the other hand, if it were an automatic it wouldn't be able to cycle in his pocket, meaning that for the moment it would be a one-shot gun. I put it out of my mind: I had no idea whether it was an automatic or not, and one shot was too much to risk anyway.

I turned my attention to his intended targets. The man had a ruddy face, calloused hands and a broken nose: a docker, I thought. The boy, no doubt his son, looked like he'd already spent a few years on the docks himself. He was skinny, gangly-legged, with sunken cheeks and a glazed look in his eyes. At his age I had been wearing a tweed jacket and tie at boarding school. Father had been in Singapore then, and I'd never worn long sleeves before, let alone a jacket or tie, but I had soon got used to it . . .

I wondered what they were doing on the Underground.

Perhaps the boy had been too weak to make it through the march? Then I noticed that the father was wheezing every few seconds. It wasn't that he was looking after the son, but the other way round.

The fluorescent lighting panels in the ceiling started flickering – and then, just like that, they went out, and we were plunged into darkness. The train screeched to a halt, and there was a collective gasp from the passengers, followed immediately by groans of frustration and anger and the murmuring of voices. Someone near me swooned and a few people lunged forward to help them – Blitz spirit and all that. I didn't have time to be chivalrous because the sniper might try to do something. He couldn't open the doors, but he could move between the carriages.

I made to step forward, but as I did the lights flickered back on. The train started moving again and the carriage returned to normal. Someone gave the woman who had fainted a thermos flask and she took a drink from it, gulping it down.

I turned my attention back to the sniper. He didn't look Russian, I realized. There was something about the way he was staring at me – he was enjoying it. There was also a bravado about him, and I put him down as a southern European. His enjoyment sent a fresh wave of anger through me. I had given Moscow more than two decades of my life, and now they had sent this thug to shoot me down like a dog. If he were taken in for questioning, he might reveal I had been his target, so I needed to kill him, and soon.

But first I wanted some answers.

The clacking of the train began to slow. The boy squinted up at the Tube map on the wall of the carriage, talking to his father. It looked like the incident with the lights had scared him, and they wanted to get off at the next stop. They started to busy themselves – they had a hold-all with them, presumably for drinks and sandwiches.

The boy helped his father up and they moved to a spot in front of the door. The sniper took a step back, but kept his aim fixed on the boy, at his midriff. I glanced at his face: he was watching me watching them. In some situations I might have tried to rush him, counting on the fact that he would hesitate before killing an innocent child. But this was not such a situation: this man had just killed the head of the Service in a very public place, and would stop at nothing to get away from me. The boy was expendable to him, and I had to act with that in mind.

We came into Barbican, and the doors opened. People rushed forward to get off the train. I made to move, but the sniper was fixing me with a frantic gaze, his nostrils flaring. The father and boy were oblivious to the danger, and were not moving. Had they simply got up a stop early to prepare? No, the father was leaning down to adjust the hold-all – it wasn't entirely closed.

He stood up, and as the boy held out his arm to help him off the train, the sniper made his move. He leapt onto the platform and took the boy under his arm, then started running, dragging the startled boy with him. There was a shout from the father, from others on the platform. For a moment, I froze.

Then I jumped forward, too, but the doors were already closing. I squeezed through and onto the platform, but the two of them had disappeared among the passengers emptying from the other carriages, and I pushed past people, furious with myself for reacting so slowly. A mother was trying to get her pram off before the doors closed and people were helping her, blocking off the entire width of the platform. By the time she had made it out I had lost several valuable seconds. I looked up the platform. There they were, at the far end of it, the sniper running towards the tunnel we had just come through, the boy's head cuffed under his arm.

I followed, but then the sniper did an extraordinary thing – he let go of the boy and ran down a ramp at the end of the platform and *into the tunnel*. For a moment I thought it was suicide, but then I remembered that there was some space next to the tracks for the Underground staff to use. As I reached the end of the platform, I could see that he was running down it. The boy was standing there, frozen in shock. I told him not to worry, to stay where he was and his father would reach him soon, and then ploughed down the wooden ramp and into the tunnel, following the sound of echoing footsteps ahead.

I had been running for only a few seconds when I stopped. The bastard had disappeared again! Up ahead, I could see the tunnel curving away towards Farringdon, but he couldn't possibly have reached the bend already. Was he hiding somewhere in the tunnel, waiting for me? I peered into the darkness, but all I could see were occasional pillars and columns at the side, and the faint glimmer of the tracks running down the middle.

Then I heard footsteps again. They were distant, but recognizably the same rhythm. He was running down a tunnel, but it wasn't this one: he was *parallel* with me. I ran back a few yards and searched the walls. There it was: another train tunnel leading off to the left, the entrance a dark chasm. I jumped over a fence at waist height and started running down the tunnel. The sound of footsteps became louder. There was hardly any light at all here, and the walls felt clammier, the air staler. The tunnel was clearly disused, but where did it lead? I put the question out of my mind and kept running, peering ahead to see where the sniper was heading. But now I couldn't distinguish any movement or sounds apart from my own breathing and the crunch of my shoes on the gravel. Had he taken another tunnel?

I registered the glint of metal a fraction of a moment before he kicked. I tried to move but I had no chance, and he caught me full square in the stomach, sending me flying to the ground. I couldn't see straight but I knew I had to keep moving whatever happened because the glint was the gun and he intended to shoot me at close range. I rolled into the wall, scratching myself against something, and screamed as loudly as I could, hoping to distract him even fractionally, because a fraction could make all the difference.

This tactic seemed to work, because he fired blindly. The shot nearly deafened me and sent a great scatter of dust and debris and Christ knows what into my eyes, but I was alive, and I had a sliver of time on my side. He was still dealing with the recoil when I grabbed his wrist. I had to get the gun away from him, because I might not be so lucky a second time and now we were very close to each other and it was very dangerous, so I didn't scream because I didn't want to panic him. I wanted him alive a little longer – I needed to know who he was and why he had been told to kill me, so I kept the pressure on his wrist and fended away his other arm as he tried to punch me, and eventually it was too much for him and he jerked free. The gun fell to the ground and I tried to follow its trajectory but it spun into the darkness, and the sniper stumbled away and the chase was on again, only now I was closer, and my blood was up, and I felt I could get him.

There were no lights, but my vision was adjusting and the tracks had a dull sheen to them. I didn't dare move into the centre of the tunnel – I didn't trust the sniper enough to know whether or not a train could come whistling down here and carry us both off to Never-never-land – but the walkway was becoming narrower. There was the sound of dripping water close by, but I could still make out the faint echo of his footsteps ahead of me, and I focussed on them.

I had been running for about five minutes when the darkness began to lift fractionally. Soon, I was entering a cavernous space, which I guessed had been some kind of goods depot. There were small trolleys and wagons filled with sacks, but everything smelled dank and part of one wall had fallen away. As I came through, I saw the sniper at the far end, racing up a cobbled ramp. I reached it a few seconds later and as I did I realized where we were: Smithfield Market. He must have taken a tunnel that had been used to transport the meat here. The familiar open space of black and green ironmongery rose in front of me, almost like a cathedral itself, and the vista of the city's life returned as I glimpsed white-coated butchers through the archways and pillars.

It was icily cold here, and I realized we had come out at an alcove away from the main body of the market – some sort of storage area. Frozen carcasses lay slapped on top of one another in metal trolleys, glowing under the neon lamps. The sniper was bounding ahead of me, but he seemed to be flagging now. He crashed into one of the carts, sending the contents flying, and I slipped on a carpet of livers and entrails. He took the opportunity and grabbed me, dragging me through the slops and the sawdust. In the distance, a butcher shouted out his last prices. But that was another world away.

The sniper kicked me several times, and then began to choke me, his hands sticky and warm. I started seeing double, Christ and Che swaying above me, and I knew that I had only a couple of seconds left before I blacked out. I had to get him away from my throat. I lunged desperately with my left arm, and caught him on the ear. His grip loosened for a fraction of a moment and I used the momentum to topple him and reverse the hold, so that I now had my hands clasped round his throat. He kicked beneath me, but I was in a strong position now and I kept pressing down. He was trying to grab something with his arm, and I realized we had moved closer to one of the metal trolleys. My eye caught sight of an object on the lowest shelf:

an electric saw. I placed my knee over the man's throat and reached out for the saw with my left hand. I flicked it on. The whine had an immediate effect on him, and the sweat started pouring off his face like a waterfall. I screamed at him to tell me who had sent him and why, loosening my grip the tiniest of a fraction for his response. After a few moments, he began repeating the same words over and over. I leaned down to catch them.

'*La prego non mi uccida . . .*' he said, and his face was creased with pain. '*Madonna mia, non mi uccida, non mi uccida . . .*'

He wasn't getting any further than that, so I slapped him, hard, and screamed at him again, but he couldn't hear over the sound of the saw, so I switched it off and tried once more, directly into his face this time, but his jaw muscles suddenly tightened and then went slack and as I watched the fluid dribble from his mouth, I realized he'd bitten into a pill and I'd failed. His eyes froze. He was gone.

*

I searched his pockets, but found nothing in them. Dazed, I staggered out of the alcove and through the market until I came to the front gates, where there was a call box. I dialled the emergency contact number, waited for the pips and then thrust sixpence in the slot. Nobody picked up. The sweat started to cool on me, and I began to shiver. I tried the number again, and then the second number, but there was nothing, no answer, nobody home.

After a while I gave up and called the office instead, telling them to send a squad down and to look for the man in the storage area with a rifle strapped to his back. I left the booth and stepped into West Smithfield. It had begun to drizzle, and a newspaper vendor across the way was dismantling his stand. I looked up for the familiar sight, but it wasn't there. Panicking, I ran down King Edward Street, desperately searching the skyline. It wasn't until I'd reached the end of the road that I saw it: the dome hovering above the city, just as it had always done. For a moment, I'd thought it had disappeared.

III

'So you will take the job?'

'It doesn't look like I have much choice, does it? If they offer it to me, of course.'

'But you said they had already—'

'It still has to be approved. The formalities won't take place for at least a couple of days. They're holding a service for Templeton in St Paul's on Thursday, and they'll push through the new appointments after that. Does that satisfy you?'

He nodded, and replaced the negatives in his pocket . . .

As the Rover skidded through the streets, I remembered my last conversation with Sasha, just three days earlier. I had told him. I had bloody *told* him where to find me.

'And he was definitely Italian?' asked Osborne, interrupting my thoughts. He was staring through the passenger window, looking rather pale and drained, as I imagined I did, too.

I followed his gaze. It was raining heavily and storms had been forecast: England's green and pleasant land was suddenly looking rather grey and sinister. The Cabinet had raised the alert level to Four: much higher and we'd have been taking the train out to Corsham, the underground city near Bath – but that was strictly for when we were facing an imminent Third World War. Political assassination didn't require a subterranean command centre, but it did require an immediate meeting. I prayed it wouldn't go on too long. I was in desperate need of a shower, something to eat and a long kip.

Osborne had asked me about the sniper's nationality several times, perhaps because it was all we had to go on, or perhaps because Italy was a NATO ally and he was wondering about the diplomatic ramifications. I told him again that I was fairly certain of the nationality because he had spoken fluent Italian on the verge of death, at which point instinct tends to take over. But it was baffling me, too, albeit for very different reasons. Had he just been a hired thug, untraceable back to Moscow? I ran through the scene in my mind for the hundredth time: Farraday's head jerking forward, the shot ringing out. There was no doubt that I had been the intended target – if he hadn't suddenly stepped in front of me, the bullet would have gone straight through my chest. The fact that nobody had picked up either of my emergency numbers confirmed it: one of those lines was supposed to be manned around the clock, without fail. I had been cut off.

'How did they know about the memorial?' Osborne asked. 'We didn't announce it.'

He was like a schoolboy heading into an exam he hadn't prepared for, and I was the swot he was desperately hoping might help him out.

23

'I don't know,' I said. 'Perhaps Fearing will have something.' Giles Fearing was head of Five, and had also been invited to the meeting.

Osborne nibbled at a fingernail. I suspected he was torn between wanting any information he could get his hands on and hoping that he wouldn't be shown up by our rival agency. Five were responsible for domestic threats, while the Service dealt with everything overseas. That could be another reason he wanted to be sure of the sniper's nationality: it offered a chance for us to head up the investigation.

If so, he'd have to manoeuvre himself sharpish, because Five had a head-start. They'd been all over the cathedral when I'd returned from Smithfield: a team had already begun examining the building from top to bottom. Farraday had been killed instantaneously – the bullet had entered just above his heart. His body had been taken to the nearest morgue, while most of the congregation had retreated to their offices to contact colleagues and plan a course of action. The corpse of the sniper had also been removed from the market.

After telling them most of what I knew, I had taken a cab to Lambeth, but Osborne had already been leaving for Whitehall when I'd arrived, so I had climbed in and was now debriefing him on the way. He was biting his nails for good reason. For two Chiefs to be murdered within two months looked worse than a lapse in security: it looked like a declaration of war. And, of course, Osborne was now worried that there might be someone training their sights on *him* – not for nothing were we travelling in one of the bullet-proofed models. I had even asked if we should travel separately, as the formalities had been overruled and I was now acting Deputy Chief and he Chief. I wished I'd kept that thought to myself, though, as it had made him even jumpier.

I was also jumpy, but trying to keep my head. The sniper had been Italian, but the whole affair had Moscow's finger-prints all over it. I had been so intent on avoiding the suspi-cions of my colleagues in the Service that I hadn't noticed the threat looming from the other flank. But I still had no idea *why* they wanted me dead. This should have been the pinnacle of my success, with their long investment in me finally paying off: even Philby hadn't made it this far. I thought back to my conversation with Sasha on Monday evening. He had told me that the Slavin provocation in Nigeria had been the work of the KGB, and that for the last two decades I had, in fact, been working for the GRU: military intelligence. I'd come away with the impression that the KGB hadn't wanted to give up control of me. Could it be that they now wanted to take revenge for my having messed up their operation? It seemed far-fetched, but there had been no mistaking the trajectory of that bullet. And Slavin had been one of their agents; perhaps they blamed me for his death. But why try to kill me in public, then, rather than simply ambush me at home? Perhaps the GRU had been behind it, after all, and someone had simply decided that I had served my purpose and had come too close to being exposed. I had taken Sasha at face value when he had told me that I was the hero of the hour, but perhaps he had just been stringing me along, keeping me sweet until a sniper could be found to deal with me. If the bullet had found its intended target, it would have made me a martyr in the eyes of the Service – and extinguished any questions about my loyalty once and for all. The Service would have closed the book on Paul Dark, and remained oblivious to the extent that I had compromised them. But as long as I was alive, I could be exposed, and if that happened I might crack under interrogation and make a list of everything I had handed over, rendering most of it worthless to Moscow in the process.

Or perhaps it was even worse than that. What if someone in the higher echelons of the GRU had decided, as a result of the events in Nigeria, that Sasha's entire network should be closed down? Or not just closed down, but terminated? What if Sasha and his whole crew had all been killed – and I was the only one left standing?

On reflection, the motivations for doing me in seemed almost infinite. But one thing was for sure: *someone* wanted me dead, and they'd gone to a lot of trouble to try to make it happen. As the car came into Whitehall, I wondered when the next attempt would come.

*

The conference room was large and well appointed, with the usual Regency furniture and chandeliers, but the blacked-out windows and whey-faced stenographer in the corner deadened the grandeur somewhat. In the centre of the room, three men were seated around a large polished teak table. Fearing was fair-haired and stoutly built, with heavy jowls; Pelham-Jones, his deputy, was a few years younger and two stone lighter; and finally, there was the Home Secretary, Haggard.

Haggard lived up to his name: a giant skeleton of a man with dark circles under his eyes and a cigar perpetually glued to his thin lips. He was considered the Prime Minister's closest ally – the two of them had risen through the party ranks together. His public image was of a straight-talking man of principle, and he was warier of spooks than everyone else in the Cabinet, with the possible exception of the PM.

As soon as Osborne and I had seated ourselves, Haggard stubbed out his cigar, scraped back his chair and walked over to one of the alcoves, from where he surveyed us like a hawk might a small cluster of overfed mice. 'Thank you for coming,' he said, not bothering to make it sound even remotely sincere. 'As you may know, John Farraday was a good friend of mine, and godfather to my eldest daughter. I also strongly recommended him for the position of Chief, and so view his murder not only as a national but as a personal tragedy.' He stepped forward and looked at us all in turn, and his voice rose fractionally. 'I also view it as a cock-up of monumental proportions. As you will remember, when the idea was mooted to hold this service in St Paul's rather than the Foreign Office chapel, my immediate concern was security. And I was assured that the place would be under closer scrutiny than the Crown Jewels.' He reached out and banged the table with the palm of his hand, making the glasses jump. 'Well, it was hardly the Crown fucking Jewels, was it, gentlemen?' he shouted, his face flushed.

He glared at us, daring anyone to reply. Fearing looked like he was considering it for a second, but then thought better of the idea. Haggard adjusted the knot in his tie and took a long, deep breath.

'The PM is currently suffering from gastroenteritis,' he said, his voice reverting to its usual chilly calm, 'so he can't be with us this morning. However, he has been fully apprised of the situation and has called a Cabinet meeting for his bedside at two o'clock, at which time I will report on the results of this meeting. He is already not best pleased with your lot as a result of the incident in Nigeria, and I need hardly remind you that John's murder came while we were mourning the death of the last man to occupy his position. So . . . can anyone tell me why I shouldn't recommend that he sack the whole bloody lot of you?' He picked his glass of water from the table and took a few gulps of it, his Adam's apple bobbing wildly. 'I want an explanation for this,' he said, sitting down again, 'and I want it now.'

Osborne glanced across at me and I debriefed for the third time, taking it from the moment of the shot until the sniper's death in Smithfield.

'What a pity you couldn't bring him in alive,' said Haggard once I'd finished. 'A capsule, you say?'

I nodded. 'He bit down on it within moments of my reaching him.'

'I see.' He took another cigar from his jacket and lit it, and a spiral of smoke wafted across the room to clog itself in the curtains. 'At any rate, thank you: we all owe you a debt of gratitude for at least trying to apprehend the killer. Perhaps your colleagues from Five can now tell us how this was allowed to happen in the first place?'

Fearing bristled at the scarcely veiled accusation. 'We took all the usual precautions and more,' he said. 'We had sixteen Redcaps stationed inside the cathedral—'

'Who were a fat lot of use,' said Haggard.

Fearing paused for a moment and decided not to pursue it: 'And we conducted a thorough sweep of the building before the service began. There was no indication—'

'"A thorough sweep"?' Haggard jumped in again. 'How on earth did the sniper get in, then? And what about the climbing ropes Paul's just told us about – how did he manage to bring them in unnoticed?'

Fearing's nostrils flared. As the head of Five, he was unused to being given a carpeting. But he deserved it: it had happened on his watch. 'We're looking into the first matter urgently, sir,' he said. 'But he may simply have walked in during the service.'

'I'm sorry,' said Haggard quietly, 'but did you just say that he might have *walked in?*'

'Yes. He was disguised as a priest. We did consider the security situation extensively, but St Paul's is a public place of worship. If we'd closed it off completely, we would have created an enormous problem with local parishioners, so some access was a condition of holding the service there, as it has been in the past.' He glanced at Osborne to make it clear that he had raised these issues beforehand. 'The Redcaps turned tourists away at the door explaining it was a private funeral service, but there was still some toing and froing. As for the climbing ropes, the scaffolding was taken down from around the dome last year but there were still a few bits and pieces on the galleries. We checked with the Dean beforehand that this was all in order, and he told us to leave it. But it appears that he had hidden his ropes among these—'

'Pathetic!' Haggard snapped. 'I don't want to hear any more of this tripe. You should, of course, have taken the Dean or whoever was responsible up there to check. And as for creating problems with parishioners . . .' His shook his head. 'Pathetic. Do we at least have any idea who was behind it? Paul said he was Italian – are we sure of that?'

'I think we can be reasonably confident, minister,' Osborne broke in. 'He spoke the language fluently as he was dying, at which point instinct tends to come into play.'

He had a good memory, Osborne; I had to give him that. Probably why he'd made it so far.

'But why on earth would the Italians want to kill John?' asked Haggard.

Pelham-Jones took it. 'The sniper may just have been a gun for hire, sir. We don't have anything further on his identity yet, although we've shared a detailed description with Interpol to see if they can help. But we have had a claim of responsibility.'

Osborne and I both looked up. 'Really?' I said. 'When was this?'

'About two hours ago. A call to Holborn police station from a group calling themselves the "Movement for International Solidarity".'

'Credible?'

Pelham-Jones nodded. 'There is no way of concealing that something happened this morning – there were simply too many people involved, and it will get out whether we like it or not. But this was still a very quick response, and at the moment we're inclined to think it was genuine.'

'I wish you'd told us this before the meeting,' said Osborne, and I felt his shoe kick against mine under the table. I glanced across at him but he was making notes intently on his pad. I squinted at the scrawl at the top of the page: *KNOW ANYTHING ABOUT THIS OUTFIT?*

'We've been rather busy,' Fearing said icily.

I picked up my pen and wrote *NO* on my pad. It rang a bell, vaguely, but I didn't have any facts at my fingertips.

Osborne scribbled again. *EDMUND MIGHT.*

He asked Haggard if I could briefly be excused to check whether or not we had anything on the group in our files. Haggard agreed, and I asked one of the private secretaries to show me to a telephone. It took a while to get hold of Innes, but once I had I quickly explained where we were. He perked up as soon as I told him the name of the group.

'I'll be there in fifteen minutes,' he said. 'I think I might have something.'

When I came back into the room, Pelham-Jones was handing round dossiers. I nodded at Osborne, who looked relieved, then picked my copy off the table. It was titled 'INTERNAL SUBVERSION: ANARCHIST AND COMMUNIST GROUPS'.

'If you turn to page twenty-six,' said Fearing, 'you'll see the chaps we think we may be dealing with.'

I turned. The page was largely taken up with a photograph of a hand-scrawled note, which read: *'Yankee fascism all over the world — no to racism — freedom for American negros!'*

Haggard snorted. 'An educated bunch.'

'Quite,' said Fearing. 'This was found in Grosvenor Square when the American embassy was machine-gunned two years ago. They managed to ruin three of the glass doors. As you can see, it's signed the "First of May", but we think John's assassination may have been carried out by a breakaway faction from that group — perhaps even more fanatical. The First of May have sometimes claimed to operate under the banner of something called the International Revolutionary Solidarity Movement, which was founded back in '61 by some anti-Franco Spanish militants. We think the Movement for International Solidarity may be a new version of that. As best we can tell, they seem to be mainly made up of anarchists and Maoist Communists, several of whom have been involved in trying to stir up violence at Vietnam demonstrations and the like.'

I wondered if this was the information Innes was racing over here to present triumphantly to the Home Secretary as our contribution to the investigation.

'All very interesting,' said Haggard, grinding the remains of his cigar into an ashtray, 'but flag-burning and chucking Molotov cocktails about are one thing, political assassination quite another. Are you sure this lot are capable? It's a long way from occupying the LSE.'

Fearing smiled tightly. 'This isn't a lot of student rebels, sir. There are some very dangerous people in this bunch. Some may have "graduated" from other movements, such as the CND, the Committee of 100 or the Spies for Peace, but we're talking about the hard-core well beyond the peace movement. Perhaps you remember last autumn, when we were warned that extremists were plotting to use home-made bombs and the like to take over sensitive installations and buildings during one of the London marches?'

'Yes – nothing came of it, though.'

'Indeed, but only because Special Branch set up barricades at strategically important points, and because we leaked enough material to the press to scare them off. Anyway, this is the same collection of people. We think they may have also had a hand in blowing up one of the pipes carrying water to Birmingham in December. But yes, in answer to your question, this would be their first assassination. They probably had outside help.'

'Any idea who?'

'I'll leave that to my colleagues,' he said, nodding towards Osborne and me.

Haggard turned to us. 'Well?'

Osborne fiddled with his tie and made eyes at me.

'Well,' I said. 'Let's look at how it was done. His rifle was some sort of custom-made job, and he picked off his target with one shot at a distance of over a hundred yards, which I'd have found difficult fifteen years ago. We know he hid the ropes on the Stone Gallery, but when and how did he do that – was it this morning, or earlier, disguised as a workman or some such thing? Either way, he ran circles around our security measures. He was also extremely fast on his feet and knew how to lose a tail, or at least try to – I was very lucky to catch up with him. Finally, he had a capsule on him, and he used it. So I don't believe he was some two-bit revolutionary, but an elite special forces operative – and my money is firmly on Moscow.'

Osborne took a sip of water and smiled coolly at Fearing. I had decided to go hell for leather in pinning the blame on Moscow because I knew they'd come to that conclusion themselves soon enough anyway, and it might be useful to be able to remind them later that the idea had come from me first, especially if there were any renewed suspicions about me. I also wanted to stress my expertise on Soviet affairs so I would be put in charge of the entire investigation. The next step was to undermine Five.

'I think the climbing stuff also gives us a possible angle of enquiry,' I went on, looking at Fearing and Pelham-Jones to make it clear that by 'us' I, in fact, meant them. 'He was clearly an accomplished abseiler: it's quite a height, and he didn't use a harness or any other equipment – just a rope. I wonder if he might have been a night-climber.'

'Is that a euphemism for something?' said Haggard.

'It's a sport,' I said, 'popular at Cambridge. I'm surprised you didn't think of it, Giles, what with you being a King's College man. Don't you remember those undergraduates rusticated a couple of years ago for placing an anti-Vietnam banner between the pinnacles of the chapel? If I might humbly suggest, why don't you call up some of your old chums and get hold of whoever runs the society? See if they've had any Italian members in the last few years, or if they know of any similar clubs in Italy that do this sort of thing. That sort of knowledge is fairly specialized, and there can't be many people who know how to do it.'

Fearing was flustered now. 'But he used a rope, you said. I thought the whole point of night-climbing was not to use any equipment at all? And the society is anonymous. How do you propose we find out who runs it?'

'Oh, sorry,' I said. 'I thought you were the Security Service.' He scowled. Careful, or he'll explode. I softened my tone. 'It's true that they don't use ropes, but many of them go on to become mountaineers. Perhaps start with the Alpine Club or the Mountaineering Council, then, and work back.'

I was about to suggest he also contact London Transport to see if they'd had anyone suspicious working on the freight line that led to the goods yard under Smithfield Market – it couldn't have been closed that long, and he hadn't looked twice running in there. But, thankfully, Innes arrived then, a little out of breath but clutching a briefcase.

*

We all made room for him, and he unclasped the case and took out an impressively thick wedge of papers. He was halfway to the projector when Fearing told him that it wasn't working.

He stroked his moustache. 'Never mind. I'll do it the old-fashioned way.' He was a dapper little man, bespectacled and balding; he tried to hide the latter by arranging his few remaining strands of hair carefully across his pate. He looked like an Edwardian banker, but he was as sharp as a commando dagger. He headed up Western Europe Section, although he'd also been holding the fort at Soviet Section while I'd been away.

He laid his papers on the table and cleared his throat.

'As you have no doubt just been hearing from Giles, the Movement for International Solidarity is an offshoot of a group that has also operated under the names the International Revolutionary Solidarity Movement and the First of May.'

Osborne smiled: Innes knew his stuff. We were in the lead again.

'This group has several splinter groups across the Continent, and they seem to be particularly active in Germany and Italy. This is partly the result of wartime allegiances: some members of the younger generation are rebelling against their parents' devotion to Hitler and Mussolini.' He turned the page on his notes. 'One of the group's first attacks took place in Rome three years ago, when they kidnapped the Ecclesiastical Counsellor to the Spanish embassy to the Vatican. In August '67, they machine-gunned the American embassy in London, which I imagine you've covered . . .' He looked up at Fearing, who nodded. 'Right. And, eighteen months ago, they claimed responsibility for bomb attacks on the Spanish, Greek and Bolivian embassies in Bonn, the Venezuelan embassy in Rome, a Spanish tourist office in Milan, and the Spanish, Greek and American embassies in The Hague. Quite a shopping list. Communiqués received after those attacks indicated that they were all in protest at what they called "fascist regimes" in Europe, and in solidarity with guerrillas in Latin America.'

'I've heard enough,' said Haggard wearily. 'Paul seems to think they're Moscow-sponsored. Is that plausible, and if so why are they targeting us?'

'I'm getting to that, sir, if you'll give me a moment,' said Innes, gloriously oblivious to the tensions that had been building in the room. 'The man who shot John appears to have been an Italian, and Italy is currently experiencing a huge amount of this sort of activity. There have been fifteen attacks in public places already this year. Two of them took place in Milan just last week, with bombs going off at a trade fair and the central railway station. Nobody has claimed responsibility yet, but we believe the First of May and factions associated with it were involved in both attacks, along with Italian Communists.' He flashed a little smile at Haggard, which was not returned. 'Between October '67 and last May, three members of the Italian Communist party travelled to Moscow for what we think was a four-month training course with the KGB in clandestine radio communications. We have reason to believe that other Italian party members have been trained by Moscow in how to prepare forged documents and other espionage-related activities.'

Haggard had turned a few shades paler than usual. 'Are you saying that the official Communist party in Italy is working hand in glove with terrorists?'

'We've no *hard* proof of it, but we suspect some members of the party may be, yes. Our colleagues in Italy are worried that Communists and sympathizers may be planning a campaign of attacks across Western Europe to force a sort of "wave of revolution". The idea would be to bring down governments – including our own, I might add – through violent means. The student movement would get caught up in it, and before you'd know it there'd be anarchy.' He pursed his lips. 'Which would suit Moscow down to the ground, of course.'

'Do the Italians have any evidence for such a plan,' said Haggard, 'and if so why haven't I heard of it before now? It sounds fairly extraordinary.'

Innes smiled sweetly. 'Well, this is just informal intelligence-sharing. It's something that's been a background concern of theirs for a while, and it's why we have stepped up our own interest in this area. About six months ago my Section started looking at a faction of the First of May in Italy called Arte come Terrore, or "art as terror". The name is taken from the title of a series of articles that were published anonymously in a magazine called *Transizione* last year, which argued that violence against the state was a form of performance art that cleansed society, which was in sore need of cleansing. Some of the ideas espoused were simply nuisance provocations along the lines of those in Holland a couple of years ago, but others seemed to be much more serious, which is why we were interested.'

'Do you mean to say that John's murder may have been intended as a piece of . . . performance art?' He looked as though he were about to choke.

'Possibly, sir, yes.'

Haggard looked around the room. 'I've heard some nonsense

in my life, but this takes the cake, gentlemen. We are being outgunned by a bunch of art students!'

'Hitler was an art student,' said Pelham-Jones.

Haggard ignored him. 'Do we have any idea who the leaders of these jokers are?'

Innes cocked his head: he was coming to that. 'Rome Station has recently managed to infiltrate an agent into Arte come Terrore, a man called Barchetti, and he's given us an outline of the basic structure. It seems there's a central committee made up of a dozen members, all based in Rome. This is the leadership of the group nationwide, of which there are a few hundred members – we're not sure how many exactly. There are several people who we either know or strongly suspect are members of the group, but Barchetti hasn't been able to discover the identities of the leaders – he's not yet trusted enough with that information.'

Haggard slapped his hand on the table again. 'Well, he'd better bloody hurry up and *become* trusted enough!'

'Yes, sir. In fact, he seems to have made something of a breakthrough. Last night he filed a report, via dead drop, in which he said he'd heard rumours that a faction connected to the group were planning something big – imminently.'

'Obviously a warning about this morning,' I said.

Innes shook his head. 'He mentioned attacks "across Europe".'

There was a brief silence as we took this in.

'Christ,' whispered Haggard. 'That's all we need.' He took another slug of his water and scraped back his chair.

'When is Barchetti next due to report?' asked Fearing.

'First thing tomorrow morning.'

'Hold on,' I said. 'Not *Edoardo* Barchetti?'

Innes looked up. 'Yes. Do you know him?'

I nodded. I had run him when I'd been stationed in Rome in '64. I hadn't recognized the name at first because he'd been known to everyone as 'Bassetto', Italian for 'shrimp', on account of being about five foot tall. He had worked for the Service since shortly after the war, and I'd inherited him from my predecessor. He had hung around the fringes of Rome's underworld for years, mixing with thieves, gangsters and the sort of criminal not too scared to get his feet wet in the spy business. Sometimes he had picked up snippets of information on blackmailed politicians and suchlike, which he'd passed on to us, no doubt after some judicious elaboration on his part. He hadn't been terribly useful, but I had liked him: he had been lively company and I'd always looked forward to meeting up with him. But it was one hell of a move from occasional source to deep-cover penetration agent.

'How long has he been infiltrated, and how has he been coping?' I asked. When I had known him, Bassetto had been a heavy drinker, and had been so scared of being discovered passing information by one particular *mafioso* that it had sometimes taken hours to arrange meetings with him just to receive the tiniest scrap of gossip. I struggled to imagine him as a plausible anarchist agitator.

'He's holding up well,' said Innes, and Osborne gave me a fierce look — we were ahead on points, and I was in danger of sabotaging the victory. 'Apparently he always wanted to do this sort of job.'

That was even more worrying, if he'd *wanted* to do it: a Walter Mitty type. I didn't like the sound of any of it.

'You seem familiar with this man,' said Haggard.

'I ran him five years ago,' I said, 'but as an informant.'

Nobody said anything. I looked around the room and wondered who would break the silence. Then I realized that they were all looking at me. They had to be joking.

'It sounds as if he's in very deep, and I don't think sending in someone new at this stage would help. Besides, my face is too well known in Rome.'

'Not by these people,' said Haggard. 'And it's an advantage that you already know the city: you know how it works. We need to find out whatever it is Barchetti knows. What if John's death is just the start of something much bigger?'

I didn't give a stuff about Farraday, and if there had been a project to assassinate intelligence bureaucrats across the globe I'd have been all in favour of it. But I knew that there wasn't, and that Farraday had been killed in my place. I didn't want any of them to discover that fact, so I needed to stay here and manoeuvre myself into taking over the investigation. If I were in Italy, Christ knew what they might dig up.

'Of course I care,' I said. 'But I'm afraid I'm under doctor's orders not to travel anywhere for the next two months. I only came out of isolation a few days ago.'

'Yes,' said Osborne, 'Paul picked up some dreadful disease in Nigeria. Have they figured out which one yet?' I shook my head. 'He's not fully recovered, and I agree it would be extremely dangerous to send him out in his current condition. We also need him here. We need to reorganize in the wake of this, and I'll require his help.'

Haggard leaned back in his chair and cracked his knuckles together. 'Well, I'm afraid *I'm* going to require much more than this to take to the PM,' he said, gesturing at the dossier in front of him. 'What we need is action. If these people are connected with John's death, I suggest we do something that hits back at them.'

'Were you thinking clandestine or covert, sir?' said Osborne.

He squinted at him. 'Remind me of the difference.'

Osborne smiled softly and spread his hands along the table. 'Clandestine is when you don't want anyone to know what you're doing; covert is when you're pretending to do something else. Helping to instigate a coup is usually clandestine; sending an agent into a country and calling him an embassy official is covert.'

'I don't care,' said Haggard, 'as long as it can't be traced back to us. Perhaps send in the agent under diplomatic cover, as you say, and then get him to work clandestinely – is that possible?'

Osborne inclined his head, thinking about it. 'It depends on what you want done.'

'I want whoever was responsible for this to be found and killed, as quickly as possible,' he spat out. He nodded at the stenographer. 'Leave that out, please. I will inform the Prime Minister myself later today. I'm happy to take the consequences.

John was a dear friend of mine, and you have my unquestioned support to do whatever it takes to find those responsible and . . . *act*.'

I looked at him. Had he gone quite mad? The target was widening by the second. 'Is that wise, minister?' I said, and I could sense the others' anger directed at me as I said it. 'I'm all for justice, too, but if these people are planning further attacks, surely it's best to find out as much as we can about their actions first, rather than go in with all guns blazing?'

'Don't give me that! Where are your balls? The head of your outfit has just been murdered in cold blood, in front of your very eyes, while you were *worshipping*. Are you going to take it lying down, or are you going to retaliate? You have a man infiltrated into the Italian division of this group, and even know the identities of some of its members. Let's find out who the leaders are, send in a hit-man, and pay the bastards back.'

'It's not quite that simple, sir,' said Osborne. 'First of all, discovering the identities of the leaders is no easy task – it may take years before Barchetti is trusted with that information. Secondly, we don't have "hit-men", and haven't for some time. There's the SAS, of course, but I hardly think—'

'What about Paul here?' said Haggard, puffing out his waistcoat and looking me over as though I were a gladiator he was considering sending into the arena. 'Can't you do it? You chased down John's killer, ran this agent in Rome. And the report I read on the Nigerian affair said you single-handedly managed to stop this Red Army sniper getting the PM.'

I coughed into my hand. 'Stopping a sniper and doing the

sniping oneself are very different jobs,' I said. 'And I got rather lucky in Nigeria.' But it was no use – I could see he thought I was being the modest English hero. I tried another tack: 'I think it's perhaps not a very good idea for us to risk too many senior officers at this juncture.'

'Nonsense! They won't see it coming, will they? Element of surprise and all that. Go out to Rome under diplomatic cover and the Russkies will sit back and relax: a fact-finding mission from the top brass. Little do they know, our top brass is rather lethal with a telescopic lens and – bang! – you give the little Eyetie who planned this whole thing a bullet to his brain. An eye for an eye. No messing. They'll get the message then, all right.'

There was an uncomfortable pause.

'If we could find the leaders,' said Osborne finally, 'it might well be an idea, sir.'

IV

'There's no need to be like that,' said Osborne once we were in the car heading back to the office. 'Nobody seriously expects you to go out and *kill* anyone – he only put it in those terms because he was upset.'

'Quite understandable,' said Innes. 'We all are.'

I didn't reply. Haggard hadn't been in the mood to be dissuaded, I knew, but Osborne's intervention had really landed me in it. The meeting had ended with the decision that I would leave for Rome at once, subject to medical approval. I wasn't sure which would be the worse result to get back: that I was still suffering from a potentially fatal and highly contagious tropical disease that nobody was sure how to treat yet, or that I was healthy enough to be sent on a wild-goose chase of a mission to slaughter an as-yet-unidentified terrorist leader in Italy.

I had wanted to be put in charge of the investigation, but this hadn't been quite what I had in mind. Even ignoring the half-cocked assassination element, I didn't like it. Parachuting an outsider into an operation was fine: that sort of thing happened occasionally, and could help speed things along. Someone with Italian experience made sense, too. But I had last been in Rome under diplomatic cover, meaning that there was no choice but for me to go in that way again or risk being easily blown. That meant that, despite Osborne leading Haggard on, the potential for clandestine activity was, in fact, extremely limited – I wouldn't even be able to take a weapon into the country, for instance. And even if there had been any opportunity for me to take part in that sort of thing, I didn't believe there was anything I could do that couldn't have been performed with greater ease and efficiency by the local Station.

There was no way around it, though. Haggard had handed down his ruling, and to refuse to go now would only raise suspicions about my motives. Perhaps the worst thing about the development was that it took me away from London at a crucial moment. Because the other conclusion of the meeting had been that Innes was now to investigate whether or not there were any links between the deaths of the two Chiefs and 'the business in Nigeria'. That filled me with dread: given the run of Registry, and with me out of the country and unable to influence matters, there was no telling what he might dig up.

The office was in a state of turmoil, and Osborne and Innes both ran off to try to calm their respective troops, while I told my secretary to get onto Urquhart's to set up an immediate appointment, giving her the emergency authorization phrase.

As I flipped off the desk intercom, there was a knock on the door of my office and Barnes poked his head around.

He was a quiet Londoner of indeterminate age, with greying close-cropped hair and a heavily lined face. After stints in Kenya and Malaya, he had become one of the Service's bodyguards, most recently for Colin Templeton on weekends in the country. Templeton's insistence that Barnes live in the neighbouring village rather than be installed in his home, as he had been urged when he had been appointed Chief, had given me a free hand on that crucial night five weeks ago. I would never have risked killing Templeton if Barnes had been in the house that evening, and as it had been the only action available to me to head off my imminent arrest, I had a lot to thank him for.

'I'm your protection, sir,' he said. 'I'll be accompanying you to Italy.'

'Under what cover?'

'Third secretary, sir. It's already been arranged.'

My desk intercom buzzed: it was Mary, saying that Urquhart's were expecting me. I told Barnes to get his coat.

*

I sat in the waiting room in a very expensive but uncomfortable leather and chrome chair, flicking through a copy of *Country Life* and wondering who still lived it. Barnes was engrossed in a cheap paperback biography of Churchill he'd brought with him: he had told me on the way over that he was a lover of military history. I'd refrained from mentioning that he had probably lived through most of it. He was more talkative than

I'd expected, and had spent much of the journey trying to reassure me that Templeton's death had been a once-in-a-life-time lapse and that I was perfectly safe in his hands. It hadn't cut a lot of ice, because he hadn't seemed to notice the navy-blue Ford Anglia three cars behind us, driven by an intent, squat-faced man. I'd managed to lose him somewhere in Battersea, but that hadn't done anything to calm my nerves. They knew I was alive now, and that meant they could try again.

The receptionist walked over and gave me her best Harley Street smile: 'Doctor Urquhart will see you now.' Barnes followed, and the receptionist nodded at him – presumably she was used to such nonsense. I wasn't: it was like having a bloody dog.

Urquhart had been a medic with the Service during the war, and when he had set up his practice afterwards he had bagged the prestigious and, I suspected, rather well-paid job of looking after most of its senior staff. Some of his patients were bankers and barristers, but the Service was his bread and butter, and as a result there was a certain discreet level of security about the place – we had come through an unmarked entrance from a side street, and would leave by another one.

So far I'd been dealt with by his assistants, but today the man himself was there to look me over – I was definitely moving up in the world. I remembered him from previous check-ups as somewhat wizened, but he was looking almost obscenely healthy, with a glowing tan under his white beard; he looked a little like Father Christmas. I asked him if he'd been on holiday, and he surprised me by saying that he'd been to Jamaica.

'I go every other year,' he smiled. 'I love the vibrancy of the place – and the music.' I tried not to imagine Urquhart in the nightclubs of Kingston, and mentally cursed myself again for not choosing an easier, more profitable profession. Jamaica in May. What a life.

He tested my reflexes and took some blood, then gave me a test tube and asked me to go behind a screen and fill it. Barnes made to stand up to follow me, but I gave him a look and he sat down again, somewhat sheepishly. Urquhart covered the awkwardness by asking Barnes when he'd last been out to Gosport, which was the Service's training establishment. Barnes started gassing back immediately, and I peed in peace.

Urquhart took the tube from me and walked to an adjoining room. Barnes lapsed back into silence, and was no doubt hoping to get back to Churchill's preparations for D-Day.

After a couple of minutes Urquhart came back in, smiling. 'Good news,' he said. 'It looks like you've made good progress. You're not entirely out of the woods, mind you. Have you had any muscle pain since you were last here, or sore eyes?'

'Quite a lot of muscle pain,' I said. 'And my eyes sometimes throb.'

He nodded.

'How about your hearing? Have you had any more bouts of deafness?'

'No, but . . .'

'Good, good. When any of the symptoms return, take one

of these.' He handed me a plastic tube containing several small blue capsules. 'Don't take more than two a day, though. And if you lose your hearing again, stop whatever you're doing, get to a hospital and contact me through the Service switchboard. I'll let them know what to give you.' He picked up a clipboard from his desk and peered at it. 'I also see from your file that you're a smoker — a thirty-a-day man.'

'I've cut down,' I said.

'To . . .?'

'About twenty,' I admitted.

He grimaced. 'Better make it ten. And go easy on the booze as well, if you can. Otherwise, I think you're basically in good shape.'

I stared at him. 'Is that it? You're clearing me for active duty?'

'Yes. It's a bit touch and go, admittedly, but I had a call from the Home Office earlier outlining just how important your work will be in Rome and I certainly don't think you're in *that* bad shape. In fact, I'm sure you'll be fine.'

Of course — Haggard had fixed it. Urquhart gave me a couple of swift jabs with whatever medication they were trying this week, before ticking off all the necessary forms for the Italian embassy. Then I drove back to the office with Barnes to let them know I had the all-clear, stopping off at my flat for a few minutes to throw some clothes and a toothbrush into a hold-all. The office had quietened a little, and Mary booked the tickets and made all the necessary arrangements, with Smale supporting her by speeding up the red tape with Accounts and Personnel. It was all very efficient — lots of bowing and scraping. Partly the promotion, partly the order from the Cabinet, and partly, I supposed, a desire to avenge Farraday's death, or at least get to the bottom of it. But somehow the likes of Smale kow-towing made me feel even more uncomfortable, and I realized that in an odd way I missed being under suspicion, because I deserved that and could concentrate on getting through it. Now that I was in the clear, the extent of my deception was getting much harder to take. Smale was almost looking up to me – and it was a little chilling.

I grabbed a quick lunch of gristle-laden beef and boiled potatoes in the canteen and then Mary came in with the tickets, and Barnes and I headed for Heathrow.

*

We were booked on a BEA flight out of the newly opened short-haul terminal. As we sat in one of the cafés on the first floor, I wondered how long it would be before the immaculate Conran furniture would be sticky with grease and lollipop stains. At least the coffee already tasted as reassuringly foul as it did in all British airports. A Pakistani cleaner placed our cups and saucers onto his gleaming chrome trolley with a clatter and moved off, his mind elsewhere. Barnes was reading his paperback, smoking one of my Players – he didn't seem in a rush to buy his own, I'd noticed.

I replaced the dossier in the hold-all by my feet. Its seven pages contained everything the Service had on Arte come Terrore. Part of me had wondered how much Innes had been showboating, but while the evidence against them was mostly circumstantial, it was also fairly overwhelming.

In July 1962, there had been an explosion at St Peter's in Rome – no one had been injured, but the base of the monument to Clement X had been chipped. Nobody had claimed responsibility for the incident, however, and the investigation had soon dried up. Then, three weeks ago, there had been another bomb scare at the Basilica, and this time two men, Paolo Rivera and Giuseppe di Angelo, had been picked up in the course of routine enquiries. Rivera and di Angelo were suspected by Italian military intelligence of being members of Arte come Terrore: the excerpts from their dossiers that had been shared with the Service showed that both had long histories with Marxist and similar-minded groups. Both had been released without charge, but subsequent investigations had revealed that di Angelo had also been in the area of the Vatican on the day in question in July 1962, and that Rivera had visited London six times in the last year and had attended an 'International Anarchist Commission' in Tuscany in August.

The Pope had responded to the bomb scare by calling for calm and the need for brotherhood. So far, it wasn't being heeded. Since the start of the year, the Italian press had been predicting a wave of industrial action, and it seemed to be coming true, with dozens of strikes, prison riots and street clashes across the country. Last month had seen a major strike at a tobacco factory near Salerno following rumours that the place would be closed down, and the police had shot and killed one of the strikers, and then a schoolteacher who had been unlucky enough to see it happen. The government had claimed provocateurs from outside the city were trying to foment trouble, while the media had pointed the finger at Maoists and anarchists. But the authorities were still taking the brunt of the blame, and the Communist party had proposed legislation to disarm the police while on public order duty. As a result, there had been strikes against police repression in both Rome and Naples. The Communists' bill had been due to be debated in Parliament on April 28th, but on the 25th – Liberation Day – there had been the two explosions in Milan that Innes had mentioned in the meeting: one at the Fiat stand at the city's annual trade fair and another at the bureau de change of a bank in the central railway station. Twenty people had been injured, and the Italians strongly suspected Arte come Terrore's involvement.

So, the group looked to be both involved in attacks and inter-ested in cathedrals. None of it would stand up in a court of law, perhaps – but it was enough. I looked out at a jet taking off and shivered inwardly. I usually enjoyed flying, but today the idea didn't appeal at all. As well as the fact that the dossier seemed to confirm that Moscow was trying to kill me through a proxy Italian cell, I was sitting here about to leave the country while Innes was rummaging through the files in Registry with those long pale fingers of his.

And there was the small matter of the tail: the man in the dark green suit and scuffed brown brogues sitting at one of the other tables, reading *Le Monde* a little too intently as he devoured a cheese and ham sandwich. The suit was a size too small for his paunch, which along with its colour gave him a striking resemblance to Toad of Toad Hall. It was the driver of the Anglia that had followed us to Harley Street. I hadn't seen him on the way here, but he'd evidently managed to follow us.

His presence was precisely why bodyguards tended to be a waste of time in this business. I had no doubt that Barnes was a tough nut, and useful to have on one's side in a fight, but he was pure muscle, and hadn't the first idea about surveillance. He wasn't acting, either, trying to make me think he wasn't switched on or some game of that sort; I'd watched him for several minutes now, and he hadn't looked up from his book once. It just wasn't in his training. He wouldn't know a Russian spy if his life depended on it.

And the man was unquestionably Russian, despite the paper he was pretending to read. It wasn't just the cut of his suit; even his face was unmistakably Russian: a pasty complexion from too much potato in the diet, blue-grey pupils glinting through narrow eyelids, a pugilist's nose and the mouth of a coelacanth. Straight out of Central Casting. He was from one of the northern republics, I thought, Lithuania or Byelorussia. Was he going to try to kill me here, in the airport? He hadn't tried to do anything on the road, but perhaps he had been waiting for the chance.

I pushed back my chair and told Barnes I was going to the lavatory.

He made to stand up and I stared him down. 'Right you are, sir,' he nodded. He went back to Churchill.

I followed the signs to the Gents' until I was out of sight of Barnes, then headed for the WH Smith stall and took up position behind a stand of paperback thrillers. It was a perfect spot: I could see the whole concourse, so would have ample warning of his approach, and there were two entrances, so I could make my escape whichever way I chose, depending on the direction he came from. I wondered what he would be thinking now. He could either sit it out and hope I would be back shortly, or come and investigate immediately in the fear that I had spotted him and done a runner.

It took him less than a minute. He ambled over, pretending he was looking for a bin to dispose of the wrapper of his sandwich. I slipped out the other exit to the gallery of duty-free shops, stepping into the aisles of alcohol, tobacco and perfume laid out to tempt. I glanced into a display of Swiss wristwatches to see if I could catch sight of Toadski in the reflection. He was at the same thriller stand at Smith's I'd just vacated, apparently engrossed in the selection.

I turned and walked into another shop, selling overpriced knitwear. Toadski suddenly lost interest in Margery Allingham and came bumbling out into the gangway. He looked around frantically, trying to see where I had got to, and then he caught sight of me and our eyes met. He looked down, embarrassed, then tried to mask it by glancing at his watch and feigning distress that he was late for his flight. An announcement was being made, and he made a show of listening to it. He started to scurry away, but I leapt in front of him and grabbed him by the arm. A few yards further along there was a door marked

STAFF. It was slightly ajar, and I caught a glimpse of a mop handle. I looked around, and saw that the cleaner was still circling the restaurants. I shoved Toadski inside and stepped in after him. There was an overpowering smell of bleach. I grabbed him by the throat and quickly searched his pockets. He was unarmed.

'What do you want?' I said. 'And make it quick.'

He gulped, his Adam's apple throbbing wildly. I loosened my grip a little.

'"The chairs . . . are being brought in . . . from the garden."' His accent wasn't bad, sort of stockbroker London. But he still looked like he'd just stepped out of the Minsk Players.

'Why am I a target?' I snapped at him, but he merely looked at me with glazed eyes and repeated the Auden line.

I removed my hand. He didn't know anything. He was a messenger, that was all: he had given me the arranged code-phrase for 'Danger: keep a low profile until further contacted.'

'Tell Sasha to screw himself,' I said. The shot had missed me by less than an inch and he thought he could reel me back in by sending this buffoon to tell me I was in danger? What the hell did he take me for? I was going to need a little more infor-mation before I turned up for a meet and risked having my head shot off by the next sniper hired for the job.

I pushed Toadski back out of the door, smiled at the Pakistani cleaner as he came rumbling towards us, and smoothed myself down.

*

SONG OF TREASON

Barnes was waiting for me outside the lavatories. 'There you are, sir,' he said. 'I was getting worried. Our flight has just been announced.'

'Thought I'd have a look at the duty-free liquor,' I said as calmly as I could. My heart was still thumping from the fury I'd released. 'The prices didn't seem anything special, though.'

Barnes smiled and we set off for the departure gate.

57

V

Thursday, 1 May 1969, Rome, Italy

My heart rate didn't have much of a chance to recover once we were on the plane: we sat for over an hour while the ground crew worked on a frequently referenced but unspecified technicality. We eventually touched down in Fiumicino at just after seven. The air was still warm on the skin as we trooped across to the terminal building, and despite the circumstances I had to admit that there was something pleasing about being back in Italy. Perhaps it had been the double Scotch I'd had once the plane had finally taken off.

Fantasy turned to reality again the moment we stepped inside: the queues snaked around the entire Customs area.

'Doesn't look too good, sir,' said Barnes unnecessarily, as a trio of small boys in sailor suits ran straight towards us, shooting each other with toy pistols. We sidestepped them and walked towards the queue that looked the shortest, but as we were taking up position behind an extremely noisy German family, someone tapped me on the shoulder.

I turned and was greeted by a beautiful young woman: a late-period Modigliani in a green blouse and a maxi skirt. She had a badge identifying her as an employee of the Italian airport authority.

'*Signor* Dark?'

I nodded, and gestured at Barnes to hand her our passports, which he did. She inspected them for a few moments, then handed them back.

'*Da questa parte, prego*,' she said.

It had slipped my mind that there were compensations to travelling under diplomatic cover, and that this was one of them: you didn't have to waste time going through the usual checks. We followed her over to a bench, where our bags were already waiting. She briskly chalked them, before giving us each a chit to sign and handing them over.

'Enjoy your stay in Italy,' she said, flashing perfect white teeth, and then her hips were swinging away from us and she was gone.

We walked through to the main concourse and were immediately accosted again, this time by a tall, fair-haired man in a dark blue suit: Charles Severn. He was a little broader round the belly, but otherwise looked much the same as I remembered: a good tan, slightly ruddy, a firm jaw and an open, earnest look about him. The only wrong note was his eyes, which somehow didn't fit the rest of his face. One expected them to be blue, but instead they were a peculiar grey, like the colour of gunmetal.

'*Buongiorno*, Paul,' he said, taking a grip of my hand. 'Long

59

time no see.' He gestured that we head towards the exit. 'We should send a letter to The Trusty Servant,' he said. '"Two Wykehamists held a hot in Rome airport . . ."'

I groaned inwardly. We had been in the same house at Winchester; he was a few years below me. He had joined the Service after the war, and our paths had crossed a few times over the years, in Istanbul, in Paris, briefly in London. I never much enjoyed encountering him. He was bright and efficient, and generally rather charming, but he could also be very brash. I hated our shared past: the fact that he had stood next to me at Preces, knew the nicknames I had been given and so on. The Trusty Servant was the school paper, and it often featured inane letters from old boys re-enacting 'hots', the school game's surreal brand of scrum, in exotic and therefore supposedly hilarious locations. My pleasure at having made it through Customs so smoothly suddenly evaporated.

We walked out to the thick warmth of the street, where a throng of recent arrivals were negotiating fares with taxi drivers to take them into the city.

'You must be Reginald!' Severn shouted across at Barnes, the first time I'd heard anyone use Barnes' first name. 'You were in Nairobi, weren't you?'

'Yes, sir!' he shouted back. 'Among other places.'

'Capital. Wonderful to have you here. I'm afraid my car's a two-seater so there's not room for all of us – would you mind too much catching a taxi to the embassy and we'll meet you there?'

Barnes gave me a questioning glance, and I nodded my

assent to the scheme. He asked Severn for the embassy's address, repeated it back to him, then took my bag from me and headed into the fray of the taxi queue without another word.

'Sorry about that,' said Severn, as we crossed the street, now Barnes-less. 'No pool cars were available. How was the flight? Shame about the delay, but you know what they say: Bastards Eventually Arrive.' I forced a smile at the stale joke. 'How are you feeling, by the way? I heard you came down with some awful bug in Nigeria.'

'I'm fine,' I said. 'Got the all-clear just a few hours ago, in fact.'

'Quite a turn-up, all that, wasn't it? I heard they even suspected you of being the double at one point – what on earth were they thinking?'

'Yes,' I said. 'It was unfortunate.'

'Desperately sad news about the Templetons. Although the last time I saw Colin he gave me a bollocking for daring to talk to Vanessa!'

I gave a tight smile: it wasn't quite how I remembered the incident.

'And everyone's very sorry about John, of course,' he said.

I doubted many out here had known Farraday, and if they had they probably wouldn't have liked him much. But I noted that Severn's diplomatic skills appeared to have improved over the years.

His car was parked precariously on a verge, although calling it a car seemed something of a disservice: I'd never seen anything like it. It was an Alfa Romeo, almost absurdly low slung and streamlined to perfection. The front window merged seamlessly into the roof, giving it the appearance of a prototype spacecraft. Instead of the traditional *rosso corsa*, the bodywork was British racing green.

'New toy?' I asked.

'Just delivered,' he smiled, unlocking an extraordinary pair of doors that swept up vertically, meeting in the middle like the wings of an enormous metal butterfly. 'Isn't it a beauty? It's a "33 Stradale" – only a dozen or so have been built. It's nearly identical to the racing version: top speed 175 miles per hour.' He climbed in and patted the white leather. 'Custom-built coachwork.' He opened a compartment and pulled on a pair of matching kidskin gloves.

I made some appreciative noises, and remarked that he seemed to be doing well for himself.

'Look who's talking,' he laughed. 'Deputy Chief at forty-five!'

I manoeuvred myself into the front passenger seat.

'Forty-four,' I said.

For a moment I wondered whether he was on the take in some way, but immediately dismissed it: he was from an old banking family, and he'd always been a flashy bugger, even at school. As he brought us out onto the street, he veered out behind a rusty-looking Fiat, then brought the wheel round and squeezed through the gap to overtake it moments before a lorry came hurtling the other way. It was a terrific piece of driving but he hardly seemed to notice, and even accelerated. I looked on in admiration. Although the coachwork and exterior of the car were beautiful, there were few creature comforts: no radio, no carpet on the floor, no luggage space. It was a pure, brutal speed machine, and it certainly replicated the feeling of being in a race car. It took me back to Father's sorties round Brooklands. I'd done a bit of racing myself in my teens, but had never really developed the taste for it: there didn't seem to be enough of a purpose.

As we approached the centre of the city, Severn finally switched down a gear and I asked him for a situation report, which he gave as fast and as fluently as he drove.

'There have been no further attacks,' he said, 'but the police took a call on Monday from someone claiming there was a bomb in the Finance Ministry – nothing was found, though. In Milan, the *carabinieri* have questioned fifteen anarchists and trouble-makers about the bombings there, and they've charged eight of them, including di Angelo and Rivera.'

I looked at him. 'I thought they were based in Rome.'

'They were both in Milan a few weeks before the bombing. The Italians think they might have been scouting around.'

'I see.' Well, that put paid to Haggard's little idea, at least – I could hardly storm Milan's police station and bump off a couple of their prisoners.

'But it's hardly over,' said Severn. 'Tensions are rising all over the place, and strikes and protests have now become almost the norm. Teachers, civil servants and railway workers have been on strike for the last few days, and a few hours ago several thousand Maoists stormed a Soviet May Day celebration and all hell broke loose, apparently. There are also rumours flying around that there's a coup in the works. It's a fairly explosive situation.'

I looked out of the window. An Agip dog whipped past, and then I started noticing the trees: ilexes, pines, even the occasional palm. In the blocks of flats lining the street, bougainvillea caught the evening sun in the highest trellises, and as we approached the next set of traffic lights I spotted a market stall selling fruit and vegetables in one of the side streets. Not much seemed to have changed in Rome, and I wondered if there was anything particularly out of the ordinary in Severn's summary. Analysis this close to events was often prone to exaggeration, and he was, of course, trying to show me he was on top of things. Coups were forever being rumoured in Italy – one had very nearly taken place when I'd been here last – and I'd just seen London's May Day march at close quarters, and that hadn't been pretty, either. Britain had more than its fair share of strikes at the moment, and army units had even been posted to Northern Ireland after a recent spate of firebombs . . . One could probably give a similarly grim sit-rep for most Western European countries, if one chose.

'And Barchetti?' I asked. 'When's your next scheduled meet with him?'

'Oh-ten-hundred tomorrow. The National Gallery of Modern Art.'

'Good. You can brief me over breakfast.'

He didn't say anything for a moment, and I tensed.

'There's good news and bad news,' he said. 'Which would you like first?'

I didn't reply.

'The Italians say they have more information about Arte come Terrore, and are happy to share it with us.'

'And what's the good news?'

He laughed. 'That *was* the good news, Paul!' I glanced at him. 'Marco Zimotti wants to brief you at dinner this evening.'

'Dinner? Not on – I need to get some kip. I've had rather a long day.'

He smiled at the understatement. *You don't know the half of it*, I thought.

'I'm afraid Lennox is insisting – visiting dignitary and all that.'

Christ, that was just what I needed. Lennox was the ambassador, a pompous fool I'd encountered several times before, and Zimotti was the new head of Italian military intelligence, Giacomo's replacement. I had never met him, but knew him by reputation: a tough customer, by all accounts. It sounded like he'd strong-armed his way into a meeting once he'd heard I was on my way. Still, if he *did* have anything useful on Arte come Terrore's plans, I might be able to tie up everything for Haggard and get back to London faster.

'All right,' I said. 'Dinner it is, but let's try to make it fast, shall we? But tell me about yourself, Charles – are you enjoying Rome?' I didn't care, especially, but it might help to show I was friendly: I was invading his turf, and he'd naturally be a little nervous.

He beeped at a passing motorcyclist and made a face. 'Can't say I do, much,' he said. 'The summers are too bloody hot and the winters aren't much better than London. Nobody ever gets anything done and, frankly, once you've seen the monuments there's not a lot to *do*, other than get hassled by beggars and cats in the street. One might as well be in Africa. Didn't you find?'

I smiled. I suspected that in a few years' time he would be attacked by a pang of longing for the place, and would have forgotten all about the beggars. I considered telling him about what was going on in at least one corner of Africa that I knew of, but decided it wasn't worth it.

I looked out of the window again. We were approaching the centre of town now, turning into Via Cristoforo Colombo. Traffic was light on account of it being Primo Maggio, and I spotted a few students with banners wandering along the pavement. We passed a bar, and for a moment I caught the eye of a pretty young girl, who flashed a mouth full of gleaming teeth at me. It was an infuriating country, no doubt, and God knew I didn't want to be here on Haggard's wild-goose chase while Innes was asking awkward questions in London. But there was something about it I couldn't help liking. It was carefree, even in the face of political strife and bloodshed. There was something *living* about the place, and you could feel it pulsing around you, in the tooting of the horns, the policemen strutting about in their spotless uniforms, the mothers slapping their children around the head. Cooped up in that office in London I'd forgotten what living was. I'd remembered it in Nigeria – there was nothing like nearly losing your life to make you appreciate it all the more – but this was more like it. This was a place where life was appreciated. Perhaps it was time to get out, retire, buy a little villa somewhere in the south . . .

I caught myself and laughed inwardly. It was a line of thought I might have pursued a few months earlier – not any more. I glanced in the rear-view mirror to see if the girl was still visible, and it was then that I spotted the tail. It was four cars behind us, a small white Fiat with Rome plates. The driver was wearing a pair of oversized dark glasses, but it was definitely him: Toadski. I looked across at Severn, but he didn't appear to have noticed, and I wasn't about to set him right.

What the hell did the man want now? And how had he got here? I'd checked every seat on the plane. Presumably, he had watched Barnes and me walk off to our gate at Heathrow – careless of me not to notice – seen where we were headed and taken the next flight out. He'd had a stroke of luck that my flight had been delayed, but then again I had flown BEA so perhaps it wasn't so much luck as fate. But what did he want? It was a long way to come to tell me to keep a low profile again. He hadn't looked like an assassin, but perhaps I'd misjudged him and the message had been a diversion. I should have drowned him in a bucket of bleach when I'd had the chance.

As Severn drove through the embassy gates, I looked in the mirror and saw the Fiat pulling up to park about halfway down the street. Severn slipped into a space at the top of the driveway under a palm tree, and I opened my door and stepped out.

VI

We walked up to the entrance and I looked out at the grounds.

'Staff still in the sheds?' I asked, as he rang the bell.

He gave a curt nod. The original embassy in Via XX Settembre had been bombed by Zionists in '46 as part of their terror campaign against the British. Twenty-three years later, work had finally begun on rebuilding it on the original site, but most of the staff were still based here at Villa Wolkonsky, the 'temporary' embassy that had been set up after the attack. Although the ambassador's quarters were rather grand, when I'd been here most of the staff had worked out of prefabricated shacks and outhouses in the grounds of the building — and apparently still did.

'Sarah's found you a room,' Severn said. 'Not terribly opulent, but I hope it will do.'

'Sarah?'

'The Station's radio officer. We married last year.'

I remembered. I'd even been asked to sign off on it by Personnel, which I had done, naturally. 'Keeping things in the family' was approved of: it tended to make life easier. From past knowledge of Severn's girlfriends, I imagined she would be very pretty and very pliant.

A butler in tails came to the door and led us inside. There was no lighting: there had been a power cut. 'You see?' Severn muttered to me under his breath. 'Africa'. The butler gave us each a torch, and we walked past the copy of Annigoni's portrait of the Queen to the reception desk, where a young man asked for our passports. Severn handed over his, and I remembered that Barnes had mine. Severn vouched for me, and the guard produced a form for him to sign to that effect. As well as having worked out of temporary quarters for over two decades, the embassy had a giant chip on its shoulder about security that dated back to the Twenties, when one of the local employees had passed hundreds of documents to the Soviets because he'd been trusted with keys to all the safes. As a result, the security precautions were often insufferable. They had annoyed me intensely in '64, but right now I was delighted they were still in place: I couldn't have picked a safer place to stay.

We climbed the staircase to the top floor, where Severn led me to a room roughly the size of the broom cupboard I should have strangled Toadski in.

'Well,' he said, 'here we are.'

An iron bedstead had been made up with linen, and someone had sprayed cologne about, presumably to banish whatever unpleasant smell had previously occupied it. A rust-stained mirror and a washstand faced the bed, beside which sat my hold-all.

'Where will Barnes sleep?' I asked.

'His room's further down this corridor. Shall we go down now, or would you like a shave and a shower first?'

I walked over to the window and peered out. The street was largely protected from view, but I could just make out one corner of it. A tiny bubble of whitish grey stood out against the darkness: the Fiat.

I turned back to Severn. 'No,' I said. 'Let's get this over with.'

*

Downstairs again, members of the household were scurrying around lighting candles. From what I could make out, the place hadn't changed much: the same candelabra and carpeting, the same paintings of dead dignitaries and the same smell of varnish.

We walked through to the dining room, where twenty or so people were seated, their faces quivering in the candlelight and their voices merging into a low babble. Lennox, the ambassador, was at the head of the table, talking to an elderly woman I vaguely recalled was married to the French cultural attaché. On seeing us, he touched her lightly on the arm and stood, placing his napkin on the table. The room hushed, and he slowly began clapping his hands. A few moments later, the others followed suit, scraping back their chairs and facing me.

'Bravo!' Lennox called out. 'Bravo!'

It took me a moment, and then I realized that they were giving me a standing ovation for chasing down Farraday's sniper. I wished I were the man they thought they were applauding

– but I wasn't. A wave of shame swept over me and I gestured for them to stop, but it only encouraged them to applaud with greater gusto. I quickly stepped over to Lennox and he shook me by the hand and, slowly, the circus died down.

'Welcome, Paul,' he said. 'It's a pleasure to see you again, although I wish it wasn't under such tragic circumstances.'

The last time we'd met had been at a particularly unpleasant meeting in London three years earlier, at which he had complained that my Section was interfering in his affairs – but no mind. 'We wanted to have something a little grander,' he was saying, 'but what with the dreadful news about John, not to mention all the demonstrations taking place in town today, it wouldn't really have sent the right message.'

I told him I quite understood and thanked him profusely both for the honour and for putting me up, and then let Severn lead me around the table. I shook hands with Cornell-Smith and Miller, two of the old hands at the Station. Then we came to Barnes, who looked up at me with evident relief that I hadn't been kidnapped on the way from the airport. It seemed that everyone was ahead of me: his taxi driver must have been luckier than us with the lights, or known a short cut. He was seated next to a good-looking man with brilliantined grey hair, to whom Severn now introduced me: Marco Zimotti. I shook his hand.

'A pleasure.'

'The pleasure is mine,' he said. He was wearing a crisp black suit accompanied by a white shirt that heightened a very dark tan, the whole outfit worn with a sort of studied nonchalance:

he looked more like a film star than a director of military intelligence.

'I've been hearing about you from Reginald here,' he said with a disarming smile. His English was faultless, with just the faintest tinge of a Neapolitan accent. 'He tells me you went to the same school as Charles. Who, may I ask, was whose "fag"?'

I glared at Barnes. Severn was blushing to the roots of his hair – I wondered whether it was because he knew the American expression or because it wasn't the sort of thing one talked about in polite company.

'Charles was mine, in fact,' I said. 'Although we didn't call them that. He was my "jun man" – "jun" meaning junior. He had to make me tea and toast in the morning and that sort of thing.'

Zimotti raised an eyebrow meaningfully. 'And now? I imagine you could say he is still your "jun man" . . . no?'

Severn laughed rather too loudly and Zimotti joined in, and somehow we moved past it and everyone pretended it hadn't been said. Severn took me by the arm and indicated a woman seated to Zimotti's right.

'And this is my wife, Sarah.' She stood, and he leaned over to kiss her on the cheek.

Well, she was more than pretty. The few women I'd encountered in the Service who had escaped the typing pool had either been buck-toothed bluestockings or had done their best to appear so in order to be taken seriously. Not this one, though. She was in her late twenties or early thirties, tall and slim, with a sheet of honey-blonde hair that looked like it had been lifted from an advertisement for Sunsilk. She wore a white evening gown that had holes cut into it, discreetly revealing segments of golden-brown skin. It looked very expensive: the Gucci, Pucci, Cucci brigade. She had a high-boned face, with deep blue eyes heavily accented by kohl and a wide jawline leading into a perfectly shaped chin. Her lips were a little thinner than the fashionable Bardot pout, but otherwise she had the instantly recognizable look of the international jet set: one of the beautiful people for whom life was an endless round of cocktails and fun, fun, fun.

She offered me a hand sparkling with diamonds. 'You must be Paul,' she said. Her voice was low and cool, the accent Home Counties. 'Charlie's been telling me all about you.'

'You've got a head-start on me, then,' I said. 'He only mentioned you ten minutes ago.'

She tilted her head to one side and smiled. It was the sort of smile that managed to say a lot of things at once, and I imagined she used it often, and found it very useful. I took a seat between her and Zimotti, and Severn pecked her on the cheek again and squeezed past to make his way to the far end of the table.

A white-jacketed steward brought round some wine and bowls of cold asparagus soup, and I turned to talk to Zimotti. He threw out a few questions about my previous experience of Rome, and I answered some of them and parried a few more.

'I was sorry to hear about John Farraday,' he said after we'd exhausted the preliminaries. 'It is truly a tragedy, and I am deeply ashamed that one of my countrymen appears to have been responsible for it.' His jaw clenched, marking the bones in his cheek. 'But you have my assurance that we will discover who was behind this – and these Communist filth will be made to pay for what they have done.'

I thanked him for his support. 'Charles told me you may have more information about Arte come Terrore. Do you have anything that specifically links them to this?'

We paused as the waiting staff came round with the main course: over-cooked venison, by the look of it. Zimotti sawed into his meat, his eyebrows knitting at the toughness.

'We haven't heard from our colleagues in Milan yet,' he said, 'but there is no question in my mind that these people were behind it. We have been watching this group for some time. They spend a lot of time here, as well as in Sardinia.'

'Sardinia?'

'Yes, they have some kind of a base there, we think. We are working on discovering more about it.'

That was something, at least. I asked him who he thought was sponsoring the group.

'Moscow,' he replied without hesitating, 'although only the leaders of the group would be aware of that, of course.' He nibbled off another chunk of meat.

'Of course. But what makes you so sure it's not Peking?'

'All our evidence points to Moscow,' he said. I was about to ask him what that evidence consisted of when one of the stewards walked over and told him he was required on the telephone. He excused himself with a smile and left the room.

So much for his briefing me. Dessert was served: a rice pudding, of all things. I had a spoonful, then pushed it to one side. I called back the steward and asked him for a grappa. He brought it to me a couple of minutes later, in a rather large glass. I leaned across and told Barnes I was going to grab some fresh air, and then headed onto one of the balconies over-looking the garden.

*

There was a faint breeze, and I could smell the mimosa and magnolia trees. I looked down, trying to catch another glimpse of the street, but I wasn't high enough. Perhaps he'd gone home. Perhaps it hadn't even been him.

No. It had been him, all right.

I took a sip of the drink, welcoming the fiery sensation it caused in my chest, and gazed out at the lights of the Eternal City: the Alban hills were just visible in the distance. Somewhere not too far away teachers were striking, students were staging sit-ins and factory workers were planting explosives. Rome itself, so Severn claimed, was on the verge of burning. And here we were, watching and waiting . . .

My thoughts were interrupted as I became aware of someone behind me. I turned to see Sarah Severn standing in the doorway.

'Mind if I join you?' she asked.

'It's a free country.'

She stepped onto the balcony and flashed her Mona Lisa smile again. 'Is it?'

She took a pack of cigarettes from her purse: Nazionali, one of the more popular local brands, rather rough on the throat as I remembered. You could buy British tobacco everywhere here, so I took it she wasn't overly attached to home-grown products, as expatriates sometimes were. She shook a cigarette into her fingers in one graceful movement, and I leaned over with my lighter. She looked up, and as our eyes met I felt the familiar flicker of interest. I stopped the thought dead. No more women.

'Zimotti's back,' she said, and exhaled a stream of smoke in the direction of the Colosseum.

So that was why she had come out here – to shepherd me along. I didn't say anything and she glanced downward, showing off her long, dark lashes. 'Sorry,' she said with a hint of sarcasm. 'I just thought you might want to know.'

I placed my glass on a balustrade and lit one of my own cigarettes. 'Thanks.'

She looked up again. 'The head of the Service has just been murdered. Don't you want to find who was responsible?'

'I *know* he was murdered,' I said. 'He was standing a couple of inches in front of me when it happened. Perhaps you could let me decide how to do my job.'

She turned away and I immediately regretted my tone: my promotion was turning me into a pompous arse.

'Do you treat everyone this way?' she said. She paused for a moment. 'Perhaps the bullet hit the wrong man.'

She was looking at me calmly, brazenly, as though daring me to slap her, and I realized I was being a fool and smiled.

'Perhaps it did,' I said, reaching for my drink again.

The tension eased away. We finished our cigarettes in companionable silence and headed back indoors. But instead of returning to the dining room, she grabbed me by the arm and led me through a door and into a long corridor.

'Where are we going?' I asked.

'For a walk!' she laughed gaily, and I followed her, a hazy configuration of white silk and brown skin moving down the unlit hallway. I wondered if she might be drunk.

'I heard you were very brave,' she called out, 'chasing the sniper across London.'

'Not really,' I replied, dragging my eyes away from her figure. 'It was just instinct. I didn't find out much.'

We were heading into the heart of the embassy now. Candles had been placed in sconces along the walls, and I could make out the gatepost for the entrance to the Station at the far end of the corridor.

'Still,' she said, 'not many people would have risked their own skins like that.' She had slowed down and turned back to face me. 'And you found out something, or you wouldn't be here.'

What was she getting at? I didn't get the chance to ask her because there was a loud humming sound in my ears, and lights were flickering on.

'Finally!' she said. 'Now we'll be able to see where we're going.' She took my arm in hers and gestured ahead of us. 'Do you fancy a tour of the Station? It's changed a bit since your day, I think.'

'It's rather late,' I said, 'and I'm sure I'll see it tomorrow. What did you mean—'

I looked up to see Charles Severn standing a few yards ahead of us, a drink in his hand.

'Hello, lovebirds,' he said, stepping forward and placing a hand on Sarah's shoulder. 'Can I join, or is it a private party?'

*

I found Barnes hovering anxiously outside my room. Severn had said he'd become worried and gone looking for me. It was still early – not yet nine o'clock – but I was shattered, so I had asked Severn to make my excuses to Lennox and he had headed back down to the dining room for coffee, his arm around Sarah's waist. He had seemed to believe her story that we had simply been stretching our legs, but I didn't. She had wanted to take me into the Station: why? She wasn't *that* forward, surely.

I told Barnes I was going to call it a night, and he nodded and headed for his room down the corridor. I walked into my broom cupboard and threw my jacket onto the bed. On an impulse I looked out of the window and down at the street, searching for the grey bubble. It was still there. Christ. Was he planning to stay there all bloody night?

I made a decision – sleep could come later. I drained the rest of the grappa from the glass and caught Barnes up in the corridor, making a show of patting my pockets. 'Damn it, I seem to have lost my cigarettes. They must have dropped out in the car on the way over. I'll just go and get them.'

'Yes, sir.'

I walked downstairs and headed outside to confront Toadski. This time, I'd make sure I got some proper answers.

VII

The street was quiet and deserted, and I ran down it looking for the Fiat. Yes, there it was. As I approached it, I smashed my glass against a wall, then yanked open the front door and pressed the jagged edge to Toadski's throat.

'Move over!'

He glared at me with a mixture of fear and fury and jerked his head desperately towards the back of the car. I looked: there was someone sitting there, hidden in the shadows.

I glanced down the street, then up at the windows of the embassy. No one. I pulled the glass away from Toadski's throat, opened the rear door and climbed in. There was a strong smell of cheap Russian tobacco, and something sweet I couldn't place.

'You've got two minutes,' I said, thrusting the glass forward. 'Why are you trying to kill me?'

I didn't know who he was, but I knew *what* he was: the head of Rome's illegal GRU station. Toadski would have called him on landing at Fiumicino and this, no doubt, was his car. He spoke to Toadski in Russian now, calling him Grigori

Mikhailovich and telling him to take a walk and come back in five minutes. His voice was high-pitched – reedy and fluting, with a slight lisp. Without a word, Toadski opened his door and climbed out.

As the echo of his footsteps faded, the man in the shadows leaned forward, bringing his face into the orbit of the nearest streetlight. It was long and slender, with bloodless lips and watery eyes hidden behind large lids: it reminded me of the husband in the Arnolfini portrait. He was young, early or mid-thirties – one of the new generation coming out of Moscow's training schools – and he seemed to be chewing or sucking on something. I looked down and saw a small blue and silver box in his lap: *Baci Perugina.*

'Good evening, Mister Dark,' he said, inclining his head a little. 'My name is Pyotr Yurevich, and I currently have a pistol aimed at your heart. However, I assure you I have no intention of using it.'

There was no trace of a Russian accent except for when he'd said his name: I'd have guessed he was French or Swiss. Pedantic sort of tone, but that seemed to come with the manual. A black-gloved hand appeared in the small pool of light available in the car, and enclosed within its grip was the gun, a nine-millimetre Makarov by the look of it. Another hand appeared and swiftly unloaded it, and then the voice continued: 'Now, kindly remove that glass from my face and tell me why you think someone is trying to kill you.'

I considered for a moment, then opened the door, leaned down and placed the glass on the pavement.

'A bullet,' I said, closing the door again. 'About an inch from my face.'

There was silence for several seconds.

'How do you feel?' he said, eventually. 'I understand you recently suffered an ordeal in Africa.'

I stared into the darkness. I recognized the question from having run agents in the field myself. They sometimes lost it, either through fear or injury or simply fatigue. He thought I was still suffering from the fever I'd caught in Nigeria – and that it had made me delusional!

'You don't know what happened in London?' I asked.

He chewed his chocolate treat and waited for me to continue.

'At eleven o'clock this morning the new head of the Service was shot in the chest by a sniper in St Paul's Cathedral. The bullet was meant for me. The sniper was an Italian.'

He stopped chewing. 'No, I did not know this.'

His surprise sounded genuine, but then it would. Spying is acting, and acting of the hardest kind: you're never allowed off-stage to remove your make-up, never get to re-take a fluffed line, and your life depends on your performance. I'd been acting for over twenty years, and had become so good at it that I even managed to convince myself some of the time. Perhaps he did, too. Because if he were acting, he'd given a very good line reading, inflected with just the right degree of innocent surprise.

'What did Grigori Mikhailovich tell you?' I asked, jerking my head towards the empty driving seat. 'He must have given you a message from Sasha.'

'He did not tell me anything about this. Do you really think

I would have come to meet you in front of the British embassy if I had just ordered your death?'

He had a point. As a deep-cover agent, he was taking an enormous risk just being here at all. Then again, so was I. Was it possible Toadski didn't know about St Paul's, either? He was a bit player, admittedly, an errand-boy, but surely Sasha would have briefed him nevertheless? Unless the GRU hadn't been responsible, of course . . .

'What about the KGB?' I asked. 'How are your relations with your colleagues there?' The infighting between the KGB and the GRU made the Service and Five look like something out of a Mills and Boon.

He hesitated for a moment. 'As far as I know, neither we nor any of our colleagues had anything to do with the incident you mention.'

As far as he knew – very reassuring. It was a legalistic sort of answer, and the hesitation didn't help make it any more convincing.

'Why don't you tell me what you *do* know,' I said, 'because I'm starting to wonder if I've stepped into the wrong car.'

He looked aggrieved, then sighed deeply, an Atlas of the spy world. 'I am a mere cog in the machine, Mister Dark. You cannot expect me to be privy to every operation we undertake.'

'We have a saying for that,' I said. 'The left hand doesn't know what the right hand is doing.' But, again, he had a point. The sniper had been Italian, but that didn't mean he had just flown in from Italy. I remembered how surely he had run into the tunnel at Barbican. Local knowledge? Pyotr here might not have been informed about a plan to kill a British double agent in London – especially if it were by another agency. Then again, if the KGB were out for me, he wouldn't want me to know that either. I glanced down at my wristwatch. I'd already been gone three minutes, and Barnes would soon be wondering where I was.

'I think we should start again,' he said. 'You are my agent now, and I would—'

'*Your* agent?' I laughed, and turned to open the door.

'If you leave this car,' he said, his voice immediately hardening, 'I will expose you.' His eyes glinted beneath puffy lids. 'Without hesitation.'

He reached inside his jacket, and for a moment I thought he was about to pull a second gun on me. He smiled at my panic and immediately opened his hand so I could see what it was he had reached for: the negatives. So it was that again.

'These are copies,' he said. 'The originals are in a safe in Moscow. If you do not do precisely as I say, my superiors will send them to your colleagues indoors. If I don't like the way you behave, they will send them. And if anything happens to *me*, they will send them. Is that clear enough for you?'

I let my hand drop from the door handle. He gave me a smug little smile and replaced the negatives in his jacket.

'Why are you in Rome?' he said. 'Is it because of Edoardo Barchetti?'

Another surprise. There were only two ways he could have known I was here to investigate Barchetti: either through a leak at the very highest level of Five, the Service or the Cabinet, or . . .

'He's been blown,' said Pyotr. 'He is a British agent, and he has infiltrated a little group of ours that operates here.' He unwrapped another chocolate and popped it in his mouth. 'We need you to kill him at once.'

*

There was a sudden sound from the street, but it was just Grigori coming back from his stroll and Pyotr sent him away again. I should have heeded his advice in Heathrow – this was hardly low profile. Had Sasha known this assassination scheme was waiting for me in Rome and tried to warn me off?

'Kill him?' I said, to buy some thinking time. Part of me noted that hidden in the absurdity of it all had been the admission that Arte come Terrore was a Moscow front: so Zimotti had been right about that. 'I think you've got the wrong man,' I said, finally. 'You're looking for an assassin.'

Pyotr pursed his lips. 'You had no such qualms in Nigeria.'

A lot of people seemed to have got the wrong end of the stick about what had happened in Nigeria. I suddenly missed Sasha. Oh, I hated him – his tweed suits and his stamp collection and his patronizing manner – but I missed him nevertheless. This chap was too smooth by half, and he was giving me the bloody creeps.

'Why me?' I said. 'Why don't you get someone in the group to do it?'

'That is our concern, not yours. But, as you ask, the group

is not aware of our sponsorship, and we would prefer it remains that way. We also do not trust them to perform a job of this delicacy.'

So they were not just running Arte come Terrore, but they were doing so as a false-flag operation. Again, Zimotti had been right, although it was fairly standard procedure. Interesting that Pyotr felt they couldn't handle a hit, though.

'It doesn't add up,' I said, staring him straight in the face. 'You didn't know I was coming.'

He shrugged. 'That is true. But the man who was to have done the job is no longer available, and you are here in Rome to meet Barchetti – it is providential.'

I could think of other words for it. The man who was to have done the job was no longer available . . . because he had recently died in Smithfield Market? Was I being targeted by the GRU after all? And if so, why did this man not seem to know about it?

'Why do you want Barchetti dead?' I asked. 'You just said he'd been blown—'

'He was carelessly given some very important information, after which he immediately contacted London. Which is why they've sent you, I suppose – to find out what it is he knows?'

'Among other things,' I said. 'What was the information?'

He looked down at the box in his lap and started rummaging around in it. He wasn't in any sort of a rush, this fellow, and that was unfortunate because I was. I'd find it rather difficult to explain to Barnes what I was doing in this car. He was armed, but he'd put his gun away and I wondered whether I should rush him, try to strangle the information out of him. Dangerous: he didn't look like he could put up much of a fight, but there would be Grigori to contend with, too. And so far I didn't seem to be having much luck getting information out of people by force.

'Look,' I said. 'Could you just forget the fucking chocolates for a minute and tell me what's going on? I don't have a lot of time.'

He winced at the obscenity. 'It is information that could expose you,' he said.

'Then it's no dice. He'll run a mile the second he sees me – we used to work together.'

'He doesn't *know* it exposes you. But I will tell you no more. It is better for your sake.'

'I'll be the judge of that.' He didn't reply, so I tried another tack. 'Severn is scheduled to meet Barchetti tomorrow morning. If I insist on taking his place and Barchetti winds up dead, how do you propose I avert suspicion?'

'Tomorrow morning will be fine,' he said, though I hadn't been asking for his approval on that score. 'As for the other matter, you will find a way: the consequences of him remaining alive are much worse. Kill Barchetti, and you will be helping both yourself and us. Everybody wins.' He smiled.

'Except Barchetti,' I said.

He leaned forward. 'I understand your reaction,' he said, in what I think he meant to be a confidential tone. 'Believe me. I have only survived in this game myself through my ability to find opportunities where none seemed to exist, and for repeatedly turning the most hopeless-seeming situations into victories. I have studied your file, and I think the same could be said of you.' His tone turned cold. 'We have a saying in Russian: "Among wolves, howl like a wolf." Do not mistake us for puppy dogs, Mister Dark. We expect you to howl with us, all the way. This time it really is the end of the road: there are no exits, and we have the winning hand. If you do not do as I say, I will expose you. I am afraid it is checkmate. Kill Barchetti tomorrow morning,' – he patted his jacket pocket – 'or I will make sure Charles Severn receives these by lunch.'

*

Barnes was waiting for me at the top of the staircase, wearing a dressing gown.

'Everything all right, sir?'

'Fine,' I said, taking the pack of cigarettes from my pocket. 'They were in the glove compartment.'

I threw him a couple of sticks and he grinned. He went back into his room to smoke them, and I went into mine. I undressed and climbed into bed.

VIII

Friday, 2 May 1969, Rome, Italy

I woke with a start. Something had touched me. I opened my eyes and saw Barnes seated on the bed, his hand shaking my shoulder.

'I'm sorry, sir,' he said, looking embarrassed. 'But it's time.'

I thanked him gruffly and rubbed my eyes. He left, and I went over to the basin and washed my face. Slowly, the nightmare of the previous evening returned. Curiosity killed the bloody cat, I thought: if I hadn't left the building, I wouldn't have found myself blackmailed into an assassination job I couldn't see any way of completing. But I had left the building, and complete it I must. Pyotr had mixed a few metaphors but I didn't think he was bluffing, and deep down I knew he was right: I could rattle my cage all I wanted, but there was no way out. I'd read plenty of reports about blackmailed agents, but until now had never really appreciated what it meant, I suppose because I'd never believed it might apply to me.

I went through my fitness regimen, then bathed, dressed in a light linen suit, and collected Barnes from his room. Downstairs at the Station, Severn came to the barrier and told the man on duty to let us through.

'Good morning,' he said. 'Sleep well?'

'Yes, thanks,' I said.

I said hello to Cornell-Smith and Miller, and a couple of others who I'd glimpsed but not been introduced to at dinner the evening before. Sarah was seated at a desk in the middle of the main area smoking a cigarette, wearing a crisp white blouse and a dark skirt that showed off her long golden legs. She caught me looking at them and smiled, pushing a wisp of hair away from her eyes.

I looked around. She had been right: it had changed since I'd last been here. There was significantly more radio equipment, some fancy Scandinavian-style furniture – her doing? – and even a *cafetière*, from which Severn was currently pouring himself a cup. But the layout of the place was basically the same, with the heavy wooden doors to the offices. Severn was in my old one, I saw.

'There's been a change of plan,' I told him. 'I'm going to meet Barchetti.'

The cup clattered in its saucer as he looked up to see if I were serious. 'But you can't,' he said when he realized I was. 'You're under diplomatic cover.'

'So are you.'

He placed the cup on the table and wiped his hands against his trousers. 'Well, yes. But I've been running him . . .'

'I've run him, too,' I said. 'It's set for the modern art museum, isn't it? That's just by the Borghese Gardens, if I remember rightly.'

He started stammering about unorthodox procedures and prior notice, so I pushed a little harder, reminding him that I was Deputy Chief and claiming for good measure that the Home Secretary had instructed me personally to report 'from the spot'. It took me a few minutes to make him understand that he had no choice in the matter – the fact that I hadn't either made it easier to do.

'I also want you to send a telex to London,' I said. 'Message to read as follows: "Rivera and di Angelo in custody in Milan. Italians claim Moscow backing group, possible base on Sardinia, but as yet no evidence. Await further instructions. Dark."'

'Did Zimotti give you that bit about Sardinia?'

I nodded. 'But that's all I got, unfortunately. He disappeared to make a phone call just as we started talking.'

Severn pursed his lips. 'I see. Shame. Sarah, did you get all that, darling?'

'I'll send it at once,' she said, standing and walking over to the coding machine. I headed for the door.

'You won't be needing me, then, sir?' asked Barnes, and I shook my head. Slowly but surely, he was catching on.

*

I walked down Via Appia Nuova and found a small bar. The street was emptier than I expected for this time of the day, but then I remembered it was the Friday after a holiday. Many people would have *fatto il ponte*: made the bridge to the weekend. Half the city would be at the beach, or enjoying a picnic in one of the city's parks.

I felt for my money clip: ten pounds at the bureau de change in Heathrow had got me just shy of fifteen thousand *lire*. I went inside and bought a couple of bread rolls and a double espresso, then took one of the outside tables. It hadn't yet gone nine o'clock, but the sun was already blasting down and my eyes started to throb from the glare. I hoped it was a result of chasing snipers about rather than my Nigerian fever returning. I reached into my jacket pocket for a pair of ancient sunglasses I'd brought along, and as I did my hand brushed against the packet of capsules Urquhart had given me in London. I wondered for a moment if I should crack it open and take one, but decided against it.

I put the glasses on and looked around, just in case Severn had decided to be clever and send someone after me. I also scanned the roofs of the buildings opposite, checking for the glint of a telescopic sight. Whatever Pyotr said, the bullet in St Paul's had been meant for me, and I had no doubt that whoever had ordered it fired meant to try again.

But, at least for the moment, the coast looked clear.

I had my breakfast, savouring the rich flavour of the coffee and vowing never to have another one in a British airport. Then I left a few coins as a tip and walked over to a kiosk across the road, where I bought a copy of the *International Herald Tribune*. I rolled it under my arm and hailed a taxi.

As the driver manoeuvred through the morning traffic, I

considered my old friend and informant 'Bassetto' Barchetti. Pyotr had been lying through his teeth about him, of course: whatever information he had managed to pick up, it didn't have anything to do with me. They'd already been planning to kill him before I arrived, and they couldn't care less whether I was in danger of being exposed; someone or other was intent on killing me, in fact. No, Pyotr had thrown in that bit about the information as bait to grab my attention. It must be something else, something big that they didn't want the Service to know, and it had got them into an almighty flap and desperate to get him out of the way for good, and sharpish. So sharpish that they had reached for their stash of negatives and tried to force *me* into doing the job for them.

I had agreed to report to Pyotr in the Borghese Gardens at noon, but I decided I would have to fob him off somehow, tell him it had been impossible to set up at such short notice. It was a plausible enough excuse, I reckoned. Assassination takes planning, and planning takes time. A museum was not a location I'd have picked, for example. I was not an assassin, but I had assassinated before, and I had studied my targets for weeks – in the case of Cheng in Hong Kong, months. If I had been doing the job I would have needed a weapon, preferably one that was completely untraceable. Thallium, for example, as the French had used with Moumié in Geneva, or a poisoned dart, like the Red Hand had done with Léopold in '57. Neither was readily available in the centre of Rome on two hours' notice.

The taxi arrived at the museum, and I paid the driver. As I

was walking up to the entrance, a better way out flashed into my mind: discover what Barchetti knew, then use it to blackmail Pyotr! It was an unlikely scenario, but a possibility nonetheless, and I skipped up the steps with a little more gaiety at the thought.

*

From the outside, the Galleria Nazionale d'Arte Moderna looks like most other temples of great art around the world: a neoclassical façade with grand pillars and a general aura of solemnity and depth. Inside, however, the museum is largely taken over by the imaginings of the deranged fringe of the modern art world. I could understand why Barchetti had picked it. If he were being watched by his Arte come Terrore chums, they wouldn't be in the least surprised that he would visit this place. And it would be much harder to follow him through than a café or park.

I took off my sunglasses and checked for signs of surveillance. The immediate area looked to be clean, but no doubt Severn or one of the Station staff would be here shortly. Severn had arranged to meet Barchetti in the twentieth-century section of the museum, so I paid for a ticket at the front desk and followed the signs until I came to it.

I spotted him right away. He was standing between a sculpture that resembled a segment of a dinosaur fossil and a painting in which arrows from a large black 'Z' pointed towards the number 44 and an 'X'. Dressed in a dark suit and porkpie hat, he was peering at the canvas as though trying to figure out the solution to the equation – he looked more like a bank clerk on his day off than the infiltrator of a terrorist cell.

As I approached him, he turned and gave me a twitchy grin. His forehead was coated in sweat and his eyes were darting about to an unsettling degree. I recognized the signs at once: he was in far too deep.

'Hello, Edoardo,' I said, holding up my copy of the *Herald Tribune*. 'Long time no see. Charles couldn't make it today, so they sent me instead.'

'Not here,' he said. 'Follow me.'

No greeting, no memories of old times. All right. We walked through to one of the other halls, and he hovered by a velvet-covered bench before finally seating himself on it.

'I thought you worked in London now,' he said.

'So did I. What is it you've discovered?'

He looked around again.

'They know,' he whispered. And then, more urgently: '*They know!*'

'You're blown?' I didn't follow – why agree a meet, then?

He shook his head furiously. 'About the attack in the dome.'

'They know we suspect them, you mean? Or you have proof they were involved?'

His head swivelled and he looked up at me, his expression one of undisguised shock. There was a strange moment when our eyes met, and then I realized what he was going to do. He stood up from the bench and began walking away from me, fast but not so fast that he would attract attention. I had no choice: a shout would have ruined everything, and he wouldn't have turned back anyway. I walked after him.

*

He headed into the next room and then took a right through a curtained archway into another one. As I got closer I realized that it was a dark room – some sort of installation. A few people were straggling by the entrance, either waiting for companions to emerge or contemplating going in themselves. Barchetti had already gone through, so I plunged into the darkness.

An old jazz number was being piped through the space, but it sounded like it was being played through several amplifiers at the wrong speed, giving everything a woozy, underwater feel. After a few seconds, my eyes adjusted and I began to get my bearings. There were objects descending from the ceiling, coloured shapes. They looked like pieces from a child's mobile, sparkling as they turned through the air.

As I moved deeper into the room I started to make out the far end of it: there was a line of strip lighting running across the middle of the wall, half-obscured by some artificial fog spraying up every few seconds from the floor. I suddenly had the impression of being in a shower facility in a concentration camp, and had an urge to run back out into the main gallery. But I had to find Barchetti first. Did his information relate to me after all? Had he somehow realized who I was?

The floor started to shift gently, like a conveyor belt, adding a layer of nausea to the claustrophobic air: the artist was evidently some sort of sadist. A man wearing a hat moved past me, and I stepped forward to grab him. But he'd already gone.

The music was getting louder and louder, throbbing strangely, and I felt completely lost. I came across several tree-like sculptures, their thin branches glowing and twisting around me. I reached into my pocket, hastily unwrapped one of Urquhart's pills and swallowed it whole. I immediately regretted it, as the thing tasted foul, bitter and chalky.

The music intensified, turning atonal: the sound of clocks ticking, crashing cymbals and a bass cello seemingly scraped at random. And then I saw him, just a foot in front of me, his face clearly lit for a moment by one of the fluorescent branches: Barchetti. I lunged forward and grabbed him by the arm.

'*Vattene, idiota! Sciò!*' he snarled, lashing out at me with his arms. There was a flash of light and I realized he had a knife. I leapt away and sensed the blade pierce the cloth of my jacket, but he'd missed *me* and I leaned forward again, kicking out towards his legs. I made contact with bone and he fell to the ground, cursing. The knife fell from his hands and I watched it skitter across the floor, the blade catching the light from the mobiles hanging from the ceiling. I immediately knelt down and grabbed it. He managed to get a foot under me and aimed it at my solar plexus and I was pushed back against a wall, winded.

But I had the knife.

There was more movement around us now: people were starting to become restless, perhaps wondering what the disturbance was. Through the speakers, a gospel choir had begun competing with the underwater whale music, and it was becoming louder by the moment. Barchetti leapt on top of me and started trying to scratch at my eyes and throat. My instinct was to use the knife on him, but I needed to get him away from here, alive. I tried to fend him away, but he was surprisingly heavy for such a small man. He was now sitting on my upper chest, restricting my breathing. The music was almost deafening, and I willed my mind to block it out. I reached out and managed to grab hold of Barchetti's shirt, and then pulled him towards me with all the force I could muster. It shifted him forward a little, but it wasn't enough and I could feel my lungs reaching their limit, so in desperation I threw my other arm up to his throat and squeezed it. He let out a scream and tried to bite me, but my chest was burning up and he didn't seem to be aware that I needed him to get off me, until there was no choice and I squeezed and squeezed and then his head jerked forward and his muscles slackened and I could roll him off me and, finally, breathe. I felt for his carotid and checked his pulse: nothing. The music took another unexpected turn, the woozy whale sounds switching to a jumpy jive, and I stood and reeled towards a sliver of light, my throat dry and my chest thumping and my hands wet.

I pushed the curtain aside and came into the adjoining room. I had to stop for a moment to gather myself, and someone came out right behind me, knocking my shoulder.

'Esilarante, no?'

I nodded dumbly, and then moved away, heading towards the exit.

IX

I walked down the stairs and onto the street, gulping fresh air into my lungs. Behind me I heard the muffled sound of screaming — someone must have stumbled over Barchetti's body. I looked down and my heart froze. The pavement was covered in spots of blood. I glanced back toward the entrance of the museum and saw a trail of it leading from the doors straight to my feet.

Panicking, I started running, but when I looked down again the blood had vanished: there were just a few small brown stones on the pavement. Was it a return of my Nigerian hallucinations? I slowed down again and reached into my pocket for another of Urquhart's pills. No. Leave them.

I picked up the pace again, and as I did I caught sight of a tall, slender figure striding up a flight of steps into a park on the opposite side of the road. Something about the way he was moving made me look at him again. He was wearing a dove-grey three-piece suit and pointed suede shoes, also grey — all rather well made. And he was taking something from his pocket and placing it in his mouth.

I hadn't seen Pyotr in daylight, but I knew instantly that it was him. My body felt as if it had been given a gigantic jolt. Had he seen me kill Barchetti? No, I thought. More than likely he had hung back in one of the adjoining rooms, watching, just to make sure I turned up for the meet. And when he had seen me coming out of the dark room, the installation or whatever the hell it had been, he had quickly made his escape. Not quite quickly enough, though . . .

I stopped for a few seconds to take some deep breaths and to let him get ahead: I didn't want him to see me. Interesting that he had come, I thought, rather than sending a lackey. Either it really was important or he didn't trust anyone in his team enough to handle it, or both. My God, I wished it had been his neck I'd wrung instead of Barchetti's. If it hadn't been for him I wouldn't be here at all − and what a damn fool I'd been for turning up on his say-so. I'd bought into the idea that he was some sort of master-spy pulling all the strings, but he was just a pathetic bloody amateur. Something I'd said back there had spooked Barchetti out of his skull, so much so that he had fled from me.

Well, enough was enough. I checked my watch. It was quarter past ten: I was due to debrief with him in the Borghese Gardens in an hour and three-quarters. So where was the bastard going now, then? I decided to find out.

It was time to rattle the cage.

*

I doubled back and made to cross the street, but the traffic seemed particularly chaotic on this stretch, and with a start I realized why – several police cars were trying to make their way down it, but were struggling against the flow. As their sirens grew louder, I started crossing and made it to the foot of the stairs I had seen Pyotr take – he had now disappeared over the top. I had to get as far away from the museum as possible, and I didn't want to lose him.

I walked briskly up the stairs, passed between a couple of fountains and finally saw Pyotr twenty or thirty yards ahead, his hands thrust into the pockets of his trousers. I breathed out and fixed my eyes on the top of his head as he wove among the pedestrians enjoying a stroll in the Borghese Gardens. He suddenly decided to cross the street, and as he did he glanced over his shoulder, and I ducked into the midst of a group of American tourists, frightening an elderly lady with a blue rinse.

'Scusi,' I said, and her anger softened at the manners of the charming local.

I manoeuvred my way through the group in order to catch sight of Pyotr again. He was striding ahead, more confidently now: he hadn't seen me. I began walking a little faster, making sure to keep several pedestrians between us in case he made any more sudden movements. But I didn't think he was going to. He'd forgotten his training, and had arrogantly presumed he wasn't being followed. The thought stung me, and I suddenly remembered Severn – could he have been at the museum as well? I stopped and looked around me, more carefully than

Pyotr had done. Tourists, businessmen, students . . . I couldn't see Severn or anyone else who looked like a potential tail, but that didn't mean a lot.

I had started sweating again, because I realized I was stumbling into traps without thinking first, letting my anger guide me. I wanted to follow Pyotr – but only if I was not being followed myself. There are several ways to spot a tail, but I didn't have the time for them: if I loitered somewhere and waited to see who came looking, for example, I'd risk losing Pyotr.

I decided to take the chance that I was alone. If Severn were following me, I could always tell him I had seen Pyotr in the museum and felt that he might have been responsible for . . . Yes. Of course! Pin Barchetti's death on Pyotr. It was perfect. I started after Pyotr again.

He was still walking straight ahead, down Viale Folke Bernadotte. I had to pray he was headed somewhere nearby, because if he got on a bus or tram I was done for. There was no way I would be able to hide from him in such a small space. And if he hailed a cab, the whole thing was off. Luckily, so far it looked like it was going to be a walk away – he was still striding along purposefully.

He reached a roundabout at a grotto and I squinted to see which turning he would take. A bus tore past me just as he rounded the grotto and I lost sight of him for a moment. But then the bus was gone and I saw that he had taken a right into Viale Giorgio Washington and my pulse quickened – he was heading for Piazzale Flaminio, where there was a tram stop.

I walked a little faster, down a cobbled footpath shaded by overhanging trees, past wooden benches on which young lovers were draped over one another. As I came into the crowded square, I saw that a couple of trams were already waiting at the stop. But Pyotr didn't even glance at them. It seemed he was walking to the end of the street, and I wondered if he was looking for a bar to find a telephone.

A tram at the front of the queue moved off, blocking my view of him again, and I leapt into the street and in front of a taxi so I could take up position on the pavement behind him on the other side of the road. But he had gone. I looked around frantically, but as I made it to the pavement I saw the outline of the back of his head and shoulders in the rear of the tram pulling out.

Damn. Damn, damn, damn.

I raced up to the next tram waiting, which was on the same line, and climbed aboard, paying the driver the fare and asking him when he was going to leave. Not for a few minutes, *signore*. I tried to calm myself and looked at the situation again. On the plus side, I knew where Pyotr was, and he could only go at a certain pace, on certain tracks. And I was still following him, from a vantage he couldn't see. But unless we left very soon, I wouldn't be able to see where he got off. What were my options: bribe the conductor to depart earlier? I dismissed it: he would be more likely to kick up a fuss or report me, and we'd probably end up leaving even later and I'd have lost Pyotr. I'd just have to hope I'd be able to see him when he got off.

I took a seat up front and kept my eyes glued to the tram

ahead. After a couple of minutes, it slowed for a stop. An elderly lady disembarked, helped by a younger man. No Pyotr. It started back up again, veering in the direction of the river.

The driver of my tram started her up and we began following in leisurely pursuit. Soon we swerved around the corner, skirting the parked cars, and came to the same stop. A young mother tried to bring her baby carriage down the aisle, and berated a long-haired boy in jeans and an embroidered shirt who was standing in the way. Their argument became more heated, and the young man called the woman '*Fascista*'. I moved out of the way to avoid them, but they were blocking my view of Pyotr's tram, which was now slowing for the next stop.

There! He was getting off. I pulled the cord.

'*Scusi!*' I cried, and leapt out of the doors as they were closing.

He was walking at a normal pace down the street, and I followed him through a cluster of parked motorbikes and Vespas, past fruit stalls and newspaper stands and shuttered restaurants. A *gattara* glared at me as I passed her feeding crumbs to an emaciated tabby. We were now on the outskirts of Trastevere, a once very down-at-heel neighbourhood that was becoming increasingly visited by tourists. A man in a leather jacket and a cap approached me. '*Tabacchi*,' he said, as though it were a greeting. Black-market cigarettes sold for about two-thirds of the usual price here, and I was running low – but now wasn't the time. I shook my head and carried on walking. Where the hell had Pyotr gone? I looked around frantically, and finally spied him. He was at the far end of the street: he had stopped at the entrance to a restored medieval house. A block of flats now, it seemed. And he was letting himself in with a key. So he had gone home – perhaps to signal Moscow that I had completed the job?

It was approaching eleven now, so he would have to leave again reasonably soon if he wanted to make our appointment in the Borghese Gardens at noon. There was a bar across the street and I walked into it. Roy Orbison was wailing from a jukebox in the corner, and two old men in cardigans and twill trousers sipped cloudy aperitifs as they studied a wooden chessboard with great solemnity. The owner, moustachioed and stout, stood behind a long mahogany-effect bar polishing glasses with a cloth. Posters advertised Cinzano and proclaimed support for a local football team. There was no sign of Severn or anyone else.

I ordered a sandwich and an orange juice. I could have done with a cold beer, but this was no time for alcohol, and the sugar in the juice would give me energy. I found a table from which I could watch the front door of the block of flats through the reflection of a mirror, and waited for my quarry to reappear.

He emerged, looking a little flustered, twenty-three minutes later. He was wearing a different suit and his hair was wet – had he just gone home for a clean-up then? Perhaps the proximity to murder had made him squeamish.

He walked back up the street in the direction of the tram stop, presumably to head off to his appointment with me. I waited a few minutes to make sure he wouldn't double back, and then headed into the building.

*

I rang the doorbell and waited. Through an iron grate I watched as a stout old woman in black shuffled out of a back room towards me. She pressed her face to the grate and glared at me with undisguised suspicion.

'I am a plain-clothes officer of the Servizio Informazioni Difesa,' I said. 'We are currently engaged in an important investigation into a man who has just left this building.'

I spoke with a pronounced Milanese accent, because it is much harder to convince someone you come from the same part of the country as they. She asked me for my papers, and I patiently explained that it was not customary for plain-clothes officers to carry identification, for obvious reasons, but if she chose to call Marco Zimotti, the chief of the SID, at headquarters, he would be able to vouch for me. I gave her an invented number and smiled sweetly, praying she wouldn't call the bluff.

She looked me over for a few moments more, and then reached into the folds of her capacious dress and took out some keys. 'That will not be necessary,' she said, unlocking the door and letting me into the cool, dark vestibule. 'How can I help you, *signore*?'

I described Pyotr and she nodded. The Swiss gentleman, Pierre Valougny. I told her that was an alias and that he was, in fact, a Communist agent, and after her eyes had widened and she had howled a bit, she spat over her shoulder and said she had known there was something wrong with him all along. I nodded soberly and asked her to show me his rooms, and she took me up a very creaky lift and along a dank corridor.

There was a large, well-furnished living room, with a window looking out onto the street and a telephone – he must have lived here a while to have arranged the connection, especially in this neighbourhood.

'Three years,' said the landlady. 'Always paid the rent on time, and kept to himself. But I never liked him. I should have known. Please don't tell anyone of our misfortune here. Was he planning a coup?'

I told her that was state business and asked her to leave. Once she'd gone, I got to work: I wouldn't have too long before he realized I wasn't coming to the meet and started heading back.

I began by just walking around the place, trying to get a feel for who I was dealing with. He'd done well, either through Moscow's funding or his own business acumen, or a combination of the two. There were some hideous modern art paintings on the wall, but they were originals, and a few of the names were familiar. A desk by the window was home to an Olivetti typewriter and stacks of books – these were mostly hardbacks and, again, the subject was modern art. What was his cover, I wondered. Art dealer? That would bring him into contact with Arte come Terrore.

After rummaging around for a couple of minutes, I spotted a ladder next to one of the bookcases. Looking at the ceiling, I saw there was an attic. I pulled out the ladder and climbed up, pushing open the door.

I tugged a piece of string, and a naked bulb lit a small room containing a wing-backed leather chair and a rusty-looking filing cabinet. There was a mousetrap by the wall, loaded with a small triangle of cheese.

The filing cabinet was unlocked. The top drawer was filled with magazines, and I picked out a few. The first that came to hand was called *La Classe* and was dated today: the headline read 'LOTTA DI CLASSE PER LA RIVOLUZIONE': 'Class struggle for the revolution'. The rest of the pile contained other underground magazines, with names like *Carte Segrete*. Interesting. And slightly odd. Pyotr didn't strike me as a flower child, in or out of cover, so what the hell was he doing with these in his flat? I opened the next drawer down. More papers, but these were mostly invitations to showings at local art galleries: La Salita, Dell'Ariete. But there were also magazines here, and one of them, I saw, was called *Transizione*. Even more interesting – but not really enough to hang anyone for.

I turned to the bottom drawer and jerked it open. The radio transmitter stared up at me.

Bingo.

It was a simple short-wave set with a high-speed transmission converter, the kind you could buy from most electronics outfitters. He was presumably using it to communicate with the Station in the embassy here – they, in turn, would send out messages based on his information via telegraph or diplomatic bag to Moscow. Hidden behind the set was a Praktina camera and several neatly bundled wads of money: *lire* and dollars. I considered pocketing the lot – it would certainly be satisfying – but decided I would need all the evidence I could get.

As head of Soviet Section, I'd read the reports from Five on the Lonsdale Ring, which they had rounded up in '61. This wasn't quite as damning as the material they had found in the Krogers' flat in Ruislip – everything from cellophane sheets tucked away in a Bible to a microdot reader in a tin of talcum powder – but it was close. A radio transmitter, a camera and significant sums of money all spelled out 'foreign agent' in capital letters. He'd been caught red-handed – or he soon would be . . .

I stopped. There had been a noise. Was that him returning already? I stood very still for a moment, breathing as shallowly as possible, wondering what the hell to do. I wasn't armed, and he'd have his Makarov . . .

Then I saw the mouse, scuttling across the floorboards – the noise had merely been its nails scratching against the wood. The tiny creature paused for a moment, looking up on its hind legs with its snout twitching, before dropping back onto all fours and scurrying forward again.

Snap!

The trap sprung with brutal velocity, catching the mouse at the base of its neck. There was a tiny, almost inaudible squeak and then its eyes froze.

I made my way back downstairs and replaced the ladder next to the bookcase. A bookcase, I now noticed, that was built into the wall. I knelt down and inspected the skirting board. A few inches from the floor there was a sharp line in the board. I pressed the base of my hand against it and pushed. It slid upwards, revealing a small metal knob beneath, rather like a light switch. I flicked it, and the lowest shelf of the bookcase moved a few inches. I pulled it all the way out. Hidden behind it was a small space, inside of which sat a blue and silver cardboard box with the words '*Baci Perugina*' printed on it.

The chocolates had long since been eaten, but in their place was a sheaf of papers bound with an elastic band. The front page was embossed with a red star in a black circle, and a string of reference numbers lay beneath the typed heading: '   '.

The world around me suddenly hushed, and everything narrowed to the field of my gaze. It was as if a mouse had scuttled its way across my scalp, and that one word had snapped the spring shut. The last time I'd met Sasha I had asked him what my codename was, and he had told me: 'NEZAVISIMYJ', meaning 'independent'.

This was *my* file.

I picked it up and slowly turned to the first page:

INDEPENDENT was recruited in the British Zone of
Germany in 1945 — please see Appendix 1 for
details of the operation . . .

Well, hadn't Sasha been clever? He'd realized I might not listen to his message at Heathrow, so he had given Toadski a copy of my file and told him that if I didn't come in with him he should follow me and hand it over to the local resident wherever I arrived. Presumably the photographs were in here, too? Yes, there they were, in a small plastic pouch beneath the file.

I shook them out and saw that, as well as the pictures with Anna that completed the nasty little honey trap that had brought me into this mess, there were around a dozen surveillance shots that had been taken of me over the years, in London, Istanbul and elsewhere. My anger at not having spotted the tails was somewhat mollified by the fact that I was now sitting in Pyotr's flat looking through their photographs.

I turned back to the file itself. The typeface was raised and glossy, almost like Braille, and the paper thick and crested. The pages were torn in places, with official stamps placed haphazardly over them and the words *Glavnoe Razvedyvatel'noe Upravlenie* everywhere. So I was under the control of the GRU: Sasha hadn't lied about that, at least. There was a long biography that focused mainly on my military service and relationship with Father, and detailed reports of every single meeting I'd attended. There was even a brief essay on my character, dated 12 December 1948, by one Nikolai Pavlovich Vasilyev – presumably Georgi's real name:

When meeting with INDEPENDENT, be advised to choose your words carefully: he has a sharp tongue and his temper cools slowly, so you will waste valuable time antagonizing him unduly. Do not make the mistake of trying to become his friend or sharing your views on the wider world with him. INDEPENDENT is intensely irritated by anything that he senses as prevarication or skirting around an issue — you would be much better advised to take a direct approach.

> INDEPENDENT is prone to questioning any state-
> ment he regards as unclear or euphemistic. He
> is also insistent that he will only give us
> information on matters of principle, so every
> request for information must be framed in such
> a way as to make him believe that it is of
> crucial importance, not just to our own efforts
> but to the benefit of all humanity. This is,
> naturally, sometimes a difficult task ...

Quite an astute assessment, on the whole. Had I really wanted everything to be of benefit to humanity? I couldn't really deny it, absurd as it looked in black and white. Still, Pyotr hadn't taken this advice to heart: his approach had been direct, all right, but it had certainly antagonized me, and unduly at that.

I checked my watch again: it had just gone half eleven. He would be at the gardens soon, and wondering what had happened to me. I calculated I had at least an hour before he would be back. I read on, transfixed. There was a bundle of correspondence from early in my career that made for very curious reading. Skimming through as fast as I could, it appeared that Moscow had not initially believed that they had succeeded in recruiting me. They had become convinced that the Service had *knowingly* let me be recruited, so they could then use me to pass disinformation over. This suspicion appeared to stem from one of the earliest reports I had given. In 1949, Georgi had asked me to note down everything I knew about the Service's efforts to recruit agents in the Soviet Union. As far as I knew there were no such efforts, and so I had said so. But that hadn't been good enough for one Anatoli Panov, an analyst in the Third Department of the First Directorate:

No British agents of note have been exposed as a result of INDEPENDENT'S assistance, although he would certainly have access to such information. Are we expected to believe that he and others have chosen to fight for our cause, and yet the British have failed to recruit a single one of our men to theirs? Ours is clearly the more desirable ideology, but this is nevertheless not a plausible assessment. The truth, of course, is that INDEPENDENT has come up against a piece of information he cannot divulge without hindering the British more than they would like, and has stubbornly insisted on this fatuous line in the hope that we swallow it whole. Let us not fall for such a simple trick. It proves comprehensively that he is a plant: a triple agent.

I read the last line several times, my temple throbbing. It seemed this idiot had been incapable of accepting that I might have been telling the truth. I was even more shocked to see that his report had been counter-signed by Stalin himself, who in the margin had even scribbled '   '– 'Investigate further'. It took me several moments to take it in, and I realized my hands were shaking. After the whole rigmarole they had gone through to recruit me, the extraordinary organization and time and resources that must have gone into that operation, after all the meetings in London and the precautions taken, and all the files I had passed over and reports I had written . . . After all of that, Uncle Joe hadn't believed I was a genuine double agent! Flicking forward, it wasn't until November 1951 – over two years later – that they had finally given me the all clear:

> We are now satisfied that INDEPENDENT is secure
> and that no disinformation is being passed to
> us. Please renew contact with this highly valu-
> able agent.

Thinking back, I realized that this coincided with Sasha's arrival in London. After several frustrating years of intermittent contact, I finally had a regular handler again, and he had pumped me for information in a way Georgi had never done. But, it seemed, to very little purpose. I searched in vain for reports on the operations I had betrayed at that time. It looked like Sasha had decided not to pass any of it on. But why on earth not, if I had been cleared? One reason immediately sprung to mind. Even in the Service, information that inconveniently contradicted a widely held theory – especially if it were also held by a Head of Section – was sometimes skimmed over or quietly dropped for fear of the messenger being shot. It looked like that might literally have been the case for Georgi: a brief note at the top of a file from 1949 explained that he had been classified as an 'undesirable'. He had been recalled and sent to the gulags, of course – perhaps Sasha didn't want to make the same mistake.

I didn't know whether to laugh or cry. So it had all been for nought, or as near as dammit. My recruitment and handling hadn't been some grand game of chess, but a muddle of crossed wires, paranoia and office politics. I'd spent twenty-four years deceiving everyone around me, but it seemed that for several years the men I had thought I was serving hadn't even been given the information I had obtained, let alone used it.

I straightened up. Did it matter, ultimately, that they had failed to take advantage of the material? Did I really need a tally of my own treachery, a count of the dead men? No. I had done it. I was a traitor, no matter what the cost had been.

But a terrifying thought suddenly occurred to me. The analyst Panov would have vanished from the scene long ago, of course, no doubt sent to the gulags himself for not having tied his shoelaces the right way. But his way of thinking had been accepted for two years, and clearly something of it had survived because it looked like much of the information I'd handed over subsequently still hadn't been passed up the ladder. What sort of an organization could have allowed that to happen? What if there was a new Panov in Moscow, or a group of them even, and they had decided that my actions in Nigeria proved I'd been a triple agent all along? After all, they had lost two long-serving agents at my hand. Could *that* be why I had been targeted? Yes, of course it bloody could.

I looked at my watch again. I'd been in here nearly an

hour already, and Pyotr would soon be boarding a tram on his way back. I took the file and chocolate box and walked over to the desk by the window. There was an old Olivetti typewriter on top of it. I lifted the cover, took a sheet of paper from the drawer and rolled it into the machine. I began typing.

A couple of minutes later I scrolled the paper out, folded it, and placed it in my jacket pocket. I walked back to the book-case and replaced the chocolate box, then glanced around the flat again, checking that everything was in order, picked my file from the desk, turned off the lights and quietly closed the door behind me.

*

I took the lift back down and thanked the landlady for her assistance. I warned her that I might return with some of my colleagues, but that whatever she did she should give no signal to Signor Valougny that he was under suspicion. She promised heartily to uphold her patriotic duty.

I went back into the bar across the street and asked for the lavatory. The barman pointed down a flight of rickety stairs. Once there, I locked the door and tore each page of my file into strips before feeding it into the bowl. Then I flushed it all away. There would be copies in Moscow, of course, but this would do for the time being. And there was a strange sense of satisfaction in watching the words dissolve and disappear. A plan of action had started to form in my mind. I went over all the scenarios I thought it could lead to, and decided that, while it was certainly a risk, it was one worth taking. Or perhaps I simply no longer cared.

I went upstairs again and asked if I could use the telephone. The barman looked at me, and nodded his head imperceptibly to the left. I gave him 100 *lire*, received two tokens and ten *lire* in change, and walked over to the machine. Severn picked up on the first ring.

'Where the hell are you? You've been gone over three hours, and Zimotti just called to say a body has been discovered in the museum—'

'It's Barchetti,' I said. 'But I've got him. I've got the bastard . . .'

'Slow down. Got who?'

'The man who arranged Farraday's assassination. The head of Arte come Terrore. Barchetti was scared at the meet, insisted I follow him into a dark room at the end of the gallery. But by the time I got in there, someone had already strangled him.'

There was a short silence, and I imagined Severn's face turning paler.

'Did you manage to get anything from him at all? What about his European lead?'

'Nothing. But I saw this chap leaving the museum in a hurry and he looked fishy, so I trailed him and he came running back to a flat in Trastevere. I waited until he left, and broke in. It's him,' I said. 'He's our man. Call Zimotti and tell him to bring a few of his men around to Viale Trastevere as fast as he can. Then jump in your car and come here yourself. I'm in a bar called' – I picked up a menu from the top of the telephone set – '*La Maddalena*, about halfway up the street. I'll tell you about it when you get here.'

X

'I demand to see a lawyer.'

Zimotti offered him an insincere smile. 'I'm afraid we can't extend you that right, *signore*.'

Pyotr glared back with contempt. I didn't blame him: his flat was suddenly looking rather cramped.

Severn had arrived in his race car fifteen minutes after my call, accompanied by his wife. Hot on their heels had been Zimotti, who had arrived with a couple of black Lancias containing two of his men, nasty-looking brutes in leather jackets and jeans. I had explained the situation in the back of the bar and shown them the note: Severn and Zimotti had glanced at each other in grim acknowledgement. Almost as if on cue, Pyotr had stepped off the tram, walked up the street and unlocked his front door.

And we'd pounced. The landlady had fretted over what the neighbours would think, but one of Zimotti's men had taken her to one side and explained that she was performing a great service for the republic, and her massive chest had risen with pride at the thought and she had waved us through, almost in tears. Pyotr had been brewing himself a cup of coffee when we'd broken the door down. He'd protested, of course, strenuously and in fluent Italian, but there wasn't a lot he could do about it: he didn't have diplomatic cover.

I looked over at Severn, who was standing by the door watching Zimotti at work. 'Let's get him,' was all he had said in the bar. Now he looked equally calm, but his jaw was clenched tight and he was drumming his fingers against his thighs. He sensed my gaze and looked across at me, then smiled unconvincingly. It sent a shiver through me. Woe betide anyone who got on the wrong side of Severn. For a moment, I almost felt sorry for Pyotr.

Almost.

Sarah Severn was standing next to her husband, smoking her third cigarette since we'd arrived. I wished to God Severn hadn't brought her along. She was a radio officer; there was no need for her to see any of this. She also seemed to be under the illusion that I'd been some sort of a hero in London, and I didn't like having to go through this grotesque charade in front of her. But go through it I would, of course.

We'd only been here a few minutes, but the flat was already halfway to a shambles. Zimotti's men had removed the drawers of the desk and shaken the contents onto the carpet, and they were now attacking the chairs, removing the cushions and tearing off the covers. Pyotr began objecting again and Zimotti pulled him up short, leaning over him and yelling at him to sit down. Pyotr glanced at the heavies and decided to do so.

'Will someone please tell me what is happening here?' he said, pouting like a child.

Zimotti smiled. '*Va bene*. We are representatives of the Servizio Informazioni Difesa, and we are here because we suspect that you are engaged in activities that may be harmful to the interests of Italy, Great Britain and its allies.'

'Only them?' said Pyotr with a sneer.

Zimotti ignored it. 'Specifically, we suspect that you are involved in terrorist activity, or are in contact with people who are. I am now going to hand you over to this man,' – he nodded at me – 'who is a very senior member of British intelligence. He has some questions to put to you.'

I stepped forward.

'Hello. My name is Paul Dark. Could you tell me yours, please?'

He didn't answer, just glared dully at me.

'The quicker you cooperate,' I said, 'the quicker we are going to get through this. If you are not involved in the way we think you are, we will soon clear this up and leave you in peace. You can have that coffee you were looking forward to.'

I tried to keep the tone relatively light, and glanced at Zimotti several times while I was talking. I wanted to hook Pyotr into believing that the Italians had somehow caught onto him but that I had engineered my way into handling the situation and was going to extricate him from it. That I was his friend, essentially.

There were a few seconds of silence, and then:

'Pierre Valougny.'

Hooked.

'Nationality?'

'Swiss.'

'Occupation?'

'I run a small printing company between here and Geneva.'

Someone had opened a window to let the air in and I walked over to it. The noise of the traffic drifted up. I strained to make out other sounds: birdsong, a dog barking, a fountain trickling in the *piazza*. I turned back to Pyotr.

'Edoardo Barchetti,' I said. 'Recognize the name?'

'No. I have absolutely no idea what any of this is—'

'He contacted us recently, concerning a small group he was a member of here: Arte come Terrore.'

No reaction, but there was no reason for there to be, yet.

'I say "was". A couple of days ago we learned that members of this group were planning a series of attacks in Europe. I went to meet him a few hours ago at the modern art museum to find out more, but I didn't get very far. Care to guess why?'

His nose twitched, but his eyes were glued to me. He didn't know where I was heading, but his instincts were telling him it wasn't the right way.

'Because by the time I reached him, Edoardo Barchetti was dead. However, I saw *you* leaving the museum in a hurry, so I followed you here. I'd like to know why you killed him.'

I didn't like myself for saying the last part, but in a way it was true. He had forced me into it, and now I was going to make him pay the price.

'I am a printer,' he said. 'My company prints art magazines. I was interested in the exhibition—'

'Is that an attic you have?' I said, glancing upwards. He made to stand up and I stepped forward and pushed him back down into the chair. I walked over to the bookcase and pulled out the ladder. Zimotti nodded at one of his men and he began climbing up.

I looked back at Pyotr. He was starting to realize the situation. The Italians hadn't caught onto him; I had framed him. His anger was rising and he was desperately trying to keep a lid on it. He was furious with himself for letting me get the upper hand on him. He'd wanted to play the big man with the compromised agent, and I'd responded by doing the unthinkable and he hadn't seen it coming. He was holding up well, considering, but I knew that he would go to the ends of the earth to pay me back if I didn't manage to pull this off. It was him or me now, and if he'd had no problem in blowing my cover earlier, he would now be itching to do it.

There was a noise from upstairs, and I knew the Italian had found the transmitter. A couple of minutes later and it was sitting on the desk, along with the magazines and gallery invitations. Zimotti and Severn both walked over and peered at the untidy-looking heap. Severn started leafing through the notes, his face set.

'How do you explain these items?' I said to Pyotr.

'The money is for emergencies – we Swiss are prudent people, and I always keep some at home, in all currencies.' He smiled sweetly, almost in recognition of his cleverness.

'And the transmitter?'

'I have a passion for amateur radio.'

'Why is it hidden in your attic?'

'My landlady does not like the idea – and it gets much better reception up there. It is not, as far as I am aware, a crime.'

'This is a spy transmitter, Signor Valougny, and you are using it to communicate with your colleagues in the Soviet embassy. And this,' – I picked up the Praktina – 'is a spy camera, used for copying documents.'

'I don't see why you use that term. I bought it in a shop in town, and I often use it to photograph pictures from my books here to take to the office with me. Books are unwieldy.'

It was weak, but then he wasn't playing to us. He was playing to a jury. We had to be a lot more solid than this to convict him; if we weren't, he wouldn't confess. He was skating on thin ice – I had to cut the ice away from his feet and make sure he fell in.

'You say you print art magazines.' I picked up the copy of *La Classe* and placed it on the table. 'But this is a Communist magazine, calling for class struggle – for revolution, in fact.'

'We print lots of different magazines. We are not responsible for the content. You must take that up with the editors and writers.'

Printer as a cover was a new one to me, but I could see the benefits. He could hover around the edge of the underground movement, but if pressed by the authorities – as now – could plausibly distance himself.

I pointed to a copy of *Transizione*.

'Did you also print this?'

He peered at it, then nodded.

'This is the same magazine that published a series of articles last year putting forward the case for violent acts against the state.'

'Yes, I read those articles. They were purely theoretical, of course. They weren't intended—'

'We don't think so. We believe that they constituted a kind of manifesto, in fact, and that they led to the foundation of Arte come Terrore. What do you know about the assassination of the head of British intelligence in London yesterday?'

'The assassination of who? I have no knowledge of this whatsoever. I demand that you leave my home at once. I am a respectable businessman, and I do not take kindly to this treatment.'

Enough cat-and-mouse. It was time to close in for the kill.

'All of this,' I said, gesturing at the table, 'is circumstantial. I found this piece of paper on Barchetti.' I took it out of my pocket and read it to him. It was only a few lines in Italian, but I'd packed it with enough to damn him to hell and back:

```
We feel that the committee is now ready to
step up its actions, and recommend the targeting
of senior members of Western intelligence agen-
cies. Details will soon follow of a public
event in Britain. Please choose an operative
for this task from among your number. We will
provide the necessary weaponry once they have
```

```
entered the country. Further operations in Italy,
France and elsewhere are in advanced stages of
planning.
```

I threw the letter onto the table and placed a hand on the Olivetti.

'How much do you want to bet that the typeface matches the one produced by this machine?'

Pyotr licked his lips anxiously. Perhaps he was missing his chocolates. He was sweating now, and his face seemed to be turning an ash-grey. It was doubly insulting to him, because only the sloppiest of agents would have handed a contact such a note, in the clear and typed up on their own machine. But he could hardly point that out.

'I did not write this,' he said coldly. 'I have never seen it before.'

I pressed it with my finger. 'Is this why you killed Barchetti? Did you realize he was an infiltrator? Or was he perhaps blackmailing you, threatening to tell someone about your plans?' I leaned on the word 'blackmailing' and was pleased to see him flinch at it. 'Tell me!'

'This is an amusing game, Mister . . .'

'Dark.'

'An amusing game, Mister Dark. But how far are you prepared to take it?'

'All the way,' I said. 'I have no choice.'

He looked up at me sharply. 'What do you mean?'

I smiled – he thought I'd slipped up. 'A sniper killed the

head of our agency in front of my eyes in London yesterday,' I said. 'It appears they have not finished their work. I can't let it go. I can't let you go until you tell us what you know.'

'So you're a patriot, is that it? You don't strike me as the type.' He glanced down at the letter disdainfully. 'I have never seen this letter before in my life.'

'Then why was it in Barchetti's—'

'Because you *planted* it there, Mister Dark!' His cheeks were burning now. 'You planted it there because you want to prove to your colleagues that I had something to do with the death of Mister Farraday in London.'

Trapped! Severn sprung forward. 'So you *do* know about—'

'I know because Mister Dark here told me,' said Pyotr, and I shook for a moment, realizing that he had decided to go all the way, dragging us through the whole charade. Well, so be it. I had a whole heap of evidence against him, and all he had against me was his say-so. 'Mister Dark told me when I met him outside the British embassy yesterday evening,' he said, his voice rising in pitch, 'because Mister Dark is a Soviet agent, and I am his contact here.'

There was silence for a moment.

'Are you confessing to being a Soviet spy, Mister Valougny?' I said.

He laughed derisively. 'No. I am confessing that you and I both are.'

Severn took a few steps closer. 'Do you have any evidence of that?' he asked, but I cut him off before he could go any further.

'Please, Charles,' I said. 'Let me handle this. It's a desperate gambit, Mister Valougny, but I'm afraid it won't work. All you have to do is tell us what it is that Arte come Terrore is planning next, and we can take it from there. Perhaps we can make some sort of a deal if you were to work for us from now on. But please show my colleagues and me a little more respect. Throwing around melodramatic accusations is an easy game to play, but you're not convincing anyone and you're not going to disrupt this investigation.'

Pyotr smiled, but it was the grim smile of a man who knew he was defeated. Oh, he would be cursing the day he met me for a long time. It served him right. Don't blackmail someone unless you are very certain of your ground – and can lose a tail.

'Let's take him out of here,' said Zimotti, who was pacing around by the door. 'We need some time to crack this nut and this isn't the place for it.'

'What do you suggest?' I said.

'We have better facilities in town,' said Zimotti. 'Let's get this bastard into an interviewing room.'

*

We went outside and bundled into the cars. The Severns took the Alfa Romeo, Zimotti's men took Pyotr in one of the Lancias and I went with Zimotti in his own car. He didn't say anything as he drove through the early afternoon traffic, his face staring ahead grimly. I reviewed the situation. It had gone well, all things considered. Pyotr had thrown out the counter-accusation, as I had expected he might when cornered, but the timing was a little awkward: I hadn't bargained on our being split up like this. No doubt he was now telling the others in the car behind that I had been recruited in Germany or some such thing. No matter — I'd disposed of all the evidence, and I doubted they would let him say very much: Zimotti's men looked like pretty tough customers. I would have to tread very carefully now to make sure none of the mud he flung stuck to me, but if I applied more pressure on him, and quickly, I reckoned I would be in a strong position . . .

We took a sudden lurch to the left, and I caught a glimpse out of the window. Zimotti had taken a minor road, and it seemed we were heading away from the city centre.

'Where are we going?' I said, but as I turned I felt a sting in my upper thigh and saw him removing the needle. I started calling out, but it was no use, because my world was fading to black and all I could think was: *I'm finished*.

XI

I came back to consciousness slowly and realized I was lying on the floor. After a few seconds, I remembered what had happened.

I did a quick inventory of my status. I was still in my suit, but my belt, shoes and socks had been taken, and my pockets emptied. Physically I seemed to be fine, apart from a small mark on my thigh from the hypodermic and some pain at the base of my neck and along my spine, no doubt due to having slept on the floor. I was drowsy, but not overly so: probably just a simple sedative, then. Mentally, nothing was damaged – yet.

The room was bare: nothing in it at all, not even a bed or a bucket. It was about fifteen feet across and ten wide. The floor and walls were white and appeared to be made from some sort of plastic material, smooth to the touch. A sliver of light crept in through a tiny window high in the ceiling. Was it dusk or dawn? My last meal had been the sandwich and juice in the bar in Trastevere, which suggested it was at least the next day, as my stomach was beginning to gnaw at me and my throat was very dry. What the hell was going on? And where the hell had they brought me?

I didn't have to wait long for answers. Within a few minutes, fluorescent panels in the ceiling flickered on and began to brighten, until it became almost painful to the eyes. A door opened in one of the walls and through it walked Zimotti . . . and Severn. Both of them were wearing dark glasses with mirrored lenses, and Zimotti was now in a tailored midnight-blue uniform and cap. He was head of *military* intelligence, I remembered. They must have brought me to a base or barracks.

A deeply tanned man with a sharp nose followed – I recognized him as one of Zimotti's men from the flat. He was also wearing dark glasses, and camouflage fatigues instead of the jacket and jeans he'd been in earlier. He carried a couple of rather tatty-looking wooden chairs into the centre of the room, planted them down, then swivelled and marched to one of the walls, where he took up station.

Zimotti and Severn seated themselves and looked down at me. Their entrance so soon after I had woken seemed unlikely to be coincidence, but how were they watching me? The room was as smooth and featureless as it was possible to be – I couldn't even make out the edges of the door they had come through – but presumably there were film cameras somewhere, monitoring every movement I made.

I looked up, and was shocked to see a frightened, cowering animal reflected in the lenses of their glasses. I struggled to my feet and started shouting at them, telling them they'd made a dreadful mistake, that I was going to have Severn dismissed, that if they wanted to believe a Soviet agent over the Deputy Chief of the Service they were out of their minds, and so on.

'Save it for someone else,' Severn said once I'd done. 'We know you're a double.'

It wasn't so much the words that scared me as the way in which they'd been said. The tone was of calm contempt, and there hadn't been a fraction of hesitation: he was dead certain. Think. The glance between him and Zimotti when I'd shown them the typewritten note in the bar . . . It hadn't been acknowledgement that Pyotr was guilty, but confirmation of *my* guilt. But how could they be so sure about it? It must have been something I'd done, because if the Service had known I was a double before now they wouldn't have let me get on a plane – they would have interrogated me back in London. So somehow I had just told them I was a double – but how? Simply because I had tried to frame Pyotr for Farraday's death? Yes, that must be it. They knew beyond a shadow of a doubt that he hadn't been responsible for it because . . .

Christ.

Of course.

'You killed Farraday,' I said to Severn.

His eyes didn't flicker.

'Not deliberately,' he said. 'You were our target.'

I shivered. If they had suspected me of being a double, they hadn't waited for confirmation of it – they had simply arranged my assassination anyway. But why would they . . .?

Leave it for the moment. Now you need to fight back, before it's too late.

'I planted the evidence on the Russian,' I said. 'I admit that much. But that doesn't make me a double.'

'Why do it, then?'

'Because I wanted the glory, of course. Christ, you should see how they're acting back in London. Haggard sent me out here to sort everything out. I couldn't very well go back and tell him that not only had I failed to make proper contact with Barchetti but that he'd been *killed*. I saw this chap hanging around the gallery and he got careless, so I followed him. And I thought, well . . . it would be a good opportunity. I know how that must sound, but—'

'Pathetic is how it sounds,' said Severn, and my hopes lifted. Precisely what I'd hoped he would think of me. 'So, the great Paul Dark is just a little fraud. Tell me, what other triumphs of yours have you created this way? How about that business in Nigeria – was all that bravado and planted evidence, too?'

'I saved the Prime Minister, for God's sake – there were witnesses to it!'

'I don't believe him,' said Zimotti, and my hopes sank again. 'It was too calculated, too fast. He knew this Soviet, and I think the man was his controller.'

Evenly matched. Could I convince one of them to go the other way? Zimotti looked firm, but perhaps I could play Severn off against him?

'Let's find out,' said Severn, and then uttered three words

that I knew meant I would never be able to change anyone's mind again. 'Let's break him.'

*

They left, taking the chairs with them. The chairs had been brought in from the garden, I thought, remembering Toadski's warning in Heathrow to keep a low profile. Well, I hadn't listened, and here I was.

The lights began to flicker, then dim, before extinguishing completely. There was a thin buzzing sound above me as a panel moved across and covered the tiny window. I was in complete darkness. I stepped forward until I reached the wall opposite – the door had to be somewhere here. I felt along the surface, but couldn't find it. It was completely flush. I made my way around the room, frantically running my hands across every inch of the walls I could reach. Finally, I came across the thinnest of seams – was *this* where they had come through? It must be. But there was nothing else there: no hinge, no handle, just the shallowest of grooves. I tried to dig into it with my hands, but I couldn't even get my nails in.

After several minutes searching the rest of the cell in vain for anything to get a handle on, I fell back onto the floor, exhausted from the effort. As I did, the lights flickered back on again. Had it just been a power cut? They kept flickering, and I realized that it was deliberate. The cell itself was an instrument of torture, a state-of-the-art environment that could be used to manipulate the occupant: me. I moved to one of the corners and seated myself as comfortably as I could, waiting for whatever they would throw at me next.

It came about ten minutes later. A blast of music suddenly erupted from hidden speakers in the ceiling. The song was vaguely familiar, the singer wailing about the world being on the eve of destruction – a little joke on Severn's part? The song became louder as it went on, until eventually I had to place my hands over my ears to try to muffle it. Then, just as suddenly as it had arrived, it was cut off. I realized I was breathing hard, and my heart rate had shot up.

Over the next few hours they continued with this game, suddenly introducing the song – always the same song – at a very loud volume, only to cut it off again abruptly. Sometimes the song lasted several minutes, sometimes just a few seconds. The result was that the music became indistinguishable noise to me, and I began to fear its return.

I knew they were trying to soften me up and that if I succumbed now I would never be able to get back, so I put all my effort into resisting, keeping my mind busy. I certainly had a lot to think about. The one question nagging at me above all was: why? Why had they tried to kill me? I'd cleared myself of being a traitor, and Osborne had even approved my promotion . . . But no, that must all have been for show, I realized, a front they had put on to lull me into complacency while they made arrangements for a sniper to take me out. They had evidently decided at some point that, traitor or not, they didn't want to take their chances with me. I could still expose the plot they'd cooked up in Nigeria, and that alone was reason enough to have me swept out of sight.

They must have planned some of it while I'd still been in isolation at the hospital recovering from the fever. Where would they have met, I wondered. The conference room on the third floor? The basement bar? No, both were too conspicuous. Not everyone could have been in on such a plot, and they'd have wanted to keep any meetings not just discreet, but completely off the radar. So they'd probably met at one of their homes after work – perhaps even Farraday's. That would have been ironic. But no, Farraday couldn't have been part of it, I realized, or he wouldn't have been stupid enough to stand in front of me in St Paul's. Then again, he hadn't been the brightest of men. But no, I reckoned Osborne was the brains behind it, in which case his house in Eaton Square would have been their base. I could just picture the scene: Osborne, Innes, Dawes, perhaps Smale . . . the whole clutch of them drinking Scotch and smoking cigars and plotting into the night. The old guard, the robber barons, protecting the Service. I had never entered that little world, had deliberately stayed apart from it. That had been my undoing, I saw now.

At some point in the fug and the smoke, as they had debated what to do about the fact that Wilson was still alive despite their best efforts, the conversation would have swung round to me. *'What the hell are we going to do about Paul?'* Well, it wouldn't have taken them long to come to their decision – I was best out of the way. They could have just given me a swift injection, of course, and nobody would have been any the wiser.

'Yes, the fever took him. Dreadful affair. He caught it out in Nigeria.' But someone had been more imaginative than that, had seen a way to get more mileage from me, even in death. By doing the deed in St Paul's, in full view of two Cabinet ministers and half the Service, they would have killed two birds with one conspicuously Soviet-manufactured cartridge. I would have died a hero, a convenient martyr in the Service's struggle against anarchists and Communists, and the ministers, spooked at seemingly having come so close to being killed themselves, would jump to treble the Service's budget to deal with the menace. A nice fringe benefit. The Service would never come under suspicion, of course, and neither would Five. They were the investigators, so they could make certain the evidence showed just what they wished it to. And who would suspect them of plotting to kill one of their most senior officers? I hadn't.

They'd had to improvise, certainly, putting it all together in so short a time. Presumably the sniper had been one of Zimotti's men, completely unconnected with Arte come Terrore. Did Arte come Terrore even exist? Yes, I reasoned. Barchetti had clearly infiltrated them, and even with their elaborate plot to kill me I doubted they had the imagination to create something quite so outlandish out of whole cloth. They had simply used Arte come Terrore as a decoy, a convenient Moscow-backed group to pin the blame on. No doubt Five had been in on it, too: that was how the sniper had been able to 'smuggle' his rifle into the cathedral so easily. I added Giles Fearing into the scene at Osborne's house, his jowls wobbling with mirth as each of them had put successive ideas into the pot, stirring it until it came to a boil. I could just imagine how they had rubbed their hands with glee and patted themselves on the back when they'd come up with the thing. A bold and fitting move to counter the Nigerian disaster. Checkmate in one.

But it wouldn't have been easy. They'd had to find a sniper, train him, rehearse his getaway route in case something went wrong. Show him the tunnel leading to Smithfield, perhaps. And, luckily for me, something *had* gone wrong: Farraday had moved his head at just the wrong moment.

Worse, from the point of view of the conspirators, was that I had taken the initiative. I'd chased the sniper down, and he'd said something in Italian. They'd had to improvise anew then – Osborne biting his nails in the Rover – and they had decided to reveal their great foresight in predicting that this was the first of a wave of attacks across Europe, stemming out of a group in Italy. I thought back to the meeting in Whitehall, playing it again in my mind. Christ, Osborne had even had me call Innes to prepare their story!

I discounted Haggard as being part of the plot – there was no feigning that depth of outrage, and his suggestion that I go to Italy to hunt down and kill those responsible for Farraday's murder wasn't a script they would have wanted to play: it might have made me think a little more carefully about who had tried to kill *me*. I cursed myself that it hadn't; the thing had been staring me in the face. But I'd been sure that I was finally in the clear. The idea that they would try to assassinate me simply hadn't crossed my mind.

And, despite killing the wrong man, they'd got away with it: I hadn't suspected their involvement for a moment, and I doubted Haggard had, either. They hadn't intended for me to visit Rome, of course, but when Haggard had given them little choice in the matter they'd been happy enough to send me on a wild-goose chase — with Barnes watching over me to make sure I didn't stray too far. Barchetti must have wanted to meet about something else entirely. If I hadn't insisted on going in Severn's place, no doubt he would have returned from the museum and fed me a suitable story that would have led me somewhere else.

My thoughts turned to the here and now. Where had they brought me? I presumed from Zimotti's presence that we were still in Rome, or somewhere in Italy, at any rate. But why had they not already flown me back to London to face Osborne et al? Zimotti might want a piece of me, if the hatred of Communists I'd glimpsed at dinner were any indication — but that couldn't be the answer. There must be some other reason. It was also odd that they had waited for me to interview Pyotr first and then brought me in, instead of simply carting me off the moment I'd shown them the note. Perhaps they had wanted to see how far I'd take it. No, of course: they must have realized Pyotr was a Soviet agent, too — my handler, Zimotti had surmised. They had let me run ahead and lead them to him. Two for the price of one . . .

The music suddenly shut down, bringing me back to earth. There was a noise coming from somewhere outside the cell. It was dulled by distance and the walls, but there was no mistaking it: screaming. So they had brought Pyotr here, too, and were torturing him. How long before it would be my turn? I shivered, and my stomach clutched anew.

The record started up again, at ear-splitting volume, but after a few seconds it began repeating the same fragment over and over: '*Destruction . . . destruction . . . destruction . . .*' Either the record had become stuck and there was nobody manning the machine playing it, or they had put it on a loop deliberately to drive me mad. Probably the latter. How long were they planning to keep me here? There was no bucket, no slops . . .

Wake up, Paul. They're not planning to keep you here at all. They're going to *kill* you. They had tried in St Paul's and narrowly missed. Yes, but they hadn't been certain I was a traitor then. It made little difference. They would squeeze everything they could out of me, then finish me off with a bullet through my skull. Severn would report back to London that the deed had been done, and Osborne would no doubt furnish a plausible story for Haggard. On reflection, perhaps I hadn't been so lucky that Farraday had moved his head.

The music stopped again, just as abruptly as the other times. This time, though, it didn't start up again. It was what I had been craving, but as the hours passed the silence became worse than the noise it had replaced: the room was suddenly twice as cold and lonely. I was desperately tired, and knew I needed to sleep if I had any chance at all of surviving. But the fear of being woken at any moment had blocked my brain, and all I could see around me was death, and death at my own hands: Colin Templeton's face as he handed me the drink, sometimes interspersed with the sniper closing his eyes on the floor of the market, or with Barchetti, choking. The images played in my mind on an eternal loop, and I tunnelled ever deeper into them.

XII

I jerked awake, my ears ringing. As the echo faded, I realized it had been a shot.

Had they just killed Pyotr?

I kept listening, but there was nothing else for several minutes. And then I heard the clacking of shoes. The door opened. I struggled to catch a glimpse of how the mechanism worked, but they had turned the lights up again and it was impossible to make out.

My eyes smarting, I squinted as Severn stepped into the cell. He was still wearing the mirrored glasses, and he had someone with him. Not Zimotti this time, but Barnes.

I'd forgotten about Barnes.

Severn took a pack of cigarettes from a pocket, shook one into his fingers and lit it, then slowly blew the smoke into my face. 'How are you doing?' he said. 'Ready to confess yet?'

'It'll take a bit more than a few flashing lights and some pop music,' I said. 'Try harder.' It was a stupid thing to say, and I don't know why I'd reacted that way. The cigarette, perhaps.

He smiled, almost jovially. 'Oh, we will. We will. You're forgetting that Reginald here worked in the camps in Kenya. He knows how to get information from a suspect, don't you?'

'Yes, sir,' said Barnes quietly. His jaw was locked tight, and his pale blue eyes drilled into me. No sunglasses for Barnes: he wanted to look at me unvarnished. 'We used to use a bucket, sir. Put it over their heads, then hit it with a club for a few hours. That was one trick we used to use, sir, with some of the harder-core elements.'

They'd told him, of course – that I'd killed Templeton.

'All right,' I said. 'I confess. I'm a double.'

It was a relief to say it after all these years, simply to say the words aloud. But it evidently wasn't what they wanted to hear. Barnes suddenly lunged forward and began pummelling at me, his fists crashing into my stomach and a deep animal roar bursting from him. As I tried to shield my head and body from the blows, I caught a glimpse of his face, his mouth in a rictus, the veins at his temples throbbing, and I just held my hands up meekly and waited for it to end. Fighting back now would only make it worse. Let him tire. Let him tire.

He didn't tire easily.

When it was finally over, my face felt like it had been inflated like a balloon. Through barely open eyes I saw him salute Severn and march out of the room. I prayed he wasn't going to fetch a bucket.

'Poor Dark,' said Severn, and laughed at the weak pun on my name. 'Got yourself into something bigger than you understood this time, didn't you?'

I looked up. Two versions of him floated in front of me. Part of my brain registered that this might mean a damaged retina, but the rest of it was busy trying to bring the two of them closer together, and failing.

I let my head hang down and wondered whether I could muster the strength to hit him, possibly even to kill him. It might be worth it, just for the cigarettes. I smiled at myself. I knew I didn't have it in me to pull it off, and what good would enraging him do? It would get it over with, perhaps. Make him kill me quicker. *No.* Hold out. What have they done? Music, lights, a beating up. You can handle that. Hold out. You might yet survive this, you might yet . . .

Severn threw his cigarette to the floor and crushed it with the heel of his shoe. Then he grabbed me by the hair and pulled me up until I was standing. It was his turn to have some fun now. He removed his glasses and I stared into his eyes. They were cold, dead: the gunmetal had turned to stone. I could smell his cologne – Floris? – but it was covered with the sharp tang of sweat. Anger – or excitement?

'I hate scum like you,' he sneered. 'I don't know how you can live with yourself, lying to your colleagues and friends day after day, for years. How do you do that, Dark, tell me?'

It was best not to answer that kind of question. And yes, true, I was scum. But there are grades of scum, and I was beginning to feel that he might be at least on the same grade as me.

'Betrayal, deceit . . . What a life. You *Judas*.' He spat out the word. The veins in his forehead were standing out, his throat muscles constricted. His body had released adrenalin into his system and he was beginning to experience tunnel vision, seeing red. He was seeing a Red, in fact: me. He seemed to have derived a vicarious thrill from watching Barnes beat me up, but he was no weakling himself.

'Tell me about school,' he whispered under his breath.

I stared at him, not understanding. *School?*

'You know about it,' I said slowly. 'You were there, too, remember?'

'Tell me about it anyway.'

It was then that I noticed his hand. Why hadn't I seen it before? It was gripping something I recognized, but had never expected to see again. A cat-o'-nine tails. He lifted it and I caught a closer look: it had a thin black leather grip, opening into the plaited thongs.

'Did you enjoy it?' he said, seeing that I had begun to understand where we were heading. 'Did you take pleasure from seeing me suffer?' His voice rose and he loomed over me, the cat waving in his hand. 'Oh, I know you didn't take part in the fun yourself, but you stood by and watched readily enough, didn't you? *You didn't do anything to stop it!*' The intensity of his rage seemed to be growing by the second. I had to calm him down before he completely lost control and killed me.

The cat's tails came down, and as the agony shot through me I finally understood what was happening inside the mind of Charles Severn.

In 1942, shortly before I left to join the army, I had been made a praefect at Winchester. One of my first duties had been to sit in on the 'Notions Examina', the school's initiation ceremony for new boys. Like most such ceremonies, it involved an element of humiliation: stupid games, coarse questions, name-calling. I'd experienced it myself, but had forgotten until this moment that Severn's test had gone horribly wrong: a few of the praefects had whipped him with a cat and somehow bones had ended up broken.

He had spent a few days in the San, but as far as I knew had suffered no lasting damage. Three months after sitting in on his Notions test I had gone to Oxford, before being sent to train with SOE. Just over a year later, I had seen men mown down by machine-gun fire in a village in Normandy. Severn's ordeal was small beer compared to what the rest of the world had gone through – though not, of course, to him. He had been recruited into the Service after the war, but would still have seen his share of men injured and killed over the years. But this had been his injury, and it had been deeper than anyone could have guessed.

I hadn't been one of the boys who had hurt him, but it didn't look like that was going to mean much now. And he had a point. He had been whipped brutally, and I hadn't lifted a finger to stop it. He had been thirteen then, and I had been seventeen: old enough to act. I hadn't realized how badly it had been going – none of us had – and I certainly hadn't enjoyed it. But it hadn't occurred to me to try to *stop* them. Severn had been having a worse time than most, certainly, but that was just hard luck. Someone had to. I hadn't felt ashamed of my inaction then, or in the intervening decades. I did now, although I suspected that if I had tried to stop them, they would have simply laughed, and quite probably turned on me.

But that was easy to say now, and not much of an excuse when it came down to it. That way led to mob rule, to Eichmann and his 'following orders'. I had stood by and let it happen. Yes. I was just as guilty as the others had been.

I became dimly aware of the sound of singing. It was Severn.

> *Domum, domum, dulce domum*
> *Domum, domum, dulce domum*
> *Dulce, dulce dulce domum!*
> *Dulce domum resonemus . . .*

It had always struck me as a strange kind of school song, one that remembered and glorified home. He was singing it very loudly, and flat. His face was scarlet and the tendons on his neck were bulging like tree-trunks. He had clearly gone quite mad, and the reason I was here and not in London was because he wanted to exact his revenge on me, in private. There weren't going to be any letters to The Trusty Servant about this particular reunion.

'What do you want to know?' I managed to gasp out.

He spat in my face and then leaned forward and kicked me in the stomach, winding me. I crashed to the floor.

He raised the cat again.

'What did she tell you?' he hissed.

I looked up at him, lost.

'Who? About what?'

'*What did she tell you?*'

His eyes stared out from his head as he screamed at me, and then he lifted the cat higher, above his shoulder. 'I'm going to destroy you, Dark,' he said. 'First I'm going to break you into little pieces, and then I am going to destroy you. Nobody . . .' he whispered, spittle foaming at the edge of his lip.

'. . . touches . . .'

His hand twitched.

'. . . my *wife!*'

He brought it down, and I let out a long scream. He kept going, bringing the thing up and then down, I don't know for how long, and then I started falling back into the abyss again, and my mind clouded over.

*

Something was terribly wrong.

That was my first thought as I came back to consciousness. The whole of my back throbbed with pain and, as I opened my eyes, my vision was still blurred. But I was *alert*. That should have been good news, but I knew it wasn't. Presumably they had drugged me again, but this time with some sort of stimulant.

I was strapped to a table. My arms and legs were in iron cuffs, making it impossible for me to move them. I couldn't lift my neck more than half an inch, but I could make out that we were in some sort of an operating theatre. Someone was hovering near the table, but all I could see was a slash of white sleeve.

I had spent twenty-four years in almost constant fear of being exposed, but I had never envisaged it ending like this. Interrogation, prison, perhaps even the chair, yes. Prolonged and sadistic torture, no. But it seemed fairly clear that that was their plan. Well, I didn't have anything to complain about – I *had* betrayed them. I'd had it coming to me.

I looked up. Neon lights lit a frame of steel instruments that was suspended from the ceiling, waiting to perform whatever form of punishment Severn and his friends had thought up for me. I tried not to think about water, food or cigarettes.

'He's come to,' said a voice I didn't recognize.

There was a delay of a few seconds, and then Severn's face loomed in front of me, his eyes expressing mild concern. They turned to stone again as soon as he saw I was conscious.

'Be brave, Paul,' he said with a grim smile. 'This will hurt you more than it will me.'

He patted me on the wrist, and I clenched it out of instinct, even though I couldn't move it away. Sweat ran down my forehead as I watched a hydraulic arm descend from the ceiling: it was clutching a needle, and I had a good idea that it would contain more than a sedative this time. Here came the squeeze of the syringe. Here came the part where I spilled out every secret I had ever betrayed. And after that they would shoot me, as they had Pyotr . . .

I looked up at the ceiling and then away, clamping my jaw as the needle plunged in, desperately searching for something in the room that would take my mind away from what was happening and give it something new to focus on as the drug pulsed through me.

Yes. There it was.

The room itself. The whole thing. Like the cell they'd kept me in earlier, it was immaculate, state-of-the-art. Glistening machines hummed, and the walls were made of the same strange plastic material. The thought leapt into my mind that it must have cost a fortune. Followed by 'Yes – but whose?' The Italians surely couldn't afford such a facility alone. Had the Service helped fund it? A stretch, I'd have thought: mechanical syringes and doors that disappeared into walls. The Americans, then? All three? I had been a Head of Section for four years but had never even heard mention of such a place. But to keep something like this so secret, it had to be operating at the very highest level. What was it Severn had said earlier? Something about me getting myself into something bigger than I understood.

And what had all that been about Sarah and me? He seemed enraged by jealousy, apparently for no other reason than he'd seen her touch my arm. But he also thought she might have told me something, which was interesting because it meant she had something to tell, and that he suspected her loyalty. I thought back to the Thursday evening, on the balcony. 'Perhaps the bullet hit the wrong man.' Had she been trying to tell me something then? No, surely she had just been angered by my over-reaction to her trying to help me. Help me, yes – she had wanted me to talk to Zimotti ... But that didn't get me anywhere either, because Zimotti was in on the game. But she had said something else, in the corridor. That I had managed to find out something, or I wouldn't have been in Rome.

Perhaps she'd been trying to warn me. Perhaps she had wanted to show me something in the Station. But what? Evidence of the plan to kill me?

'What is your name?' It was Zimotti's voice.

'My name? You know my—'

A shard of agony pierced my chest, and I realized they had wired me up to some sort of electric shock machine. In my peripheral vision, I glimpsed pieces of coil dangling from the table.

'That was just a warm-up,' said Severn, as though we were playing tennis and he'd aced me on the first serve. 'I will now increase the voltage. Please answer the question.'

I hesitated for a moment and another jolt shot through me, a sheer blast of pain that made my bones shudder and my heart palpitate madly.

'Paul Dark,' I said, gasping.

'Age?'

'Forty-four.'

'Where were you born?'

'London . . .'

They were softening me up, getting me to talk about innocuous subjects so my mind would offer less resistance. They wouldn't be innocuous for long. It was the standard technique. They would have asked me all these questions before they had injected me, but I'd forgotten what answers I'd given them. The drug was already starting to take hold and I could feel my thoughts drifting away from me like pieces of an ice floe. I had at most a couple of minutes before they disintegrated completely and I lost control of my own mind, after which I wouldn't be able to stop them probing it for every last secret they wanted. But there was something wrong, and I had to find out what it was. I had to interrogate *them*.

'Bill Merriweather told me about this,' I said. 'There are several phases to it, aren't there? The first—'

'Who's Bill Merriweather?' asked Severn.

'Porton Down,' I said. 'Don't you know him? Our chap there. Flaky skin, plays golf with Chief, used to anyway.' Steer clear of Templeton – you'll be confessing to murder next. 'Met him a few times, first in '65 after I'd been made Head of Section, and I went down to see him, took Vanessa's car, not that we were involved then' – steer clear – 'but I suppose it was the beginning of something because I took her car, and I visited Bill in his office and he told me all about how it works.'

Porton Down was the Ministry of Defence's chemical laboratory, and Merriweather was the Service's chief scientist on the staff. He had told me in gruesome detail about how the North Koreans had managed to brainwash American POWs. According to Merriweather, the Americans wanted to beat the Koreans at their own game, and had a project dealing with barbiturates that could break down the mind and render any subject helpless in the arms of his captors. Merriweather wanted a larger research budget, but admitted that there were ethical concerns.

Someone had obviously overruled them.

There was also Blake, of course, whose files I'd studied. One theory was that he had become a double after the North Koreans had captured him, and in the rounds of vetting that had followed his confession there had been a lot of discussion in the office about the plausibility of brainwashing, or 'conversion', as it was known. Could it really be the case, some had wondered. Wasn't all this conversion stuff simply fantasy? Let's not beat about the bush here, chaps, Blake was just a bloody Dutch Jew *traitor*. I had asked Merriweather about Blake, and he had explained in chilling detail how they might have done it, enumerating each phase, or 'plane', in the process. The first plane was to break down the mind so you got at everything there was in it, and that, I was sure, was what they were going to try with me now. I tried desperately to remember the other planes, because Merriweather had also said that no drug was perfect. The drugs simply 'opened up' the mind, enough to let the interrogator pry into it. But if you were prepared for it to happen, or knew about it, you could counter it. So I tried to counter it now by thinking about the very process I was going through, and blocking out the part of my mind that wanted to cooperate.

'What have you used?' I said. 'Amytal?'

Severn looked at Zimotti anxiously. He didn't know Merriweather, but he knew that a subject who was aware of mind control techniques was going to be a lot harder to crack.

'You met Barchetti,' he rapped out. 'Do you remember?'

'Yes,' I said. Volunteer nothing. It's his interrogation.

'What did he tell you?'

'He was scared,' I said, unable to help myself. 'He ran away from me. I followed—'

'What did he say to you?'

The voice was firmer, urgent, and it rang alarm bells. Why did they want to know this? Instinct warned me not to tell them.

'He didn't say anything. He didn't get the chance.'

There was silence, and then I thought I heard a fluttering sound far off in the distance: a helicopter in flight? There was suddenly fierce whispering between Severn and Zimotti. I couldn't make out what they were saying, but I knew what was wrong now. They were going about this all the wrong way. They were asking *the wrong questions*. I had been a double agent for over twenty years, but they hadn't shown the faintest interest in any of the secrets I'd revealed in that time. They didn't want a confession. Instead they were asking me about Barchetti, and what he had told me. That suggested that something was still running, that they were in the midst of some kind of operation. So the sniper in St Paul's was not the whole picture, just part of it – part of something wider. The wave of attacks Innes had mentioned back in London? Only Arte come Terrore hadn't been responsible for Farraday's death in the first place, *they* had, so why would—

Christ.

The bombs in Milan: the Fiat stand and the other one. They hadn't been Arte come Terrore either, of course. Zimotti's lot had been responsible, and they had framed Arte come Terrore and others for it, just as the Service had done with Farraday's death. It was part and parcel of the same thing, a continuation of the shenanigans Osborne had been up to in Nigeria.

Italy had the largest Communist party in Western Europe: what better way to keep them out of power here than by carrying out attacks on civilians and blaming them on Red groups? The Communists' support at the ballot box would plummet, and any security measures Zimotti and his cadre wanted to introduce to counter the threat would be welcomed with open arms.

So there *was* a plan for a campaign of attacks: a campaign to be committed by Italian military intelligence. And the Service was providing the support – with American help, perhaps? As Deputy Chief, presumably they would have considered indoctrinating me into the operation, to stop me asking too many awkward questions if I came across material that didn't make sense. But in the end they had decided they couldn't trust me at all, and that I was better off dead. Better off, in fact, as another rung *in* the plan. Kill me and blame it on the Communists – perfect. Only they had missed.

And now? Now they wanted to know whether Barchetti had told me about any of this – but why were they so desperate? There could only be one reason, I realized: another attack was imminent.

I turned my focus back to Severn and Zimotti. I guessed they had tried to find out from Pyotr if he knew anything about the plan. Perhaps they hadn't been successful, but they had shot him just in case. Now all they wanted from me – apart from the personal satisfaction of tearing me limb from limb – was to discover whether Barchetti had unwittingly revealed the conspiracy to me, and whether or not I had told anyone else about it. Well, perhaps I should just tell them he had. What difference did it make either way? I couldn't stop whatever it was they were planning, for the simple reason that I didn't know what it was. But no – if I revealed I knew about the plan, they would kill me. The other night in the embassy Sarah had told me I was brave, that not many people would have risked their own skins chasing down a sniper. But, of course, the only reason I had chased him was to save my own skin. All I cared about was saving my own skin.

There was a noise and I looked up at Severn. I suddenly noticed another figure standing behind him. He was wearing flannel trousers and a dickie bow, and he looked very angry.

'Hello, Paul,' he said. 'Thought you could kill me, did you?'

It was Colin Templeton.

Ignore. It was a hallucination caused by the drugs, that was all: mental pictures fished from the parieto-occipital region of the brain, my visual mechanisms out of control, creating scenes that the subconscious had been avoiding, that the core of my psyche was terrified of confronting. Pink elephants occurring to a man terrified of elephants, a man in the pink . . .

I was entering Plane Three now – thoughts disrupted, difficulty in forming new thoughts. This was their access area, their point of penetration. But Plane Three only lasts a few minutes. It can be prolonged with further injections – how many had they given me, I wondered – but not for very long. I had to get through the next few minutes without giving away that I was on to them. I had to pretend to be . . . what? Well, they knew I was a double. Tell them about that, then. Bore them with it.

'I was recruited in 1945,' I announced. 'By a woman called Anna Maleva. She was a nurse at the Red Cross hospital in—'

'We know about all that,' snapped Severn. 'We want to know about more recent events. Why did you meet with this man Valougny?'

'That was his idea,' I said, unable to stop myself from blurting it out. 'He met me.' Change the subject. You're a double agent. Bore them. 'He's the local control, you see. Sasha couldn't make it in London. He didn't answer the call, nobody answered the—'

'What did Valougny want from you?'

'He wanted me to kill Barchetti.'

'Why?'

They didn't even care. Didn't care that I'd killed one of their own.

'Because . . .'

'Yes?'

Think.

'Because Barchetti knew about him.'

'What do you mean? That he had blown his cover?'

'Yes. Exactly. Pyotr – that's his name, or the name he gave me anyway – was worried, because Barchetti had discovered his identity and he was sure he was compromised, so he needed him killed. I told him you were due to meet him and he ordered me to go instead, said it was the perfect opportunity.'

Silence again. Then more whispering. The prick of a needle. And darkness.

*

I came back to consciousness to discover I was being dragged by my feet. I lifted my head as much as I could, as my back scraped against the floor. The man carrying me was panting and grunting, and I could hear shouting in guttural Italian. Above me swung a never-ending stream of lights, and I realized I was being dragged down a long corridor. Finally there was the jangling of keys, the clicking of a lock, and I was plunged into darkness again.

'*Bene*,' I heard a voice say. 'Leave him there.'

My body fell, bones crunching as my spine hit the floor.

I opened my eyes. My vision was still somewhat blurry, but I could see a fierce-looking brown face with a beak for a nose and bloodshot eyes. He was deeply tanned all over, like polished mahogany, and his eyes were sharp little pellets in his skull. Zimotti's chief enforcer and chair-carrier. Behind him was Barnes, gripping a brutish-looking sub-machine gun. They talked between themselves for a few moments, but too low for me to hear, and then they went out, leaving me in my private world of pain.

I managed to sit up, and touched the back of my head: it was sticky with blood. I was dizzy from hunger and thirst, although it was still the craving for tobacco that hovered utmost in my mind. I knew if I even thought about any of that I would go mad, so I rocked back and forth on my haunches, whimpering lines from a hymn I'd sung at Templeton's service:

> O still, small voice of calm.
> O still, small voice of calm . . .

My vision gradually began to clear, and I looked around. It looked very similar to the first cell, only the dimensions seemed slightly different: a little squarer. There was a pile of grey matter in one corner of the room, and I crawled towards it frantically, hoping it might be food or drink. But as I got closer, I saw with horror that it was a body, laid out like a corpse. At first I thought it might be Pyotr, but then I saw a curl of blonde hair, and realized it was her.

XIII

'Sarah,' I whispered.

No response.

I lifted myself onto my elbows and slowly crawled nearer, willing the pain in my neck and spine away. Her nostrils flared as the breath came in and out: she was alive, but either in a deep sleep or unconscious. She was wearing the same clothes I'd last seen her in, back at Pyotr's flat, only they were now torn and spotted with blood. Her skin was yellowish, and mottled and dark under her eyes. Finally, I saw the deep welts that criss-crossed her shoulders and neck. He had used the cat on her, too. A wave of revulsion swept over me, which swiftly turned to a cold rage. He had tortured his own wife.

I retreated slowly to the nearest corner to gather my thoughts. I wondered how many Severn and Zimotti would kill to get their way. Hundreds? Thousands? The goal would be a dictatorship, with Zimotti either the head of it or part of the leadership. It would be a coup, effectively, albeit a gradual and undeclared one. Italy had seen coups before, of course, but nothing like this. After a few large-scale attacks and swift arrests, Zimotti and his men would be able to introduce whatever measures they felt necessary, while a pliant and terrified public would greet them with open arms. And the British were apparently lending a hand, through their man in Rome. It seemed extraordinary, but I realized that I hadn't been paying close enough attention. There was a very powerful right-wing faction operating within the Service. Perhaps more of a movement than a faction. They had tried to take control of the government but failed — because of me. Perhaps they were planning a similar series of attacks in England, blaming everything on the First of May or similar groups. Perhaps Italy was just the beginning . . .

Something in me turned. This wasn't where my life should end. I hadn't *helped*. I had spent it trying to divine the difference between causes, but I hadn't seen the forest for the trees. East and West, I now knew, were just two frightened children spurring each other on to greater and greater acts of excess. But I was no better, standing on the edge of the field pointing out their mistakes. I had to get onto the pitch, into the game. I had to put aside all my cynicism and stupid bloody English pride and admit that there were choices here, and that I could make a difference to the situation. Where was the shame in that? Why was I so afraid of it? Here was the opportunity: a chance to save others, and atone for all the men I'd betrayed.

No. That was still selfish thinking. I glanced across at Sarah, her chest rising and falling. I wondered what she would think were she to know who I really was. Utter contempt, I was sure.

Nothing could wash the blood from my hands or atone for those I had betrayed – for Colin Templeton, or Vanessa, or Isabelle. But I could save others from their fate, and stop a gang of power-hungry men taking this country over, simply because *it was the right thing to do.*

Moscow hadn't tried to kill me, after all – but they would now. I had deliberately exposed one of their men and got him tortured and, it appeared, killed as a result. Even if they were prepared to let that go and still wanted to use me, I didn't want them any more, and they no longer had anything to blackmail me with: the Service knew who I was now. I realized that I had become unmoored from both sides and no longer had anyone to blame for my actions but myself – that I was, finally, living up to my codename: independent, a free agent. But what to do with that new-found freedom? Run to ground? Or fight back – and create my own side? I had to, or I was lost forever.

I shook my head suddenly: the only thing that was unmoored was my mind. I wasn't free at all, and had no way of creating any *side*. I was not only imprisoned, but hours or perhaps minutes from death. The guards would return soon, and for the last time.

I looked across at Sarah again, and wondered why had they put me in here with her. On the face of it, it was a weak move, as we could conspire together, perhaps even help each other escape. On the face of it. In reality, of course, we were in a secured cell inside a military base that was doubtlessly manned by hundreds of soldiers; she was unconscious; and I was nearing the point of physical and mental collapse. There was no bucket or bed or food or anything else in this room, so it looked like they were only planning to hold us here for a short while before killing us. Severn had thrown me in here with her because it no longer mattered to him if she knew of his plans, or that she might tell me them. He had discarded us both.

So how would they end it, then? A bullet to the head, like Pyotr? That might well be the plan. But where had Severn and Zimotti disappeared to in the meantime? Perhaps they had left to oversee the next stage in their grand scheme, the next attack. Or perhaps it was now the middle of the night, and they were simply catching up on their sleep before returning for some more games in the morning. Yes, a bullet to the head would be too easy. They would have a slow and painful death in mind for me . . .

Perhaps it was the awareness that I hadn't long to live, or perhaps my nascent conscience, but my mind latched on to the idea that they had disappeared to execute the next attack, and refused to let it go. Hypothetically speaking, it asked, if you *were* somehow able to escape, how could you help, how could you stop them? What would the man you might have been do? What would the man Colin Templeton had believed you were do? Well, perhaps he'd try to get in touch with London, reach Haggard and tell him what was happening. No, I realized at once, that would be pointless. I was an exposed double agent. Haggard would never believe me. Yes, but exposed in what way? The only proof they had of my treachery depended on their admitting that they had murdered Farraday. A chink of understanding opened in my mind. Was that why they needed a confession from me – to block any remaining chance I could expose them? Was that why I was here, and not in London? They could extract a confession, then see that I didn't live much beyond it. And sort out the paperwork later.

Perhaps. But my confession hadn't seemed paramount. Regardless, I didn't trust taking this to Haggard, or anyone else. I would have to find out what they were planning and address it myself.

I stopped, and glanced at Sarah once again. I thought of her walking down the corridor, her hips swinging in front of me, asking if I wanted to see the Station. She must have wanted to take me there for a reason. Could it be that she knew what they were planning?

I crawled over to her and stared at her face, pale and gaunt from the stress and fear. I felt her pulse. She was sleeping, not unconscious. She needed her rest. I shouldn't wake her.

But somewhere outside these walls, a bomb might be ticking down.

I shook her shoulder gently, and her eyes opened. The moment she saw me she started sobbing.

*

It took some time for her to stop, but when she did it was almost frightening how calm she was, as if utterly detached from the world. I left her alone, fearing the worst, but eventually she called out to me. 'I think we need to talk,' she said, and I couldn't help smiling at the matter-of-factness of it.

At first I insisted we only communicate in whispers. I was afraid that the whole thing might be some sort of a set-up so Severn could learn what it was she knew – the place was almost certainly bugged. But it soon became clear she had told him everything already. She didn't say what he had done to extract the information, and I didn't ask, but we both knew we had been left here to die, and therefore had nothing to lose from telling each other all we knew. Her voice was hoarse, as was mine, and we spoke quickly and frantically, uncertain how long we had before Barnes and his friend returned.

It transpired that Severn had used her as a courier, giving her packages to deliver to dead drops around Rome. She told me how she had gone about the job quite happily, not thinking too much about what it might mean – until the bombs had started going off.

'In Milan?' I asked.

'No,' she said, 'this was earlier than that. They were smaller scale. Charles had been frantic and nervous enough already, but now he was at fever pitch. I noticed one morning that he was reading the newspaper very intently over breakfast, and then rushed off to use the telephone. I looked at the page he'd been reading: it was about a bomb somewhere in the north of the country. A few people had been killed, and the thing had been blamed on some Marxist group. Bits and pieces of conversations I'd overheard suddenly seemed to make sense. The next time he asked me to do one of his late-night deliveries, to a churchyard in the south of the city, I opened the package.'

'What made you do that?'

'Well, he'd insisted so much that I never open any of them, and I was worried that they might have something to do with these bombs going off. I thought he might be involved in something . . . outside the remit of the embassy.'

'Working for someone else, you mean?'

She held my gaze for a moment. 'Yes.'

I considered this. 'All right, so you opened the package. What was in it?'

'Codes,' she said. 'Lots of documents in code: one-time pad stuff. I panicked because I couldn't find a way to reseal it so it didn't look like it had been opened. But eventually I did, and I thought the chap who picked up the message wouldn't notice. But he did, and he told Charles about it, and Charles went completely mad. He screamed at me, asking me dozens and dozens of questions until I just broke down and told him I'd been curious but hadn't understood any of it. That seemed to calm him down a bit. He made me promise never to mention any of it to anyone else or he'd . . .' She grimaced. ' . . . or he'd kill me.'

I tried not to think about what sort of marriage they had had, and what had happened to her in this cell. I asked her to carry on.

'Well, he never mentioned the packages again after that, and I tried to put the whole thing out of my mind. But then the message came through that you were being sent over from London, and Charles seemed to panic a little. Towards the end of Thursday afternoon I found myself alone in the Station: Cornell-Smith and Miller had gone home to get ready for dinner in the embassy, and Charles had left to collect you from the airport. Last year, he gave me the combination to his safe as a contingency — if anything ever happens to him, I'm to take everything out and burn it. So I went into his office and opened it. I just had to know what was going on. After looking through several dossiers, I found some one-time pads and documents that contained photographs of some of the drops I'd been sent to. And there were numbers — lots of them. Dates. I recognized them.'

'The dates when the bombs had exploded?'

'Yes. But the thing that really scared me was that some of the documents I saw had been stamped with Service seals. Charles isn't working for anyone else: it's an officially sanctioned operation, codenamed "Stay Behind".'

I stared at her, and let the silence envelop me for a moment. A chill crept through my bones.

Stay Behind. Was it possible?

Yes, I thought. Of course it was . . .

XIV

Saturday, 16 June 1951, Istanbul, Turkey

'Breakfast in Europe and lunch in Asia!' cried the ambassador's wife as the motorboat drew up to the landing-stage. 'I shall never get used to the decadence.'

'We do our best,' smiled Joan Templeton, stretching out an arm to help her ashore. She alighted with an unladylike squeal, but swiftly recovered and handed small bouquets of wild flowers to Joan and her daughter, Vanessa. The ambassador made the leap unaided, then turned back and muttered instructions to the crew, half a dozen young men in starched white shirts and matching pantaloons. They swiftly removed the Union Jack from its position by the wheel, folded it away, and seated themselves cross-legged on the cushions on deck – I guessed they would wait here until required for the return journey.

On land, everyone greeted one another with polite pecks on the cheek, and the ambassador asked Vanessa how she was enjoying her final year at Badminton. His wife, meanwhile, had caught sight of me standing to the side and immediately leapt over.

'I was *so* sorry to hear about your mother,' she said, taking my hands in hers and clutching them urgently.

'It was perhaps for the best,' I told her. 'She had suffered long enough.'

She tilted her head and gazed at me for a long moment, her eyes large and liquid with sympathy. I gave a tight smile in return: I knew this was one of many such exchanges I could expect to face in coming weeks. While we spooks were housed in the city's Consulate-General – the old embassy, a magnificent nineteenth-century *palazzo* – the regular diplomatic corps were based out in Ankara, an arrangement that suited us rather well. But in summer they descended on Istanbul, their arrival presaged by a flurry of thick crested invitation cards embossed with gold type. My usual existence, in which I saw less than a dozen colleagues regularly, was about to be overturned with two months of cocktail parties and picnics.

Today was the opening of the season, the Templetons' annual lunch party, which one had to take a ferry to reach as they lived in Beylerbeyi, a pleasant suburb on the Asiatic side of the Bosphorus. Like many others out here, the ambassador and his wife had known my parents in Cairo. I had spent much of the previous summer, my first in the city, fielding anxious enquiries over Father's disappearance at the end of the war and my mother's continuing ill health. But with Mother's death a couple of months earlier I had become an orphan, so I was braced for an even higher pitch of concern.

Had she known the truth about my parents, the ambassador's wife would probably have recoiled in horror. My mother had hailed from an old Swedish family that had settled in Finland in the nineteenth century. Father had been introduced to her at a ball in Helsinki in 1923 when she was just nineteen, and they had married soon after and moved to Egypt, where Father had been Head of Station. I had been born in London a couple of years later – I was to be their only child.

Shortly after my birth, it had become clear that beneath Mother's poised exterior lurked serious problems. She suffered from continual headaches, and became increasingly demanding, rude and, eventually, hysterical. Her father had been killed in the civil war by the Red Guards, and as a result she harboured a deep hatred of the Soviet Union. She was also virulently anti-Semitic, and would often refer to Jews in public as 'vermin'.

All this proved to be highly embarrassing for Father, whose career in the Service was flourishing. In 1936, he was posted back to head office in London. As the Nazis in Germany became more powerful, he had advocated closer ties with them, becoming one of the leading lights of the Anglo-German Fellowship. He was also an admirer of fascism – he was briefly Treasurer of the Nordic League – and argued strongly in favour of appeasement. However, he had swiftly abandoned this line once it had become clear that war was inevitable, and following the Molotov–Ribbentrop pact he had publicly cut all ties with fascist groups and become staunchly anti-Nazi as well as anti-Communist. But Mother's 'condition', as everyone had started to call it, was much harder to disguise.

Things had come to a head in early September 1939, when she had announced at a party in Belgravia attended by several government ministers that Hitler was the strongest leader Europe had seen in generations and that he was fully justified in his persecution of the Jews, who, she had added for good measure, were also natural enemies of England. Father had been advised by friends in the War Office that she was a liability, and that if nothing were done the three of us could be interned. As a result, he had had her shipped off to Finland, where she was cared for by private doctors at a remote estate. I came home from school to be told that Mother was ill, and that it might be some time before I saw her again. In the event, it wouldn't be for another five years.

In late 1941 Britain had declared war on Finland, and Father had had her shifted again, this time to a clinic in Stockholm. I had visited her there briefly early in 1945, but she hadn't even recognized me: either madness or medication had frozen her mind. She had remained in the clinic after the war, and had finally passed away after a series of strokes in April. Her funeral had been a quiet affair near her family's home in Helsinki. I had attended and spent a few days there, and then flown straight back to Istanbul.

The ambassador's wife let go of my hand, and Joan Templeton led us beneath some parasol pines and into the house. We walked through the cool shade of the living room and out to the sunlit garden, where several cane chairs were arranged beside a table laden with salads, cold cuts and a large dish of pigeon with rice.

'Colin's just upstairs with some guests,' Joan said. 'Colleagues from London. He'll be down shortly, I'm sure. Can I get you both a drink? Colin made some of his punch.'

'That sounds just the ticket,' said the ambassador, and his wife nodded her approval from beneath the brim of her hat. Joan headed towards the table to fix the drinks and everyone seated themselves. Vanessa settled into the chair next to mine and gave me a mischievous grin. She was seventeen now, and had blossomed into a classic English rose. She was lively company, but my thoughts were still entirely consumed by another woman: Anna, the nurse who had treated me in Germany six years earlier, whom I had loved and had planned to marry – and whom my own father had murdered before turning the gun on himself.

Anna had been a Russian, and over the course of our love affair had tried to convert me to Communism. She had come within a hair's breadth of doing so, but her revelation that she was an NKVD agent and allegation that Father was using me to execute Soviets rather than Nazi war criminals had been more than I could accept. I had coldly rejected her, and immediately delivered a message to Father denouncing her as a spy. Her subsequent death at his hands had overturned my mind: as well as the devastation of the loss, it had seemed to confirm everything she had claimed, and I had been plunged into shock, grief and rage. The rage had soon won out, however, and it had been directed not just at Father, but at all he represented. The thought of Anna's body laid out on the stretcher in the hospital, her skin already turning grey, tormented me. And so, as I had buried Father in the garden of the farmhouse in Lübeck, I had vowed to take my vengeance, by adopting Anna's cause as my own.

She had told me that her handler was based in the Displaced Persons' camp at Burgdorf, so I had taken Father's jeep and driven there. It had started snowing, huge flakes of the stuff, and by the time I arrived at the camp there was a blanket of it across the landscape. I presented the papers identifying myself as a member of an SAS War Crimes Investigations Unit and said I wished to interview residents of the camp as part of my team's enquiries. My uniform was a mess, but I had placed Father's leather jerkin over it, and after I had filled in a couple of forms, they had let me through with the advice to tread very carefully: several former SS officers had recently been discovered in the camp and nerves were particularly taut as a result.

I had walked around the main area for several hours showing the one photograph I had of Anna. Most people had clammed up as soon as I approached, but eventually someone recognized her and told me she had been an occasional visitor of Yuri, a Ukrainian doctor whose room was on the second floor of the old barracks. I made my way there and knocked on the door. After a few seconds, it was opened by a thin man wearing a greatcoat over a pair of pyjamas.

'Yes?' he said, peering at me. His face was cracked and leathery, as though he had spent most of his life outdoors, and he had tiny eyes, like sparks in a furnace. A snubbed nose gave him a faintly childlike appearance, but his hair was greying at the temples and I put him in his mid to late forties.

'I believe we have a mutual acquaintance,' I said.

He looked me over uncertainly, but then something registered in the eyes and I guessed he had recognized me from my file. He turned to speak to someone in the room, and a few seconds later a small figure scurried past me: a girl, fourteen or fifteen years old, wearing a thin nightgown. She looked up at me for a moment with startled eyes, then wrapped the gown tightly around her waist and disappeared into the corridor.

'My daughter,' said Yuri, his voice raspy. 'I do not like to discuss my work in front of her.'

He opened the door wider and I stepped inside. The room was sparsely furnished: an iron bedstead with a dirty mattress, a couple of wooden chairs, and clothes and books laid out on the floor. But he and his daughter had a room to themselves, which meant he was a very powerful person in the camp. I had seen rooms elsewhere that had been home to two and even three families. Presumably he was using his medical skills to gain favours and influence – and to seek out potential agents.

'Anna should not have told you about me,' he said, locking the door. 'Why have you come here?'

'Anna is dead.' At first I wasn't sure if he had heard me, but then he visibly crumpled, his body hunching over and his breathing coming in gasps. I made to approach him, but he held a hand up until he had recovered. When he looked up at me again, his eyes were wet with tears.

'It cannot be,' he whispered. 'Not my Anna.'

'Was she also your daughter?' I asked, suddenly shocked at the thought.

He shook his head slowly. 'But she could have been.'

He asked me what had happened and I told him, leaving nothing out. He listened very carefully, occasionally interjecting with questions to clarify a detail. When I had finished, he walked over to one of the chairs and perched himself on it.

'Thank you for telling me this,' he said. 'Anna was one of my finest agents, but she is not the first to have been murdered by the British.' He looked up at me sharply. 'Can you believe that earlier this year your country and mine were allies? Now one would almost think we are at war.'

'I know. There were even rumours after the ceasefire that we would join forces with the Germans and take up arms against you.'

His eyes widened a fraction.

'Why have you come here?' he said.

I had rehearsed a speech in the jeep, but suddenly I wasn't so certain of my convictions. I shut my eyes. The image of Anna in the stretcher swam back into my mind, and I forced myself to imagine Father squeezing the trigger, the bullet entering her . . .

'I want to work for you,' I said.

He stood up. 'And yet you did not when Anna was alive?' he said, a touch of anger in his voice. Perhaps realizing this, he stepped forward and placed a hand on my shoulder. 'I am sorry, but revenge is not a good motivation. It burns out too quickly. It does not persist. And I need people with persistence. With *ideals*.'

'I have ideals,' I said. 'You're right, I didn't want to do it when Anna was alive. But I didn't understand the situation, not fully. I . . . I'm afraid I didn't believe what she told me.' I stared into his face, at the curious snubbed nose and the glinting eyes.

'But you do now?'

I nodded, willing myself not to cry in front of him. 'Please,' I said. 'Have some faith in me. I am ready to serve . . .' But even then, even in that moment, I had been about to say 'Anna', not 'Communism' or 'the Soviet Union'.

Yuri paced around the room for a few minutes, his hands steepled together at his lips as he considered my proposal.

'I want to make sure we are very clear about this before we proceed any further,' he said, after a while. 'I need to be certain that you understand the consequences of what you are suggesting. There is no return from this point. Once you have committed to us, we will become your home. Your family.'

I thought of the family I had been born into: Father a murderer, Mother on the brink of insanity. And I thought of Anna, and the family we might have had together had she lived.

'I am committed,' I said.

Yuri looked at me for a long while. I held his gaze. 'You must go to London at once,' he said finally, and his voice had taken on a quiet hardness. 'Nobody must ever know you have been in Germany. You will be contacted shortly.'

I was filled with conflicting emotions: elation that he had agreed to take me on, disappointment and puzzlement that it wasn't to be at once. 'How will you know where to find me?'

'Don't worry,' he said. 'We will.' He walked over to the bed and picked a book from a pile leaning against it. I was surprised to see that it was a selection of poems by W. H. Auden. He opened it and read out one of the lines, then looked across at me. 'That will be your signal.'

It didn't seem as if there were anything else to say, so I had shaken his hand and left him. My frustration at his request for me to wait was tempered by the knowledge that I had now set out on the path Anna had wanted for me. I returned to London as instructed, and told everyone I had been visiting my mother in Sweden. A few people asked about Father, and I replied that I hadn't seen him in over a year. The story soon went around that he had disappeared just after the ceasefire – nobody knew where, or what had happened to him, but as time went by most presumed he had been killed. Eventually, I cleared out his things in Chelsea Cloisters and moved in there myself.

I had expected to find another job fairly easily, but it proved harder than I'd anticipated. This was perhaps partly because I felt very uncomfortable being back in England. After three years in foreign fields, the entire country now seemed to me an ugly braggart: delighted with itself for winning the war, but ignorant of the fact that without the Soviets and the Americans it would never have happened. I hated the glorying in victory, especially as I had seen the terrible state Germany had been left in.

I was a fish out of water in other ways, too. After joining the war late because of my age I had, almost as though making up for lost time, taken part in operations under the auspices of several organizations: the SAS, SOE and a few other irregular units. But all of them had either been disbanded or were about to be, and I wasn't sure I was cut out for the Service: I was a field agent, and most of the Service chaps I knew were desk men.

I nevertheless applied for a job in the Soviet Section, which was expanding almost by the day. Unbeknownst to me, it was headed up by one of Father's oldest friends, Colin Templeton. I was given the position, and started work at Broadway Buildings in early February, 1946.

The Section's entire focus was on obtaining up-to-date information about the Soviet Union: its scientific expertise, intelligence structures and, of course, military plans. Many were convinced that Stalin intended to invade Western Europe. As reliable information was extremely scant, real war crimes investigators in Germany, Austria and elsewhere were being thwarted: many of the senior Nazis they apprehended were swiftly judged by London to be crucial counter-espionage assets, and were exfiltrated, given new names, and pumped for everything they had. But the more I heard about the supposed Soviet threat, the more determined I became to counter it from within – and the more anxious I became about the fact that I had not yet been contacted.

Just as I was starting to wonder if Yuri had simply given me the brush-off, it happened. I was walking down Thurloe Street when I felt something graze my shoulder. Whirling around, I caught sight of a slim man in a grey herringbone coat heading in the opposite direction. As he walked away I felt my pockets, but to my surprise found that something had been added to them rather than subtracted. It was a small visiting card for a café a few streets away. And on the back of it, someone had written in pencil: '*It is later than you think. Saturday. 11.00.*'

The line of poetry seemed more ominous now than when Yuri had recited it to me a couple of months earlier. Perhaps as a result, I left the flat at eight o'clock that Saturday morning. The café was within walking distance, but instead I took a succession of buses all over town, repeatedly checking my watch. I had arrived, flustered but certain I had not been tailed, just before eleven, and waited for my contact to arrive. When he did, I realized it was the man in the herringbone coat. He shook me by the hand as though he had known me for a very long time, removed his coat, and ordered a pot of tea.

This was Georgi. He was in his mid-thirties, intelligent, cultured and charming. He had worked in France and Belgium, where he had been responsible for rooting out information about the Nazis' troop movements. We got on immediately, and over the next few months met regularly in locations around South Kensington. I once asked him if it wasn't unwise to meet so close to where I lived, and he had told me that it was by far the safest option: it would be easier to explain my presence if I happened to meet anyone, and the police were less vigilant because it was a genteel neighbourhood with few immigrants. As an additional precaution, we opened every meeting by establishing the cover story for it in the event of any interruption: most of the time he was a Finnish aristocrat who had known my mother in Helsinki. But we never had to use any of the cover stories we prepared: nobody paid us the least attention. We would sit in a corner and play chess or backgammon – he was rather good at both – and he would quietly question me about my work at the office. At that stage there was very little to report, and I had the feeling he already knew everything I told him anyway and was simply testing how much I would reveal to him, and how clearly I could relay information.

At our fourth meeting, Georgi announced that he would cut contact with me for six months, barring emergencies, in which case I was to leave him a message at a dead drop in a cemetery in Southgate. I had immediately feared that I had done something wrong, but he assured me that this was a positive sign, and that it meant that Moscow now trusted me enough to leave me to advance my career without having to watch over my every step.

'Bide your time,' he said. 'Go about your work efficiently, and when we meet again you will have more to tell me.' As I had watched the back of his coat disappear through the door of the café, I had felt strangely abandoned.

But I had followed his instructions. I had continued with my work in Soviet Section, and slowly but surely was given more responsibilities. Colin Templeton now often invited me to his home, where I met his family. The six months crept by, and then it was time to meet with Georgi once more. He asked about my work, and seemed pleased with my answers. Once again, I didn't feel I was telling him anything he did not know, but was happy I was finally of some use.

My meetings with Georgi continued in this way until late 1949, when Colin Templeton called me into his office and told me he was being posted to Istanbul as Head of Station, and that he would like me to come along as part of his team. I accepted at once, and left a message for Georgi in the cemetery in Southgate telling him the news. There had been no time for another meeting, as I was due to head out to Turkey immediately.

After nearly four years behind a desk in London I had been looking forward to heading into the field again, and Istanbul didn't disappoint. The city had been crawling with spies during the war, and it seemed little had changed since. The main concern was the Soviets, with the growing American influence a close second. Turkey had been neutral in the war, by and large, and was now cleverly playing the former combatants off against one another. Despite the plans for democratic elections, the possibility that they might turn to the Soviet Union had everyone worried, and strenuous efforts were being made to convince them to come into the new NATO structure. Britain's position was that this should happen in conjunction with it joining a separate Middle Eastern security alliance, but the Americans had other ideas. Despite Britain's efforts to persuade them otherwise, the Turks were coming to the realization that the balance of power was shifting in the world, and that the United States might be better able to provide them with long-term support.

I quickly settled into my position in the Station. I loved being away from London, with its pea-soupers and boiled beef, and immediately immersed myself in the hubbub and intrigue of the city's back alleys. After a year had passed without any contact from the Soviets, I began to panic. Perhaps Georgi had not picked up my message in Southgate, and they were unaware I had moved to Turkey? But surely he would have checked the drop.

My fears had finally been put to rest just three weeks earlier. I had been wandering around the Grand Bazaar when a small boy had placed a piece of paper in my jacket pocket and run away giggling. I had followed the address to a shop that sold antique silverware, where I had discreetly been led through to a back room. To my surprise, I found Yuri seated on a pile of silk cushions. He looked much the same as he had in Burgdorf, only his hair was a little greyer and the greatcoat and pyjamas had been replaced with a smart lounge suit.

He had wasted no time in getting to the point. There had been some commotion in Moscow: several agents in the field had been recalled to headquarters for further training. As a result, all the information I had given to date had been reviewed – and been found wanting.

'What do you mean?' I asked, reeling. 'Georgi was very pleased—'

'He was mistaken. Moscow feels you have not yet handed us anything significant.'

'But I haven't had anything significant to provide!' I said. 'Georgi told me to bide my time until I was more established.'

Yuri gave a thin smile. 'Moscow is concerned about the time and resources that have been spent on you for such little reward. Unless you can provide a higher grade of material, it is perhaps best that we discontinue our arrangement.' And with that he announced the time and location of the next meet, then stood, parted the curtains, and disappeared through them.

That next meet was now less than a week away, and I still had nothing of note to report. The simple truth was that, at twenty-six years old and with just five years in the job, I was still far too junior to be given access to any great secrets – and I couldn't see that situation changing any time soon.

I took a sip of punch and looked up at the villa, wondering again what it was that Templeton might be discussing with the 'colleagues from London'. They had arrived a couple of hours earlier, not by motorboat like the other guests, but in a scratched-up jeep they had parked in the driveway at the foot of the garden, on the Asian side. Templeton had immediately escorted them inside the house and up to his office, and they hadn't been seen since.

There had been three of them. William Osborne was one of the Service's rising stars: having spent much of the war working in the Middle East, he was now establishing a reputation as an expert in deception operations. Charles Severn, the driver of the jeep, was a new recruit to the Service whom I had known at school, and not much liked. The final member of the party had not been from London at all: the head of Turkish military intelligence, a dapper man with a marvellous moustache who, for reasons I had been unable to unearth, we called 'Cousin

Freddie'. He sometimes came by the office to meet Templeton – but what was so important that he had come to his house?

'Hello, Dark.'

I looked up to see a young man stretching out his hand. He was dressed in a dazzlingly white short-sleeved shirt and navy-blue Daks, and his fair hair was brushed back with pomade. Despite the addition of several inches in height and a short clipped moustache, he was instantly recognizable as the boy I had last seen nine years earlier.

'Severn,' I said, shaking his hand. 'It's been a while, hasn't it? Do you know everyone?'

Severn made his way around introducing himself, and Vanessa blushed as he kissed her hand.

'Is this your first visit to Istanbul?' she asked him.

'Yes,' he said, settling into a chair.

'How are you enjoying it?'

He wrinkled his nose. 'Not much. Rather a scruffy-looking place. I was expecting more, somehow.'

There was an awkward silence, and I wondered whether Templeton had sent him out of the meeting early because he was too junior to hear the rest, or because he hadn't been able to stand the sound of his voice any longer. Perhaps he was nervous. I asked him if he wanted a drink, and he looked up at me with gratitude. Yes, I decided, it must be nerves. Probably his first mission in the field – I remembered how I had felt on mine.

More guests arrived, most of them diplomats. Drink was consumed, and food eaten. Conversation turned to Korea, and the King's health, and which mosques were worth visiting. Severn told me a series of anecdotes about old boys I had no recollection of, and I did my best to feign interest. But there was still no sign of Templeton, Osborne or Cousin Freddie. They'd now been closeted away for over two hours. What on earth could they be discussing?

'Pretty girl,' said Severn. 'Is she yours?' I turned to him, and he nodded at Vanessa, who was talking to a first secretary.

'No,' I said coldly. 'She is not.'

'Sorry. Didn't mean to offend.'

I decided to change the subject. 'How's London these days – do I take it you're working for Osborne?'

Severn laughed bitterly. 'That's one word for it. The man's a positive slave-driver, and I'm the one being driven. Or rather, it's the other way round – would you believe he's dragged me halfway across the world to be his chauffeur? Wish he'd got some local sod to drive him around the desert instead.'

I suppressed a smile. 'Why didn't he?'

He placed a finger to his lips. 'Hush-hush stuff. Although no doubt Templeton's given you some of the background?'

I shook my head. 'No,' I said. 'Sorry, I didn't realize. Templeton doesn't tell me that sort of—'

'Don't pull that with me. You should have heard him in there – he couldn't stop talking about you. You're his boy. Stay close to him, I would. Only reason I'm chumming up to Osborne is because I reckon he might go to the top. And his politics are sound. He says what he means, anyway.'

I made some assenting noises and went to help myself to

more punch. I couldn't work it out: was something significant going on here, or was it just the pressure from Moscow that was making me believe there might be? I found Severn's attitude mildly surprising. His family were one of the richest in England, and I had presumed the Service was simply a hobby for him. But it appeared that he was, in fact, rather ambitious, and sharp enough at least to try to judge which way the wind was blowing.

I made a note to myself to keep an eye on him, and turned to see Templeton, magisterial in a straw hat, cream linen suit and a pair of battered leather sandals, marching out of the house. Osborne and Cousin Freddie followed directly behind him. The meeting finally appeared to be over.

'Hello, everyone!' Templeton said as he approached the gathering. 'Sorry to be the absent host. Is there any punch left?'

Everyone laughed, and he kissed his wife and daughter. More introductions were made; glasses clinked; the sun beat down. A *hookah* appeared from somewhere and Templeton offered it to Cousin Freddie, who nodded in appreciation at being given his own amber mouthpiece to use. Some felt that Templeton had gone native, but I suspected that this sort of thing was simply solid tradecraft, an extension of the idea that a good agent always listens twice as much as he speaks. Cousin Freddie certainly seemed to become more talkative as he inhaled from the water-pipe, and Templeton sat cross-legged opposite him, nodding his head every once in a while.

The shape of the party shifted, with separate circles forming.

Osborne ambled over to speak to Severn, who noticeably stiffened as he approached. Osborne gave me a nod – we had met briefly during the war. He had put on a lot of weight since then, and the heat seemed to be getting to him: his hair was plastered to his forehead and his cheeks were flushed. I couldn't see his eyes, as they were hidden behind small dark glasses with gold rims.

'What's the story with the missing diplomats?' Vanessa asked him. 'Is it true they were spying for the Russians?'

I glanced across at Templeton to see whether he had heard, but he was still deeply engrossed in conversation with Cousin Freddie. Templeton tried to shield his daughter from any discussion of his work, but it had had the opposite effect: Vanessa was fascinated by the espionage world, particularly its more sensationalist aspects. She had been talking incessantly about the diplomats since they had vanished from their jobs at the Foreign Office a few weeks earlier.

She wasn't the only one. I had never met either man, but both were well known to the community here. Donald Maclean, the son of a Liberal MP, had been head of Chancery in Cairo, while everyone seemed to have a story to tell about Guy Burgess. He had been in the Service before the war, worked for the BBC during it, and afterwards had joined the Foreign Office, eventually being posted to Washington as a second secretary. The rumour was that he and Maclean were Soviet agents who had been on the brink of being exposed by Five. Their disappearance was the talk of the town, and as a result, several diplomats within earshot turned to see how Osborne would reply to Vanessa's question. Such subjects were not generally broached in public, but if ever you were going to pick up a titbit it would be at the Templetons' party.

'It doesn't look good,' Osborne admitted *sotto voce*. 'The bad news is that Five now want to interrogate Philby about the whole affair.'

'Really?' said Vanessa, placing her hand over her mouth. There was an almost audible intake of breath from people seated nearby. Kim Philby had been Head of Station here before Templeton, leaving for Washington in '49. We were sitting less than a mile from his old house: he had been the first from the office to live out in this neighbourhood, and several others had followed suit, the Templetons included. I knew Philby and Burgess had been friends: the regulars at the Moda Yacht Club still hadn't forgiven either man for the time they had become royally drunk in the bar on one of Burgess' visits out here. But that hardly seemed enough to hang him for.

'They don't seriously suspect him?' I asked.

Osborne removed a handkerchief from his jacket and wiped the back of his neck with it. 'Apparently, yes. They claim he's the only person who was in contact with Burgess and also knew Maclean was under suspicion. But the whole thing's absurd. Everyone's blaming everyone else, and it looks like Five want to blame us.'

'I heard they were queer,' said Severn, who was now on his fifth glass of punch by my count. 'Part of the Homintern.' He gave a braying laugh, and Osborne glared at him. 'Well,' Severn trailed off, 'they're snakes in the grass anyway.'

'We once had a snake in our garden in Cairo,' said Joan Templeton brightly, and polite titters rippled around the chairs. 'No, really, we did! What was it, Vanessa — a cobra?'

'No, Mummy, it was an adder! And the snake-charmer brought it there especially, remember?'

The conversation moved on. People began reminiscing about the embassy ball in '47, when the Fleet had visited, while Severn continued to knock back the punch and Osborne turned more and more scarlet. The heat was starting to get to me, too, and I excused myself to stretch my legs.

I wandered through the house and back to the landing-stage. The boat crew were busy chatting to one another, and looked up at me with surprise.

'Does anyone have a cigarette?' I asked, placing my fingers to my lips.

One of them smiled and produced a packet. Although disappointed I couldn't get hold of Players in the city, I had gradually become accustomed to the taste of Turkish tobacco. As I gratefully accepted the cigarette, I pondered the conversation about Maclean and Burgess. By the sound of it, they were indeed doubles. I had occasionally wondered whether there might be others, but had been grateful I didn't know who they were any more than I imagined they knew of me, working on the well-established principle that the fewer people who were in on a secret the more likely it was to be kept. But it seemed the two men had planned their flight together, so perhaps they had been aware of each other's secret beforehand — and then there was the extraordinary possibility they might have been aided by Philby. I had nobody to confide in but Yuri, or whomever else Moscow sent to run me. Once away from a meet, I was on my own.

I chatted to the boat crew for a while, then wandered back into the house. Joan had decorated it with her customary good taste: elegant silk screens, mementoes from the family's time in Egypt and a few artfully placed carpets. I smoked my cigarette and eyed the staircase that led up to Templeton's study. I knew from the office that he often left the last thing he had been working with on his desk. Perhaps he had done the same now. Everyone was sitting outside, enjoying the party – would anyone be likely to notice if I were away for a few more minutes? I thought not. I headed towards the staircase and started walking up it.

As I reached the top, I heard raised voices – they were coming from Templeton's study. I pushed open the door and saw Templeton towering over Severn, his eyes bulging out of his head and his face flushed. He looked like he was about to hit him. He spun round on his heels at the sound of my entering, and I immediately hid my cigarette behind my back – he disapproved of smoking.

'Paul,' Templeton said, his jaw clamped together in quiet fury, 'I wonder if you would be good enough to put Charles up this evening? I fear we're a little short of room here.'

'Of . . . of course, sir,' I said, and Templeton bowed his head at me and stalked out of the room.

I stepped forward and helped Severn up – he had slipped to the floor.

'What the hell did you do?' I asked in wonder. I'd never seen Templeton lose his temper in this way.

Severn looked up at me with clouded eyes. 'Search me,' he said, slurring the words. 'I only placed my hand on her leg, I swear.'

After a decent interval, I took him by the arm and led him downstairs.

*

By the time we reached my flat in Pera, Severn's head was lolling against the side of the jeep. As I had helped him downstairs, Templeton had discreetly taken me to one side and given me the keys to the vehicle, telling me to return it to the Consulate-General transport park as soon as I was able. Then he had placed a hand on my shoulder, thanked me, and trudged back to the party. I didn't get the chance to see Vanessa before leaving to check if she was all right.

I managed to drag Severn up the stairs and hoisted him onto the couch in my tiny living room. I took his shoes off and went back down to the jeep to lock up. As I did, my eye fell on a flap of yellow material peeking out of the underside of the driver's seat. I jimmied the seat up, slid it out, and squinted at it in the glare of the afternoon sun. What on earth . . .?

It was a large-scale fold-out map of Turkey, and someone had drawn small black circles at several points on it: I counted thirty of them.

I quickly considered my options, and came to the conclusion there were two: I could either make a copy of the map and give it to Yuri at our next meeting, or I could replace it under the seat and forget I had ever seen it.

My first instinct was to copy it, of course. Here, finally, was something substantial to give Moscow. But *was* it, and if so just how substantial? I had no way of knowing. It was a strange sort of morality, perhaps, but it was mine: I was uncomfortable with the idea of handing over a secret I didn't even know myself. And there would be nothing lost if I replaced it. After all, it was only thanks to Severn getting blotto that I had seen it at all. I might just as easily not have done – and it might not be important at all.

No, it had to be important. Osborne had come out here because of this, and Severn had obviously driven him, Templeton and Cousin Freddie to some or all of the marked locations.

Perhaps, it occurred to me, there was a third option. I could find out what the map meant myself, and then decide whether it was something I felt I could pass to Yuri. I glanced down at it again. The nearest circle was positioned just outside Izmit, a town about sixty miles away – if I took the jeep, I could be there and back in a couple of hours. Severn was passed out, and everyone else was still at the party in Beylerbeyi. I had a jeep at my disposal . . .

I walked back up to the flat and into the living room. Severn was snoring now, his head tilted back. I went over to the dresser and wrote a quick note explaining that I was returning the jeep and would be back shortly. I placed it by his head, then went into the bedroom and removed a metal case from beneath a floorboard. I took out Father's Luger, which I had taken from his body in Germany six years earlier, and held it in my hand. It was heavy and cold. I placed it in my waist-band, then turned off the lights, locked up the flat and returned to the jeep.

*

Once I had crossed back over the Galata bridge, I took the road out of town, heading through a landscape of grey mosques and olive groves until I was driving along the coast, the wind blowing dust into my hair. The circle on the map was a few miles short of Izmit, and as I reached the spot I saw a wide earth track heading off the road and decided that it must be the location. I slowed to a snail's pace, checking for signs that the site might be occupied or under surveillance. There didn't seem to be any, so I slowly drove down the track, eventually coming to a dead-end at the crest of a hillock. I parked the jeep and got out to have a look.

It was late afternoon now, but the sun was still a glaring hole in the sky, and it beat down on my neck as I walked around trying to see what it was that Severn and the others had driven out here to see. I decided I had turned off too early, as there was nothing but scrub and a few beech trees. After several minutes of fruitless searching, I headed back to the jeep and started reversing back down the track to rejoin the road. It was probably just as well, I thought . . . But as I tried to angle one of the wheels, I saw something that made me hit the brakes: a tree stump.

If I hadn't been here with the map, it would never have given me pause for thought. But it was the only stump around, and it was setting off alarms in my head. I braked again and went to the back of the jeep, where there was a small bag of equipment: driving gloves, binoculars and a torch. I took the torch and walked up to the stump. Kneeling down, I placed my hands against the side of it, and pushed.

The stump lifted: it was on a hinge. I brushed away soil and leaves to reveal netting. Pulling that away, a dark hole about the width of a man appeared, and I saw a narrow wooden ladder leading down. I took a breath. There was still a chance to turn back, pretend I'd never seen the map, pretend none of it had happened. But Yuri's words came back to me: *'Unless you can provide a higher grade of material, it is perhaps best that we discontinue our arrangement.'* I reached out for the top rung of the ladder.

A few seconds later I landed in darkness. I grabbed the Luger from my waistband and turned on the torch. I was in a low tunnel. There was an opening to my left, and I crouched down and crawled through it.

The space was bigger than my bedroom in Pera. Most of it was taken up with wooden crates. I pushed aside a layer of plastic sheeting in one and shone my torch down on it: cold metal glinted up at me, and I caught a whiff of cosmoline.

I spent several minutes poking around the boxes, prying with my fingers and the torch. I found rifles, pistols, binoculars, a radio set and even commando daggers. The latter confirmed all my suspicions: this was a stay-behind base.

Early in the last war, several groups in England had been

secretly trained and provided with underground arms caches such as this, the idea being that if the Germans invaded a resistance force would already be in place ready to counter them. The concept of the Auxiliary Units, as they had been called, had expanded as the war had progressed. Instead of waiting until a country fell to the Axis powers and then dropping supplies to hastily assembled partisan groups, as had happened in France, men in several countries were discreetly approached and asked to commit to staying on as part of resistance forces in the event of invasion. In Singapore, these groups had initially been called 'left-behind parties' until someone had realized that it might not be the best name to inspire volunteers, and changed it to the rather more inspiring 'stay-behind parties'.

But why would the Service need stay-behind parties in Turkey? The answer was obvious: the threat of Soviet invasion. If there were to be another war, as many were predicting, Turkey was an obvious flashpoint – the Russians could slip over the mountains along the long border and the army wouldn't know what had hit it. Britain didn't fancy that idea, so had set up these bases as a precautionary measure. That meant that there must also be men who knew where the bases were and had been trained in guerrilla warfare – that, presumably, was where Cousin Freddie came in.

I made sure there was no sign that I had been in the cave, then clambered back up the ladder and hoisted myself out of the hole. I carefully replaced the netting, the foliage over it and the stump, then headed back to the jeep and drove off, my heart thumping in my chest.

I arrived back at the flat around dusk. I replaced the map under the driver's seat and entered the flat. Severn hadn't moved from where I had left him, and his snores had only increased in volume.

I tore up the note I'd left him, and headed for the comfort of my bed.

XV

A lot had happened since that summer eighteen years ago. Turkey had joined NATO, and the Americans had soon taken charge of the place. All three of the Templetons were dead: Joan from cancer a couple of years ago, Colin more recently by my own hand. And Vanessa, whose love I had ignored for so many years, then tried but failed to return . . . she, too, was gone.

My dreaded meet with Yuri had been a wash-out: I had waited in the chill morning mist outside the warren of the Grand Bazaar for half an hour, but he had never turned up. I had tried again the following day, then three days after that and so on according to the schedule, but he had never shown his face again. Part of me had been relieved, as the prospect of blowing the stay-behind bases had made me very uneasy: if the Soviet Union *did* invade, the entire security of Turkey might depend on them, and that was a measure of influence I wasn't sure I wanted to have. But Yuri's vanishing act had also seemed rather final: it seemed Moscow had carried out its threat, and discarded me.

I had been posted back to London in September, where I was given a hefty promotion within Soviet Section. I had occasionally checked the old dead drops, but to no avail. Finally, one freezing December evening someone brushed past me as I left a cinema, and my double life resumed once again.

My new contact, Sasha, was in his early forties, with a neat beard and a penchant for tweed suits and bow ties. He claimed not to know why Yuri had failed to show in Istanbul, but assured me that Moscow's previous concerns about me were ancient history. He pumped me with questions about my work in Soviet Section, and I answered them as fully as I could. He never asked me about Turkey, and I decided not to mention the map or the arms cache.

Our meetings continued over the next few years, although after a while they became much more infrequent for security reasons. The Templetons' garden party had given me my first indication that I might not be the only double, and that had been confirmed in '56, when Burgess and Maclean appeared at a press conference in Moscow. A string of exposures had followed: Blake in '61, Vassall in '62, and then Philby's defection in '63, which had, in turn, led to the unmasking of Blunt and Cairncross. The newspapers were filled with talk of spy rings and third and fourth men. I was as agog as anyone at the extent of Soviet penetration.

I forced my mind back into the here and now: a prison cell, presumably somewhere in Italy. Now, finally, I too had been exposed, but I had to figure out what the hell was going on and get out of here and stop it. When I had been appointed Head of Soviet Section in '65, I had been given access to a lot more files, but I had seen nothing about a stay-behind operation in Turkey, and I'd presumed that it had been wound down: the threat of Soviet invasion no longer seemed realistic. The idea that Severn and Zimotti's plans were part of the same operation suggested a much larger scale than I had feared. There had been thirty arms caches hidden across Turkey in '51. How many would there be in Italy now and, more importantly, how many men had been trained to use them? If my suspicions were right, this wasn't just a few spooks idly plotting, placing a bomb here or there: they had a highly trained army prepared to do their dirty work.

I turned to Sarah sitting next to me in the gloom of the cell, and let my mind absorb the significance of it for a moment.

'So this is what you wanted to tell me at the embassy?' I said. 'Your suspicions about Charles, the documents you found in his safe . . .' She nodded. 'But why? How could you be sure I wasn't a part of the plot?'

She took a deep breath and smiled faintly.

'Charles had already told me about what happened in St Paul's: that you had chased down the sniper, discovered that he was an Italian, and were coming out to investigate. He seemed very jumpy about you, so I asked him about your history. He told me you'd been at school together, and also about what had happened in Nigeria, and after – that you had briefly been suspected of being a double. We still had files in the office from your time here, so I read up on you – your missing father and your wonderful career and so on – and suddenly it just came to me, I suppose.'

'What did?' I asked. But I knew what she was going to say.

'Well, that you *were* a double. That you had gone out to Nigeria to stop that defector exposing you, and chased the sniper halfway across London because *you* had been the target, not John Farraday. As I read the files, it seemed that everyone around you ended up dead, but there you were still standing at the end of it all, and . . .' She looked into my eyes. 'I was right, wasn't I?'

I stared back at her. It was ironic, of course: I had fooled Templeton and Osborne and everyone else for all these years, and finally with barely a glance at my file a cipher clerk in Rome had guessed at the truth.

'Yes,' I said. 'You were right. But if you were so sure I was a double, why did you decide to confide in me?'

She raised a smile. 'It was a risk – but I reckoned a Soviet agent probably wouldn't be involved in a conspiracy to smear Communists. I thought you might have already guessed at what they were up to, in fact, and that that was why you had come out here, or that you were at least somewhere on the road to finding out. So I thought I could be . . .' She looked for the right word. 'Indiscreet. Not tell you, exactly, but just give you a nudge in the right direction. If you realized what was going on, you'd tell Moscow, and then they'd have to stop it.' She shrugged her shoulders simply. 'I'm not a Communist or anything.'

'Neither am I. I was, once, but that was a long time ago, and

I was . . .' What — young? Trapped? It was time to put my excuses away. 'And I was wrong about it,' I said.

We sat in silence for a while then. I wanted very much to tell her that everything would be better — to *make* it better for her, somehow. But there was nothing that could be done. For anything to move forward, we had to get those documents. Without them, this was all smoke and mirrors: nobody would ever believe it. Even with them it might be smoke and mirrors, because several governments would be very quick to discredit them as fakes, and it might be hard to prove otherwise. But the operational details would be in there, and if Sarah were telling the truth we were faced with the slaughter of hundreds, possibly even thousands, of innocent people.

Somewhere in the back of my mind, the seed of an idea was forming: Haggard. In Italy, the operation was designed to discredit the Communists and keep them from coming to power. But in Britain, the target seemed to be the Labour government. That meant Haggard couldn't be part of the conspiracy: he was one of its main targets. And as Home Secretary, he could act. Unmask the conspiracy to him and I had a sliver of a chance of not just stopping whatever blood-bath was being planned, but redeeming myself. My life as a double agent was over, but perhaps, if I could take on this lot and *win*, I could start afresh, in a new Service purged of the conspirators. A new life, a new page . . .

Well, it was a nice thought, but I couldn't unmask anyone without proof. And that was tightly locked up in Severn's safe in Rome. I squeezed Sarah's hand gently, and as I did I felt a hardness in her fingers. Her wedding band, no doubt. Only it was sharp. I glanced down. Her other jewellery had gone, but her engagement ring, dirty and bloodied, shone dully.

That meant two things. First, Severn had not discarded her entirely. My watch and everything in my pockets had been taken from me, so it must have been a deliberate decision to leave this on her. Despite imprisoning and torturing her, it seemed he hadn't wanted to remove this symbol of love from her body. I remembered his screams as he had brought the whip down on me: '*Nobody touches my wife.*' Secondly, it was a weapon. Not an ideal weapon, by any means, but then prisoners with no other hope of escape can't be choosers.

'I have an idea,' I said. 'Can you run?'

She nodded slowly. 'I can try.'

'What would happen if . . .?' I stopped myself. It wasn't the most gallant request I'd ever made. I tried to keep my voice even. 'What would happen if I kissed you?'

I thought for a moment she was going to slap me, but then she saw me nodding at the walls and felt me squeeze her ring finger, and understanding dawned on her.

'Charles . . . Yes, I see. But he might bring others with him.'

I held her gaze. 'What do we have to lose? They'll be here sooner or later anyway. Isn't it better if it's sooner?'

She didn't answer for a few moments, and then I thought I saw the trace of a smile cross her pale lips.

'"Was ever woman in this humour wooed?"'

My spirits lifted faintly: if she still had the wherewithal to make literary references, we might just have a chance. I took a deep breath, and she nodded. This was, I thought, quite likely suicide.

We stood and I moved closer to her, whispering in her ear to pass me the ring. She wriggled it off and I squeezed it onto my little finger. I made sure that the stone was facing outward: a very small, very expensive knuckle-duster.

We were inches away from each other now. I tried to keep my mind focused on the task ahead, and brushed a wisp of hair away from her face with my fingers. My stomach began to contract as the adrenalin began pumping through me. I leaned down and touched my lips gently against her collarbone.

'Does that hurt?' I whispered.

She shook her head. She was breathing rapidly now, whether in earnest or acting for the cameras I wasn't sure, and I brought my face up and gently pressed my mouth against hers. She didn't react at first, but then her lips parted slightly, and I felt the warm moistness of her tongue . . .

The door of the cell slammed open, and Severn rushed in, his face dark with rage and a low roar in his throat. I lunged at him, thrashing the ring against his face with every ounce of strength I had in me. Somehow I hit home, because he cried out and reeled backwards, stumbling into the wall and falling to the ground with a thick thudding noise. I stepped forward to finish the job, but he was already out for the count: his cheek was torn open and blood was gushing down it, but his mouth was lax and his head was resting on his shoulder.

I breathed out. It had worked. Against all the odds, it had worked.

But now we had to get out of here.

I quickly searched him: he was unarmed, but I grabbed the keys from his belt. Sarah picked the ring from the floor and threw it at him fiercely, then made to kick him. I pulled her away — we didn't have time. I opened the door and we came out into a long corridor, at the far end of which was a staircase.

We started running towards it.

XVI

The staircase led us out to a strip of concrete – we had been underground. The soles of my feet were already sore from the short run and my chest was still tight with tension. The light was bluish-grey and eerie, and I shivered as I breathed in the cool air. I could smell the sea close by. To our right, about a hundred yards away, were several Nissen huts and a line of low dark buildings, many with radio masts jutting from their roofs.

I turned to Sarah. 'Any idea where we are?'

'Sardinia, I think. Charles mentioned it once. A special base for political prisoners.'

Sardinia – I had spent a long weekend here with a girlfriend in the spring of '64, a lifetime ago. Zimotti had told me Arte come Terrore were based on the island. A strange sort of a bluff, but perhaps they'd intended to lure me out here all along. Perhaps torture had always been on the cards. Precisely how long had they known I was a double – and *who* knew, precisely?

To our left was a gate, surrounded on both sides by a fence, the top of which gleamed in the dim light: barbed wire. There was a small hut, no doubt for guards, but they would be more prepared for people trying to come into the base than trying to leave it – if we were fast enough. I reckoned we had a couple of minutes at most before Severn recovered and started coming after us. And, in a place like this, there was no telling how many he might bring with him.

There were several small military vehicles parked on the concrete: Volkswagens. We jumped into the nearest one and I reached under the dashboard, pushing against the panel to free it and quickly locating the two wires. I bridged them and the engine stuttered into life.

'That's a clever trick,' said Sarah, as I grabbed the wheel and headed for the main gate.

'It can come in useful,' I agreed. The engine was behind the vehicle's rear wheels and it felt very lightweight, almost like driving a dune buggy. I told Sarah to duck and then pushed my foot down and steered to the right of the gate, straight for the barbed wire fence, the engine squealing from the strain I was putting it under. There was a screech and crunching of metal and glass as the wheels trampled over the fence and crashed through to the other side, and then the shots started coming from behind us. They went wide, but they had reacted faster than I'd expected, and they wouldn't go wide for long.

I made to steer onto the main road leading out of the camp, but decided against it at the last moment. That would give them the advantage, as they would know where we were heading and could plan accordingly. So instead I yanked the wheel to the left. I glanced across at Sarah, and saw she had her fists curled up in her lap from the suddenness of the manoeuvre. 'Sorry!' I shouted, as we bumped across the ground and through a string of low shrubbery.

Glancing in the rear-view mirror, I saw that there were now several vehicles in pursuit: at least three, but there was a shroud of early morning mist so there might have been more behind them. There was a rough path through the brush straight ahead, but looking to my right I glimpsed a tiny segment of pale blue in the darkness and suddenly realized we were on a bluff overlooking water. There was our chance.

I started slowing the engine and shouted out to Sarah to jump out. She didn't hear me, so I told her again, screaming it out. She looked at me in terror, but nodded, and on the count of three I opened my door and leapt to the earth, hoping she was doing the same.

I landed badly, a stream of stones and grit cutting into my hands and face, but I was going very fast and managed to tumble my body for several yards, lessening the impact. Sarah had already got up and was scurrying over to join me: she must have had a better landing. The Volkswagen was already beginning to veer off course, but I reckoned our pursuers wouldn't realize we had bundled out for another second or two. We needed to get out of their line of fire in that time, and down into the rocks where they couldn't follow us on wheels.

The surfaces of the stones were ice-cold against the soles of my feet. I started clambering down the slope, taking care not to go too fast. My body was still aching from the beating Barnes had given me, and if I slipped and fell now I wasn't sure I'd have the strength to get up again. This was Maquis-type country, with the rocks interrupted by stiff brush, gorse and myrtle bushes. I picked out some scrub to step on, but it was spiky and I rapidly switched back to searching for stone surfaces. Sarah was just behind me and I could hear her panting with the effort.

We clawed our way down the bluff, conscious that we might be spotted at any moment. My hands were getting scratched and we were kicking up a lot of dust, which kept getting in my eyes. Above us the noise of engines died away and was replaced by the voices of men. I strained my ears to try to make out whether Severn was among them, but couldn't hear and didn't have time to linger. The further down we got before they realized which way we had gone, the harder it would be for them to find us. But they wouldn't give up easily, I knew. We had to get off the island entirely.

As we approached the bottom of the slope, the water stretched out before us in a small bay, and my heart lifted a little. I couldn't yet see any boats, but we should be able to swim far enough away to find one, or some other form of transport. But then I turned and saw Sarah staggering behind me, her chest shivering beneath the thin dress, and the panic rose in me again.

'You go!' she called out in a hoarse whisper. I shook my head and looked around desperately. The voices were still above us, but they didn't seem to have figured out which way we had gone yet. A large structure, a circular stone tower, suddenly loomed out of the mist on a plateau not more than a dozen feet away from us. My first thought was that it was another hallucination, but it looked far too real and it triggered something at the back of my mind. Yes, I had seen several of these on my previous trip. I couldn't remember what they were called, but they had been used by the island's prehistoric inhabitants, I seemed to recall, for shelter against potential invaders.

Well, we needed shelter now. If they hadn't seen which way we had come down the slope, we might just be in luck, as they would no longer have the chance to spot us and we'd also be able to catch our breath and perhaps get some strength back. There was, hopefully, simply too much ground for them to cover, and they would have to conclude eventually that we had got away from them. Then again, if they had already seen which way we'd gone, we might be making a fatal mistake by stopping, as they could simply come in and scoop us up.

I couldn't hear the voices any more, so decided to risk it. I took Sarah by the arm and we headed towards the narrow entrance of the shelter, and into a very dimly lit passageway. I remembered that these places were built from stones simply piled up on top of each other, and suddenly wondered how solid they were.

At the end of the passageway we came to a staircase, which we started to climb. The place was dank and cold, and the only light filtered through a few tiny windows. About halfway up I heard a faint buzzing in the background, which grew to a drone.

A helicopter was coming our way.

I looked through one of the windows. It was a camouflaged Sea King, or an Italian version of it. I turned to Sarah, who had started shaking, her breaths coming out in sobs.

'It's all right,' I whispered. 'We'll be all right.'

But the obvious lie made her even more nervous and she started making more noise. I looked through a slat again – the helicopter had started to descend, and was now hovering a hundred feet or so away, like a giant and sinister wasp.

I took Sarah in my arms, letting her bury her head in my chest, stifling her sounds. 'You must be quiet,' I said, and held her as firmly as I could, willing her to stop shaking. The sweat was pouring off me now, and I prayed that the helicopter would leave. We stayed in that position for what seemed like an eternity, but then Sarah suddenly looked up from my chest. There had been a noise down-stairs.

Someone had come in.

*

We sat, huddled, hardly daring to breathe, and listened to the footsteps below us. I realized we were on a level circling the exterior of the structure. It might take them a little while to figure that out, too, so perhaps once they started climbing we could cross to the other side, take the stairs back down and slip out. Only . . . I glanced through the slat again: the heli-copter was still there, and would no doubt be equipped with machine-guns. Our only hope, then, was that they wouldn't realize we were in here, and would leave to check somewhere else. But the footsteps sounded very sure, and were moving closer to us by the moment.

I gestured at Sarah and we started moving away from the sound, to the other side of the floor. But we must have dislodged something as we ran, either a stone or some dust, because there was suddenly a shout from below, and when I next looked up, Barnes was standing in front of me with a machine-pistol in his hands and a murderous look in his eyes.

We raised our hands, and he gestured to the staircase with the weapon.

'Down.'

*

The helicopter was hovering several feet above the ground, flattening the surrounding shrubbery and kicking up eddies of dust. In the cockpit, headphones over his ears, sat the beak-nosed guard, while standing a few feet in front of it was Severn, his fair hair swept back by the wind from the blades and his eyes locked on us as Barnes marched us towards him. He wiped his hand against the gash on his cheek, and as it came away I saw it was dark with blood.

I looked across at Sarah: she was still shaking, and her back was hunched over. Behind us, I could sense Barnes' fingers twitching on the trigger of his machine-pistol, and realized that we were probably seconds away from death. But there was no way out. My chest tightened, and I could hear my heart drumming in my head.

'Here, sir?' Barnes called out to Severn. He was itching to kill me, to avenge Templeton.

Severn shook his head. 'Inside.'

A few seconds' reprieve, then. Probably because he didn't want the trouble of carrying our corpses aboard.

We were level with Severn now. The spinning of the rotors was deafening, and it was proving difficult to walk. Barnes yelled at us to enter the helicopter, and Sarah started trying to lift herself over the ledge. She fell on the first attempt, and Barnes roughly dragged her up and pushed her up and over with one hand, the other still clutching the machine-pistol. Now? The moment I had the thought the chance was gone: he swivelled back to face me, and gestured I should follow suit.

I didn't react. I knew he would shoot us as soon as we were both on board. Once the chopper was safely over the water, they would throw our bodies out. Barnes took me by the collar of my shirt and shoved me up and in, using the machine-pistol as a prod. As I collapsed at Sarah's feet, Barnes leapt aboard, and Severn after him, and I soaked in the smell and atmosphere of the cramped space, taking in the beak-nosed guard up front, the bank of equipment he was operating, and the fact that we had already started to take off. I glanced up and saw Barnes looking over at Severn, who nodded.

'Dark first,' he shouted, pointing at me, and Barnes grabbed me by the collar again and hauled me around until I was kneeling by the door, facing out and looking down at the ground as we rose up from it and away, now already above water, my heart in my lungs and vomit rising in my throat.

This was it. This was the end. I could hear Sarah sobbing behind me, begging Severn not to kill us. She was interrupted by a loud burst of noise, static from a transmitter, and for a fraction of a second Barnes moved to register it and without even thinking I reached back and grabbed Sarah by the wrist, then pitched forward, diving blindly into the sky. The wind yanked me down, and I lost contact with Sarah and went spinning through the air, my guts in my eyeballs and my brain in my toes and a choir of gunshots ringing in my ears, and then there was a smack and a deep boom, and the water was cold, freezing, salty, and I was plummeting further and further into it . . .

XVII

It took a few moments to catch up with what had happened: my head was dizzy from the fall, my chest burning from the impact, and every injury on my body was suddenly seared by the salt in the water. But my mind was singing, because I knew I was alive.

I clawed my way up to the surface for air, but the moment I broke through machine-gun fire split the water around me, bursts of green and orange flame kicking up through the waves. I grabbed a breath before submerging again, and saw that Sarah was just a few feet away, and seemingly in trouble, her limbs flailing about. My mind stopped singing. There was a helicopter with machine guns right above us, and we were sitting ducks. I squinted through the bluey-green world and saw a formation of jagged grey rocks in front of me: the coastline.

About halfway down the wall of rocks was a large hole: it looked like some sort of passage. I swam frantically towards Sarah and managed to twist her round so that she was lying atop my back, and then kicked as hard as I could towards the cavern. It was large, and I swam through, feeling ripples from fish and sea-creatures around me as I did.

I came up for air a few seconds later and deposited Sarah next to me on a large cold slab of stone. She spluttered out water and wheezed, her body racked from the experience. I looked up – had they seen us? Apparently not. Directly above our heads was a large overhanging rock formation, and just a few feet away its twin. Between the two overhangs stretched a patch of pale pink sky. The hole was much larger than I would have liked: if the helicopter happened to fly over it, we were fish in a barrel. But if we had come up anywhere else, they would have already shot us.

The vital thing now was not to move and attract their attention. I explained the situation to Sarah, and we sat there, listening to the shuddering roar of the helicopter as it hovered over the area, circling back and forth, looking for us. With every increase in volume, my heart clenched, then subsided as the sound receded, only to clench again moments later. After a few minutes, the effort of staying still was starting to cramp my muscles, and I was worried that I wasn't going to be able to hold out much longer. If I fainted now, it could be fatal. Sarah was in the same position as I was, her muscles tensed and her stomach heaving. I suddenly noticed a line of small dark dots in the corner of the window of sky. Had they spotted us? But the dots weren't moving. My brain rearranged the perspective and I realized with a start that there was another overhanging rock between the sky and us, and that the dots clinging to it were, in fact, the heads of birds: vultures.

I squinted, and managed to make out a few of the individual heads. They were staring intently at us, and I knew why. We weren't moving: they were starting to wonder if we might be carrion.

Keep calm.

I looked beyond them at the patch of sky. No helicopter in it, but the noise was still there, so they hadn't given up yet, and were no doubt using binoculars to examine every possible hiding place we could have disappeared into. If we made any movement at all, they might catch it and then we would be finished. But if we *didn't* move, the vultures might decide we were worth investigating further.

I switched back to the line of dots. They weren't there any more! I caught a frantic flap of black feathers in my peripheral vision, and then saw them gliding down, seemingly not moving their wings, until they were circling directly above the nearest ledge. Any closer, and they might give away our position. But we were still exposed by the window, and any movement I made might alert Severn and the others.

The vultures were swooping nearer and nearer, a sinister sound emanating from their throats. An image flashed into my mind of their red eyes glaring glassily as their beaks pecked at our flesh, and I realized I had to risk it. The noise of the chopper momentarily fell away and I threw up a hand and retracted it almost as quickly, praying that the sudden movement would be enough to tell the birds we were alive but not enough to be seen by anyone in the chopper. There was a flickering of wings from the vulture at the head of the pack, and within a few moments they had disappeared from the window, no doubt moving on to the next outcrop. I looked up for any sign of the helicopter. Had they seen either the vultures' interest or my hands? It didn't seem so. The sound of the blades was fading into the distance.

Several minutes later, I realized they weren't coming back – at least not for the time being. I suddenly felt very tired. My eyes stung, my arms ached, my legs were in seizure – my whole body was racked with pain, and all I wanted to do was lie down and sleep and let oblivion do the rest. But now wasn't the time for such thoughts. We couldn't stay here – they'd have the police of the whole island awake to our presence within a few hours, which would mean we wouldn't be able to rent a boat or catch a ferry or do anything. We had to get back to the mainland, where we'd be able to slip through the cracks, and we had to do it now. I pushed myself up to a standing position and gripped the corner of a nearby rock. There was a narrow opening between two stones that led to more rocks. I helped Sarah to her feet, and we began crawling through.

It took us about an hour by my estimation, but we finally clambered through the rocks and found ourselves on a small strip of beach. The sun had come up now, and the heat was starting to beat down on us. Hidden high above the beach I could see the outline of a large white building: a hotel, perhaps, or one of the older villas.

We walked across the sand until we came to a tiny wooden jetty. Tethered to it was a boat. It was small, but it could get us off the island. I climbed up and threw off the ropes. There didn't seem to be a key anywhere, and I decided the best option would be to jump-start it. I hadn't done it since the war, but this didn't look all that different from a motor-torpedo. I was about to climb in when something stopped me dead. It was the click of a hammer.

I looked up. Standing directly above us was a man wearing a striped shirt and canvas trousers. And he was pointing a shotgun at our heads.

*

'*Che state facendo qui?*' he snarled. '*E' proprieta' privata.*'

He was young, in his early twenties I thought, and of much the same stamp as the sniper from St Paul's: long dark hair swept down over his forehead and the beginnings of a beard covering his deeply tanned face.

We raised our hands and walked towards him. He looked Sarah over in a way that made me feel queasy – her clothes hadn't completely dried and were still clinging to her in places – and then levelled the gun at my chest.

'*Abbiamo solo fatto una nuotata,*' I said. '*Non e' quello che pensa—*'

His eyes widened. '*E cosa penso?*'

'*Ascolti, mi dispiace molto di averla disturbata,*' Sarah broke in, surprising me. '*Avremmo bisogno di affittare la sua barca. In questo momento non abbiamo denaro con noi, ma lavoriamo per il governo britannico e mi accertero' personalmente che l'ambasciata la rimborsi—*'

'My God,' he said, lowering the gun. 'You're *British*! Why didn't you say so in the first place?'

Sarah and I looked at him with shock. The voice was pure Old Etonian.

'What the hell are you doing here?' he asked. 'You look a complete mess.'

'Help us up and we'll explain,' said Sarah, and gave her most winning smile. 'We come in peace, honestly.'

He hesitated for a moment, but a beautiful girl with an English accent can never be dangerous. He stuck out his hand, and helped her up, then offered it to me.

'Ralph Balfour-Laing,' he said. 'Pleasure to meet you. And yes, of *the* Balfour-Laings, before you ask!'

I'd never heard of any Balfour-Laings, and hadn't been planning on asking about them either. My first instinct was distrust, and it even went through my head that he might be a plant of Severn's, some sort of casual watchman for the base. But I dismissed it at once – he was just a rich young layabout, and Sardinia was one of their natural habitats. Gesturing at the villa, he explained that he was a painter and that the place was a private retreat where he sometimes came to discover his muse and, it seemed, host the occasional wild party with the island's jet set. He eyed Sarah up again and asked her if she had ever been painted nude. Before things got too out of hand I told him we were on urgent government business and needed to get back to the mainland immediately. Could he help?

'I can do more than that,' he said with a grin. 'I'll take you there myself. That's not my only boat, you know.'

XVIII

The face in front of me was covered in the beginnings of a beard, the bloodshot eyes staring out wildly. I looked like hell, and felt worse. There was a razor next to the basin, but I decided it wasn't a good idea: partly hidden under the beard, a long gash ran down the length of my right cheek, with grit visible inside it, and there were abrasions on my chin and throat. If I shaved, I might look even worse.

I picked up a monogrammed hand towel from a pile above the mirror and soaked a corner of it in the basin, then cleaned out as many of the wounds as I could, wincing with the pain, trying to remove as many of the surface problems as possible. Once I was satisfied, I picked up a glass from a mahogany sideboard, filled it with water from the tap, and drank down several glugs.

I walked over to one of the portholes and looked out at the island rapidly receding behind us. We'd made it. We were alive. But I couldn't help feeling it was just a temporary reprieve. The boat was going at a healthy rate of knots – but would it be fast enough? Severn would comb every inch of the bay looking for our bodies. When he didn't find us he would eventually come to the conclusion that we had escaped, and then his thoughts would turn to what Sarah might know, what she might have told me and what we might do next. Everything depended on how long he would keep up the search. He might start sending men into the nearby villages to look for us and ask around – or he might decide not to take any chances and immediately fly the helicopter straight to Rome. In which case, this would all have been for nothing, as he'd be waiting for us when we arrived.

I looked across at Sarah, obliviously asleep on a bank of padded orange seats in the corner of the cabin, beneath one of our host's works of art, a blotchy oil painting that I thought might be a Sardinian sunset gone askew. On the floor, the end of a cigarette smouldered in a terracotta ashtray.

Balfour-Laing hadn't had any food on board apart from some beans he'd found in a cupboard, which we had devoured straight from the tin, but the cigarettes had perhaps been more welcome. He had also offered us wine and beer, but neither of us was in any shape or mood for alcohol and had been more than grateful for water, and Sarah had soon fallen asleep. Some colour had finally returned to her face, and while the welts were still faintly visible on her neck, she otherwise looked in much better shape. Balfour-Laing had dug up a T-shirt and a pair of old overalls and, hunched over in them inelegantly, she looked like a child in hand-me-downs. I was wearing a pair of his trousers and a paint-flecked shirt – he hadn't had any spare underwear, but I wasn't about to complain. Both our outfits were completed by rather natty white plimsolls, part of a supply he kept on board for when the heat of the sun became too much for his guests to walk around barefoot on deck. Today was Sunday, he had told us: we had been imprisoned for nearly two days.

Perhaps feeling the force of my gaze on her, Sarah opened her eyes. She sat up and stared at me inquisitively.

'Are we nearly there?'

'Another hour or so.'

She nodded, and leaned over to pick up the pack of cigarettes from the floor. She slid one out and lit it. 'Thank you,' she said.

'Thank *you*,' I replied. 'You got us aboard.'

She took a draught of the cigarette and looked at me intently. 'That was nothing. You got me out of there.'

I changed the subject. 'We need to prepare. What more can you tell me about those documents you read in Charles' safe?'

'Nothing,' she said. 'I told you all I know. I could only risk staying in his office for a few minutes. I saw the Service seal and "Stay Behind", but there were hundreds of pieces of paper in the dossier and I didn't have the time—'

'I understand. Look, I have to stop whatever it is they are planning, so I'll need to get back into that safe and find those documents.'

'I know. I'll help you.'

'Good. I think it's best if you tell me the combination now, and that we part ways once we reach the mainland. They won't have put a stop on the airports yet and you'll be able to get a flight to London soon enough. As soon as you land, go straight to Whitehall and ask to see the Home Secretary, urgently. Tell him what you know—'

'But I don't really know anything!'

'You know enough. Tell Haggard everything you told me, and make sure to mention "Stay Behind". He'll understand. He'll ask you for proof, of course: tell him it's coming. Don't mention me.' It wasn't ideal, by any means, but I had to get her out of the country – and out of the reach of Severn.

She leaned down and crushed the remains of her cigarette into the ashtray. 'I appreciate what you're trying to do, Paul, but I want to stop this, too, and running away won't help. The Home Secretary isn't going to do anything without any evidence, and you know it. You need me to show you where the documents are – there were hundreds of them.'

'Describe them to me. I've a good memory.'

Her jaw was set. 'You're not getting rid of me.'

'Look,' I said, 'this isn't a time for heroics or impulse decisions. If this is what I think it might be, we're dealing with a conspiracy that a lot of very powerful men will do anything to protect. And I mean *anything*.'

'Don't you dare lecture me,' she said, her voice rising. 'I was already committed to stopping them, remember – I was prepared to show you the documents the other night, and I haven't found any reason to change my mind since. Quite the contrary.'

'Tell me how to get into the safe, Sarah. This isn't a game.'

She cut me off with a bitter laugh. 'Do you think I don't know that?' she spat out. She pulled the collar of her blouse down sharply, exposing one of the larger welts. 'Do you think I don't know who we're dealing with here?' Her gaze narrowed. 'I want to stop whatever it is he is planning, even it means I die running from him.'

Her voice had started to crack and she put a hand up to her face. I made to lean over, but she shook her head and stood up. She walked over to the other side of the cabin, next to a lifebuoy pinned to the wall with the name of the boat emblazoned on it: PARADISO. I could see her shoulders moving a little, and knew she was crying in both shame and fury.

I walked over and placed my hand on her shoulder, and eventually said something I didn't want to: 'All right, then. We'll do it together.'

She turned to face me, her face streaked with tears. 'Really?' She burst into unintended laughter, and I had a dreadful hollow feeling inside. But I had no choice – I had to get into that safe. For a moment, I wondered about abandoning the whole idea and just flying to London with her and going to Haggard. But I knew she was right, and that that wouldn't stop anything. I thought again of Colin Templeton and my vow to do some good finally, and my will hardened. I needed to get to the documents, and if she were prepared to take the risks I'd have to live with that, too. I didn't want her death on my conscience, but she had her own will and I couldn't force it – or I'd be as bad as her husband.

I nodded. 'Let's go upstairs and see Ralph. He might have

some more of those beans.' I did my best to smile convincingly, and passed her a towel to wipe away her tears.

'Can't we stay down here for a bit?' she asked.

'I told you, it's perfectly safe. The deck area is completely sheltered and—'

'It's not that,' she said. 'I just don't feel I've thanked you properly.'

I looked at her sharply. Something in her tone – was she toying with me?

'I don't need a reward,' I said. 'You've thanked me more than enough.'

She stood up. 'At least let me return that kiss you gave me.'

She turned and needlessly drew together the curtains behind her, affording me a glimpse of the outline of her backside through the thin cotton of the overalls.

'Look,' I said, 'we're not out of the woods yet. Not by a long chalk. And you've been through a hell of a lot and I think—'

She placed a finger to my lips, and then leaned her face over so her mouth was by my left ear.

'I liked the way you kissed me,' she whispered. 'Do it again.'

She moved my chin across to her lips. I opened my mouth and the hot wetness of her tongue jolted through me. I pressed against her. She abruptly took her mouth away from mine and started kissing my neck, then raised my arms and lifted off my shirt. We stumbled across to the padded seats and she kissed my chest, rubbing her chin against my hair there, and then flickering her tongue against my stomach.

'Sarah . . .'

She shushed me, then placed her fingers at the waistband of my trousers, and slowly slipped them down. She smiled softly at the lack of underwear.

I couldn't resist any longer. I caught hold of her by the hips and struggled to unclasp the overalls, cursing as I did. She laughed at my ineptitude but finally the clasp was undone, and she removed her T-shirt and bra while I ran my fingers down her body to her panties. I eased them down over her thighs and she gasped, clamping her eyes shut.

We stood there naked, gazing at each other, and then she pushed me down onto the seats. She leaned over me for a moment, breathing hard, and tipped her head back. Her neck and breasts glistened with sweat, and I pulled her closer to me, until we were locked tightly together. I clasped her shoulder to slow her rhythm and she cried out, then moved with me, rocking back and forth. She stared down at me, her hair covering her eyes, and I thought for a moment I could feel what she was feeling, her flesh parted by me, the shiver through her body. She began panting louder, gasping for air, and I moved more frantically, and she bit down on my hand as we rocked back and forth, faster and faster . . .

There was a fierce knocking on the door of the cabin, and we froze, our hearts thumping against each other.

'I say,' called a voice, 'everything all right down there?'

I glanced at Sarah, a film of sweat covering her forehead.

'Out in a minute!' I called back.

There was no reply for a second, then a 'Righty-ho!' and the sound of receding footsteps.

Sarah leaned forward.

'I do hope not,' she whispered, and then slowly ran her tongue along the underside of my neck. I grabbed hold of her and took her with renewed ferocity.

XIX

Sunday, 4 May 1969, Rome, Italy

We spent the rest of the journey above deck with Ralph Balfour-Laing: Sarah and he discovered that they had a few acquaintances in common, and I learned more about the London 'scene' and the Cresta Ball than I needed to know. We both declined several offers of marijuana cigarettes. But, as promised, he took us all the way to the mainland, dropping us at the main harbour at Civitavecchia. It was just coming up to eight o'clock in the morning. When we told him we needed to get to Rome, he unhesitatingly thrust a sheaf of *lire* into our hands and brushed aside all our thanks and assurances that the embassy would be in touch to reimburse him. He chanced his hand one last time by giving Sarah a card with his details, and then he returned to the boat and to the sweet life in his island retreat, and we jumped aboard a crowded bus on its way to Rome.

As the bus sped through the dusty roads, I opened the window so the sun could warm my bones. Our driver had the radio on, and sang along to the romantic ballads emanating from it in a loud and gloriously out-of-tune baritone, but about twenty miles outside the city, relief came in the form of a news bulletin. The first headline: someone had hurled a bomb from a passing car at the headquarters of the Communist party in the city the previous night, and the party had responded by pulling down the shutters and drafting in students and activists to guard the building.

'These damned Communists deserve what they get!' cried the driver in Italian, throwing out an arm angrily, and rather dangerously. Several voices in the bus grunted their agreement.

Sarah looked at me questioningly, and I shook my head. This wasn't connected, although it didn't help the situation much. Severn and Zimotti were going to use the current climate to stage something, and I had a feeling it would be more spectacular than a bomb thrown from a car. It would also, of course, be something they would blame on the Communists, rather than targeting them. She turned away, and as she did I took the opportunity to examine her profile. She looked like a Pre-Raphaelite painting, crossed with Grace Kelly. No ... that wasn't quite right. She was like nobody else, of course – utterly unique. The line of her jaw, of her nose, the positioning of every feature was so simple, so fitting, that one wondered why God or whichever artist was responsible had not repeated the trick with all women, with all the world ...

'Easy prey for any beautiful woman.' It was a phrase I'd read in my dossier at Pyotr's flat – part of the preparatory document for my recruitment in '45. But could this be different? I put it out

of my mind. My attraction to Sarah was strong – frighteningly so – but it was simply being reinforced by the position we were in. We were both on the run, and we had only each other to turn to. I had to make sure I didn't get carried away. We hadn't talked much since our love-making on the boat, but perhaps she had simply needed a release, a way to prove she was still alive and banish the thought of Charles a little. I had simply been there, that was all – I had done the same myself many times.

*

About an hour and a half later we got off the bus at the main train station, and from there we took a taxi to the embassy – Balfour-Laing's money was disappearing rapidly. There were no cars parked outside. It looked like Severn had not yet made it here. We knocked on the large iron door and were led into the entrance by the same butler as had let me in three evenings earlier. He didn't seem surprised to see us, and I breathed a tiny sigh of relief. We hurried across the marble floor to the reception desk. The clerk did look a little surprised, but then it was Sunday, and we had turned up looking like a couple of clowns.

'Good morning, Mrs Severn. Mister . . .?'

'Dark,' I said. 'I was at the reception here on Thursday.'

'Yes, sir. If I could just see your identification . . .?'

'Don't be so absurd, Harry,' Sarah said. 'I'm here every day, and this is the Deputy Chief of the Service. We're going up.'

Harry's face flushed but he didn't move from his desk, and

we quickly headed for the staircase and made our way up to the Station. The place was deserted, and it was odd to think I'd been here just two days earlier, about to go out to meet Barchetti.

'Are there any weapons in here?' I asked Sarah, but she shook her head.

'Charles has a Browning, but he had it with him in Sardinia.' She caught my look. 'There may be something hidden somewhere, but I've no idea where.'

I nodded. It was unfortunate, but we didn't have time to waste on it. She ran over to a drawer next to the *cafetière* and pulled out the key to Charles' office, which she swiftly unlocked. The morning sunlight streamed through the window and the sound of traffic came up from the street below. She went over to the painting above the desk – a portrait of the Queen, of course – and I helped her take it down, revealing a wall safe. That was new – I'd only had a locked filing cabinet when this had been my office. She dialled the combination, and then, with a click, it opened.

She hadn't been exaggerating on the boat: there were *hundreds* of dossiers, all arranged in metal shelves within the safe. Thank God I had her with me – I'd never have found the right one by myself. As the thought hit me, I noticed the look on her face.

'What's wrong?'

'It looks different,' she whispered. 'I think he's rearranged it.'

My heart sank. I considered taking the whole lot with us

for a moment, but there was simply far too much to carry. I started removing the dossiers from the left-hand side of the safe and lifting them over to Severn's desk.

'Anything you remember about the dossier?' I asked. 'About what it looked like?'

She was already bent to the task. 'Some of the pages had a black banner across the top,' she said. 'And the whole thing was paper-clipped together.'

I started going through them, wanting to set aside anything that didn't look right as fast as possible, but not so fast as to miss the crucial dossier. There were insurance papers, staff lists, files on Italian leaders . . . Some fascinating information, no doubt, but none of it threatening the imminent death of innocent civilians. I continued riffling through, looking for paper-clipped pages with black banners . . .

I had looked through and abandoned over a dozen dossiers when I froze.

'Did you hear that?'

Sarah looked up. 'What?'

I thought there had been a noise from outside. I leapt over to the embrasure of the window and peered down into the driveway. But there was nobody there. I hurried back to the desk.

'Got it!' Sarah suddenly shouted. 'I've got it!'

'Are you sure?' If we took the wrong documents, we'd be back where we started.

She nodded furiously. 'This is it.'

'Let me see,' I said, and she reacted to my tone and handed

it across. I suppose part of me had refused to believe it possible, and I needed to see it for myself. By the look of it this was Severn's own copy, and I guessed it had come through the diplomatic bag to avoid being deciphered by Sarah. The whole thing was held together with a large and slightly rusty paper clip, and a black banner across the top read 'STAY BEHIND: STRATEGY AND EXECUTION'. Beneath that was the date: 18 June 1968. I read it almost in a haze:

```
In previous papers, we outlined the proposed
new aims for STAY BEHIND in the current polit-
ical climate. In this paper, we will explore
how those aims might practically be executed
across Western Europe. We estimate that these
plans would be put into practice starting in
early 1969 ...
```

I flicked through the rest – it was in sections, but I wanted to check that the whole thing was here. I needed to be sure that it contained the details of the operation, and that they hadn't been saved for another paper. The next section of the dossier was titled 'Targeting', and I turned to it anxiously.

```
Targets should be as iconic as possible. Historic
monuments are desirable, especially as many are
poorly guarded. Smaller targets with signifi-
cance to the local population are ideal, as
one can cause less damage and thus not lose
```

> too much sympathy, but have a much greater
> effect on public morale . . .

That didn't help much. The country was littered with historic monuments. I hurried on:

> Whatever the target, we must consider whether
> to blame the attacks on Moscow or on local
> groups with particular grudges to bear, whom
> we can then associate with Moscow via falsi-
> fied documentation, communiqués, press contacts
> and other means. In our view, the latter is
> the preferable option, as newspapers and others
> will piece together a conspiracy of attacks
> across Europe of their own accord, without
> seeming to have been fed the information. We
> wish to give the impression that Moscow is
> supporting several disparate groups, to the
> same end . . .

Damning stuff, but there were still no specifics: there was no indication of *which* targets they had chosen or on what dates they planned to attack them. I flicked to the end of the document, to the final page:

> Large-scale public events also provide oppor-
> tunities for attacks. The Olympic Games, soccer
> tournaments and similar sporting events attract

> thousands of spectators, and the impact of an
> attack at such an event would be enormous.

'Soccer', I noted, rather than football. The Americans were
definitely involved, then.

> Cultural events, such as concerts or other
> performances, should also be considered.
> Transport to such events — such as train jour-
> neys — could be easier targets. However, secu-
> rity is usually extremely tight at larger events,
> so it is worth looking for smaller ones appro-
> priate to the message we want to convey. An
> attack during a performance of a play critical
> of Communism would clearly point to Communist
> perpetrators. Taking a step further into the
> symbolic, a sabotaged play about high finance
> could also be plausibly portrayed as a Communist
> attack. Going further still, an attack during
> a ballet could be seen as an indirect comment
> on Nureyev's defection, even if Nureyev were
> not in the production. This would require a
> more delicate touch, but planning an attack
> for a ballet in which Nureyev would usually
> be expected to perform but did not for some
> reason on that day could be particularly effec-
> tive. In the next part of the paper, we will
> discuss operational plans in greater detail.

Apart from the reference to soccer, it had all the hallmarks of one of Osborne's Section reports. I had misread him all along, seeing him as a little Englander, a rabid Mosleyite who thought 'the wogs start at Calais'. But even Mosley was a European these days, and it seemed Osborne's hatred of Communism was rather stronger than his distaste for foreigners. He evidently had some powerful friends, and together they had taken over the original stay-behind networks and planned to use them to forge a hard-right agenda for the Continent.

And it was as well I had checked: the report seemed to end here, followed by a sheaf of documents in completely different typefaces. So either this was merely the first in a series of reports about the operation or someone had removed whatever came next in it – either way, it seemed to be missing the details of what they were planning. I turned back to Sarah. 'Do you remember if this was the exact dossier you saw, or could it have been one of the others?'

She looked at me in despair. 'I'm sorry,' she said. 'I really don't know.'

'We need to find the next part of this dossier,' I said. 'We need to know the operational—' I stopped. A car had just driven past the window, followed by the sound of tyres screeching on gravel. Severn? I ran over and looked down.

Yes. He was parking the Alfa Romeo, and coming through the gates behind it were two black Lancias.

I glanced at Sarah, and nodded affirmation. A clanging of iron echoed up the stairs.

They were in.

I calculated we had less than two minutes. I scooped up as many dossiers as I could, about half a dozen of them, stuffed them under my shirt, and gestured to Sarah to do the same. We would just have to hope that the operational plans were among them.

We stepped out of the office, and Sarah pointed to a door at the end of the corridor. Behind it was a much narrower staircase, with no carpet and no paintings on the walls: the staff staircase.

'This way!' she said.

XX

As we reached the foot of the staircase, we met the man with the beak coming into the main hallway. He froze at the sight of us, then reached for the pistol in his waistband. I leapt towards him and aimed a kick at the lower half of his legs – several of the dossiers that had been in my shirt fell to the floor, scattering in a spread at his feet. He stumbled on one of them, but then managed to throw out his hands and catch hold of Sarah by the waist as she made to run past him. She screamed and lashed out with her feet, catching him in the jaw. He was knocked to the ground, but she had also lost a few dossiers in the meantime, and started to lean down to pick them up.

'Leave them!' I shouted at her, and she nodded and started running for the open doorway. I kicked the man in the stomach to make sure he stayed down, then started to follow her. But the commotion had already alerted the others, and as I approached the door I saw Severn coming down the main staircase, with Barnes and Zimotti directly behind him.

I leapt through the doorway as the shot scraped the nearest

wall. They would be with me in a second or two. I saw Sarah running down the driveway, heading for the Alfa Romeo. Good idea. I raced over to join her. The key was still in the ignition.

'I'll drive!' I shouted, pressing the button to unlock the doors. They opened on their hinges and we jumped in. The machine growled as I started her up, and we tore through the gates. A shot fired behind us, wild. But they would come in the Lancias soon enough.

As I turned onto the street, Sarah cried out and I glanced across at her.

'Drive on the right!' she screamed.

Shit. I looked back at the road and pulled us onto the other side just as a heavy goods lorry came rumbling towards us.

Close call.

Sarah started looking frantically through the dossiers, throwing each one onto the car's floor as soon as she had discarded it. I hoped to God we hadn't left the crucial one behind.

My plan was to head straight for the centre of town, as fast as possible: the more people there were around, the harder it would be for them to shoot at us. I squeezed the throttle and the needle shot up, and kept climbing. We passed the Fontana delle Api, and then I turned sharply down Via Druso. The car took the corner beautifully, and part of my brain was involuntarily awed by the machine under my command. The other part was desperately trying to see the street ahead, control this beast and get away from our pursuers. One of the Lancias was already in my rear-view mirror, taking the turn. A bullet ricocheted off the bodywork, and I swerved into the centre of the road for a moment. I swerved back, and reached over to open the glove compartment. Perhaps Severn had left a gun in there, or a map – but there was nothing. I looked up just as a Fiat with an enormous exhaust swerved in front of me, and I jabbed at the horn manically until it got out of the way.

I took another hard turn, into Via dei Cerchi. The traffic was starting to thicken now – evidently not everyone had taken the long weekend off. The streets were packed with pedestrians milling about aimlessly: tourists and nuns and children slobbering ice cream. I realized it had been a tactical error to head this way, because even if it made our pursuers a little gun-shy, which I was now rather less sure of, it was slowing us down terribly.

We had to get *out* of the centre – but where to? By now Severn would have made sure that all the country's ports, airports and customs posts had been given detailed descriptions of the two of us, and even if we travelled separately I didn't fancy our chances. Ergo, we had to find a way of avoiding Italian customs. If we reached, say, Switzerland, we would then be able to fly to London with little trouble: even Severn's powers didn't stretch that far. Travel between Italy and Switzerland didn't require visas, so if we ditched the car, split up and took the train we might be able to get through the checkpoints.

Switzerland it was, then straight to Haggard in London. But we needed proof first.

'Any luck yet?' I called out to Sarah.

'Not yet!'

I saw a space in the traffic and turned down Via della Greca, taking us around the bank of the Tiber. The main train station was only a mile or so away, but I had to find a way through this bloody maze of a city to get back to it. A thought hit me: the conspirators might not have dared to commit the operational details of this to paper. The strategic document could be all we had, and we would have to figure it out from there. 'Check the document we read in the embassy again,' I told Sarah. 'See if it mentions any other targets, or dates.'

She leaned down and started rummaging in the files at her feet. We came into a boulevard shaded with trees: Lungotevere dei Pierleoni, but that would take us into town, not away from it, so I took the next turn and pushed the pedal down again.

Sarah had now found the original document and was reading through it hurriedly. 'How about this?' she said. '"*In some Western European countries, especially in the south, religious events should be considered for attacks, as they provide a large crowd, easily understood and revered symbolism, shock value and, in many cases, low security. As Communism is an atheist ideology, Moscow's involvement would immediately be suspected . . .*"'

A religious event – yes, that might make sense. Could that be it, rather than a ballet or a football match? I thought back to my meeting with Barchetti. 'They know,' he had whispered. And then, when I had asked him if his cover had blown, he had shaken his head: 'About the attack in the dome.' I had presumed he meant that Arte come Terrore knew they were the prime suspects for Farraday's murder. But perhaps I'd been wrong. The sniper had stored his climbing ropes on the gallery at the base of St Paul's dome, and used that as an escape route, but the attack itself had taken place down in the cathedral, not inside the cupola. A slip? Barchetti's English hadn't been perfect, but I didn't think so. I bit my lip and cursed myself. I'd missed his real message – he hadn't been talking about what had happened in London at all. He had wanted to tell Severn that Arte come Terrore already knew of the next attack, which was going to take place *in another church entirely*.

Sarah had gone quiet, still engrossed in the document.

'What is it?'

'Charles has written in the margins on this page,' she said. 'He's circled the part where it talks about religious events and written . . .' She squinted. '"4 May."'

I looked across at her. 'That's today.'

Forget Switzerland. Forget Haggard. I swerved to the right, taking the turning back into the centre of town.

'What the hell are you doing?' shouted Sarah.

'It's going to happen *here*,' I said. 'In Rome. The Pope's noon address in St Peter's Square. They've placed a bomb in the dome. They're going to kill the Pope.'

She went quiet, and the papers slipped from her grasp and onto the floor.

XXI

I pushed my foot down on the accelerator and adjusted my hands on the wheel: they were slipping from the sweat pouring off them, as I realized what we were up against. No wonder Severn and Zimotti had been so anxious to find out what Barchetti had told me. This was on a far greater scale than the attacks in Milan, or the attempt to kill me in the middle of St Paul's.

The assassination of the Pope would, of course, shock Italy, and shock the world. No doubt they had already prepared a way to pin the blame on Arte come Terrore, or some other Communist-linked group, as outlined in the dossier. Moscow could deny it as much as they wanted but nobody would ever believe that Italian intelligence had been behind such a thing. I could scarcely believe it myself. The foot-soldiers would not be aware of it, of course. Did anyone in the Vatican know about it? They had certainly made some shaky alliances in the past – but to assassinate the Pope in this day and age? Even if they were brutal enough to sanction such a thing, Zimotti would never have trusted them with the information: one slip of someone's conscience and the whole operation would fall apart.

So there was a chance, if I reached the Vatican in time and warned them. I looked at the clock by the speedometer: it read ten o'clock. We had two hours. That would normally be plenty of time to get to the Vatican, but of course we were being pursued, and heading straight through the centre of the city.

I cursed the car. It was a racing model, or close enough, but that wasn't much help in this situation: we were being chased on very short stretches in a built-up area by cars that were not that much slower anyway. Even if I could have increased my speed, it wouldn't have been a good idea, because I didn't want the *carabinieri* on our tail as well. But the Lancias, perhaps because they were being driven by the two Italians, were snaking expertly through the traffic. The one in front, driven by Zimotti, was now less than a hundred yards behind us, and the traffic was, if anything, slowing.

We crossed the Tiber, the Castel Sant'Angelo to our right, and came into Via della Conciliazone. And there was the dome, reaching up into a cloudless blue sky. It was tantalizingly close, but traffic in the street was at a complete standstill and in my rear-view mirror I could see the Lancia gaining ground. I decided drastic action was needed, and veered right into the nearest side street, Via della Traspontina.

A three-wheeled scooter loaded with flowers in the back cart squealed around the corner, and I swerved to avoid it, then took the next left down Borgo Sant'Angelo. I just needed to find a left turning somewhere down here to get ahead of the traffic in Via della Conciliazone and come into the square. The entrance to Via della'Erba was blocked by an idiotically parked van, and the tip of the dome had now vanished behind one of the buildings ahead, making it harder for me to judge the distance. But the next turning or the one after that should do . . .

I glanced in the mirror again and saw that one of the Lancias was now just three cars behind us. I took a sharp right. It was taking us away from St Peter's, but I had to lose them and if I could take a few quick turns I might be able to. The street was narrow, leaving barely enough room for us to squeeze by, so I put my foot down and tooted the horn like a born Roman. Pedestrians jumped out of the way, a few of them shouting or waving their fists at us.

I turned left onto Borgo Pio. It was slightly wider, but had an outdoor *caffè* in it. I swerved to avoid it, but just as I did the sun broke over a building, blinding me for a moment, and Sarah gasped as one of our rear wheels crunched against a metal chair.

To the left was Vicolo del Farinone. A sign read 'SENSO UNICO', but it was the wrong way. No matter. I turned in. Vespas and motorcycles lined the left-hand side, while in the centre of the street a party of pigeons was flapping about a crust of bread. They scattered at the sound of the engine, and I hugged the car to the right wall. There was an archway at the end of the street, but as we approached it I saw the nose of a car just coming into view. It was one of the Lancias. *How the hell had they got there?* I glanced in the mirror: the other was now right behind us. And there were no turnings in the street.

I put my foot down, hoping that I might scare the Lancia ahead into reversing. But it kept nosing further into the archway. The walls on either side of us seemed to be closing in, and even the sky above was obscured by laundry hanging from windows: underwear and shirts. The sun was blazing – they wouldn't take long to dry. I saw that the street widened a little before the archway, and as I looked over to the right I saw why – there was some sort of gate there. Something sparked in my mind and I reached for the button for the car doors. The hinges clunked and began moving out and then upward, just avoiding the walls of the passing houses, until they were almost touching each other above the front windscreen.

Wind was rushing into the car, and I started slowing down. We were a couple of seconds from the end of the street now, but we had to get there before the Lancia could block us off completely. I slowed the car some more, and we hit a cobble or something and landed a little off course: a corner of my door sheared against a drainpipe and got caught for a moment, metal screeching against metal. I righted us, then unbuckled myself from my seat. Now we were coming up to the end of the street, and the gate. A sign above it read '*Proprieta Privata*', but I could see that it was slightly ajar.

We were now travelling at just a few miles an hour, and the Lancia behind us thumped into the rear of the car. Someone – Zimotti? – took a shot, but it hit the metalwork. Even at this speed, we were a moving target. There was an awful whistling

noise emanating from the engine, and one of our back tyres
had gone, a victim to speeding over the cobbles.

I turned to Sarah and gestured at the documents in her
hand. She nodded dully and thrust them into the pouch of
her overalls.

'Now!' I shouted, and she bundled herself out of the door,
pushing the gate open as she did. The Lancia ahead of us was
now in the archway, but it was stuck – they had no room to
open *their* doors. I let go of the wheel and dived after Sarah
through the open gate. There was a crunch as the Lancia bull-
dozed into the front of the Alfa Romeo, but I was already
racing up stairs and down a small alleyway, passing the backs
of houses. A few feet ahead there was another gate, and it was
closed. Was it locked?

No. Sarah reached it and opened it, and a few moments later
I joined her. As I stepped into the street I was nearly run over
by a horse-drawn carriage coming the other way. The horse
whinnied and lifted its legs and the tourists in the carriage
shouted abuse at me. I took a moment to catch my breath,
then looked up at the street sign on the archway. Via del
Mascherino. I had momentarily lost my sense of direction, so
I took a few more steps into the street and glanced to my left
– the Lancia was reversing out of the archway a few feet away.
But to my right was a curving colonnade, and just visible
above it was the ball and cross of St Peter's.

I took Sarah by the hand and we started running towards it.

*

I'd forgotten how vast the square was, and how crowded it could become. The first part of it was reasonably easy to cross, but by the time we reached the Obelisk we had been absorbed into a heaving mass of people, chattering, jostling and fanning themselves in the heat of the morning. Believers of every age, nationality and colour were here, wearing paper hats and sporting binoculars so they'd be able to get a better look at the action. I pushed past a group of African nuns and squinted up at one of the clocks on the Basilica: it was coming up to half past ten. There was just over an hour and a half left before the Pope was due to address the crowd.

The great church stood in front of us, the dome now just visible, framed by a cloudless blue sky. It looked even more impressive than St Paul's – but was it any more invulnerable? Sarah and I elbowed our way through the crowd, muttering 'Scusi – emergenza!' People let us pass, reluctant to show anger in such a place and perhaps sensing our urgency.

Sarah pointed towards a flight of stairs on the right-hand side of the colonnade, and we headed that way. Several Swiss Guards were posted as sentries around the entrance, their absurd costumes offset by the short rapiers holstered in them and the long halberds they held in their hands. I pulled away a low wooden barrier and we ran up the stairs. The nearest of the Guards turned to us, alarmed.

'We need to speak to someone on the Pope's staff immediately,' I said, still panting. 'It's an emergency.'

He gave us a frozen look, and I became conscious that we

were bruised, battered and wearing Ralph Balfour-Laing's paint-flecked clothes.

'Do you have any identification, please?' said the Guard, a pug-faced man sweating beneath his ridiculous plumed helmet.

'We're from the British embassy,' said Sarah. 'Ambassador Mazzerelli will be able to vouch for us.'

He wasn't impressed. 'Ambassador Mazzerelli is not here, *signora*. Do you have any identification from your embassy?'

Sarah touched my arm, and I turned to see Severn and Zimotti making their way through the crowd, followed by Barnes and the beak-faced soldier. They were now just a few dozen feet away, and heading straight for us, holding up wallets as they made their way past: they had identification, of course.

I faced the Guard again. 'Please,' I said. 'We are representatives of the British government and we need to speak to someone on the Pope's staff at once. You must stop the address at noon.'

'*Signore*, I do not care who you are. We cannot allow anyone through simply because they claim to have an urgent matter. Please wait here.'

He made to leave and I leaned forward and grabbed his tunic by the sleeve. He swivelled round sharply, and I turned to Sarah.

'How are those documents keeping?' I said. She looked at me blankly, and for a terrifying moment I thought we might have lost them on the way, but then she reached into her overalls and removed the sheaf of papers. At my prompting she turned to the page she had been reading from in the car and thrust it into the hands of the Guard.

'Just look at this,' she said. 'It's a proposal by foreign governments to commit terrorist attacks in Italy and blame them on Communists. Here' – she pointed to the relevant paragraph – 'it mentions that ideal targets are religious events. May the fourth is circled in the margin—'

'And that's today,' I broke in. 'There may be a bomb in the church.'

The Guard's momentary anger seemed to have calmed: perhaps he was used to such claims and was now certain he was dealing with a couple of cranks. I glanced back into the crowd. Severn and the others had already reached the first flight of steps.

'This is not possible,' the Guard was saying, and he handed the documents back to Sarah. 'We have very good security measures here, and I myself was involved in the search of the Basilica this morning. But if you would care to wait here— '

'You don't understand! The life of the Pope and everyone in this crowd may be at risk.'

He wasn't budging, so I took Sarah by the arm and made to leave, then at the last moment turned with her.

'Come on!' We ran through the gap between the Guards, through the massive arched doorway behind them. They let out a shout and began running after us.

*

We were in some sort of a hallway, with a thick red carpet and glittering chandeliers. A tall man in flowing robes with a red sash was already bustling towards us, the slapping of his slippers echoing against the marble floor.

'What is this, please?' he said. He had a narrow, ascetic face: a thin mouth, high cheekbones and deep-set eyes. The Guards were now stationed behind us, their halberds drawn.

'These people just broke in—' our Guard started to explain, but I cut him off.

'We are from British intelligence. We have information suggesting that there may be a bomb in the Basilica.' I nodded at Sarah again, and she withdrew the papers and handed them over, pointing to the paragraph in question. The man took a pair of spectacles from his robe and began reading, but after a few seconds he handed the wad back officiously.

'I have no way of knowing if these are genuine or not. Do you have any identification?'

'That is what we asked, Cardinal—' the Guard broke in, but the cardinal silenced him with a glare.

'No,' I said, 'but there really isn't time for that. You need to tell His Holiness to cancel his address.'

The cardinal started. 'Impossible! Look at the crowd outside, *signore*. Many people have come a very long way to see His Holiness, and they will be very upset if he does not appear.'

'They'll be even more upset if he's killed. Send these Guards out to explain that he's not feeling well. The people will be disappointed, of course, but they will understand. What do you have to lose? If you find we have tricked you in some way, you can make a formal complaint to the British government and I assure you we will make a full public apology. But please – this is a very serious threat.'

He was quiet for a moment, then put out a skeletal hand to Sarah again. She returned the papers, and he looked down at them once more.

'Impossible,' he muttered.

I looked at him in despair, and started wondering if we could perhaps risk running past *him*. But then I remembered something. 'Last month,' I said. 'There was a warning about a bomb here.'

He looked up at me, surprised. 'Yes – but nothing was found.'

'Because they didn't know where to look. Someone *planted* it then, and it's due to go off today.'

His eyes widened. He looked back down at the document, and then he seemed to reach a decision.

'Do you know where they have placed it?'

I nodded.

He gestured to the lead Swiss Guard. 'Take this man wherever he wants to go – and quickly!'

'The dome,' I told him. He glared at me for a moment, then bowed to the cardinal and showed us to a door at the side.

'Follow me, please.'

*

The Guard took us quickly up a flight of stairs, then down a long carpeted corridor. We passed a magnificent statue of a horse and then pushed through a doorway into a small courtyard. There was a long queue of people waiting to take the lift up to the top. I had thought that the Pope's address would have thinned the crowd inside the church, but by the looks of things it hadn't made much difference. We rushed to the front of the line, and the Swiss Guard pulled aside the rope and asked the clerk in the ticket booth how long it would be until the next lift arrived. The clerk shrugged expansively.

'Five minutes?'

Too long. I nodded to the Swiss Guard, and the three of us raced ahead to the staircase. I reached it first and started climbing the narrow steps, turning past walls scratched with names and dates: tourists who wanted to leave their mark for posterity, I supposed. There were several other people making their way up the stairs, and I weaved my way around them, wondering how far behind Severn and Zimotti were.

I came out onto another courtyard, and there was the dome directly ahead, the cross and ball lit by the morning sun. To the left, beyond some pieces of scaffolding and canvas, the statues of the Apostles gazed out over the city. Could the bomb be here somewhere? I didn't think so – not enough impact. *In* the dome, Barchetti had said. Keep going.

I could hear a low burring noise behind me and realized it was the lift descending – Severn and Zimotti might soon be coming up in it. I crossed the courtyard to the next flight of stairs, which was surrounded by white railings. A short flight up and I reached a narrow balcony that gave spectacular views both down into the church and up into the dome. Tourists were pressed along the balcony deciding which to photograph first, and I squeezed past them to the next archway. The stairs led down, confusing me for a moment, but then I saw the archway on the right. The sign above it read 'INGRESSO ALLA CVPPOLA', and I leapt through it and saw the next flight leading up.

Christ, it was narrow. There was barely room to move, and as my leg muscles started to pulse with pain I regretted not taking the lift for the first part of the journey – I'd be lucky if I had any energy left by the time I reached the top. Then again, if we had waited for the lift Severn and Zimotti might already have caught up with us. I had to climb at a slower pace now because I was stuck behind an Australian woman complaining to her husband that she hadn't had any breakfast and couldn't climb on an empty stomach. I heard shallow breathing behind me, and turned to see Sarah, the palm of one hand resting against the wall for support as she climbed.

The staircase began spiralling, and through narrow slits in the walls I caught glimpses of pink tiles, white statues, green trees. The stairs straightened again, and then started angling to one side as we squeezed between the inner and outer drums of the dome. It was getting warm, and a surge of dizziness flooded through me – I blinked and shook it away.

There was another spiralling stairwell, now with a rope instead of banisters, but it was mercifully short and we came out onto another balcony, this one in the open air. A mass of tourists stood by the low railings, and beyond them the city stretched out in the sunshine. I turned to see both Sarah and the Swiss Guard and raised my chin. The Guard pointed ahead, and I saw an iron ladder a few feet away, hanging almost verti-cally. I pushed through the crowd of people and grabbed hold of it, my heart racing. How long did we have until the bomb went off? I climbed hand over hand, until finally I was right in the copper-plated ball. I took a few seconds to recover my breath, then looked around.

There was nobody here, just a wooden bench, smooth from a billion tourists' arses, and tiny slats looking down at the city. And somewhere, I was sure, a bomb. But where? Had I guessed wrong? Perhaps they had placed it in the church itself, or on the balcony the Pope would be standing on shortly . . . No. Barchetti had specifically mentioned the attack *in the dome*.

There was a clanging at the ladder and the Swiss Guard climbed into the space. Sweat was pouring down his face, and I felt a pang of sympathy — I hadn't made the climb in that outfit. He glanced at me and immediately registered my confu-sion.

'I told you, *signore*,' he said. 'We checked thoroughly this morning.'

My sympathy vanished. Triumphant little shit. But he was wrong. It *had* to be here.

There was another clang, and Sarah emerged, very out of breath.

'What's the programme now?' I asked the Guard. 'The Pope's address is at noon, and then what? Mass?' Perhaps they hadn't planted the bomb yet, but would do shortly.

The Guard shook his head.

'It is a much shorter Mass today, because at one o'clock there is a special service for the feast day of Santa Sindone.'

'How much shorter?' I asked. 'Will the Pope be . . .' I stopped. 'What was that? The feast day of what?'

'Santa Sindone.' I stared at him blankly. 'The Holy Shroud of Turin – the cloth Christ was buried in.'

May the fourth was the feast day of the Shroud. That was an iconic religious event, all right – even more so than the Pope's regular Sunday address.

'The Shroud. Where is it?'

'In Turin,' said the Guard, exasperated at my ignorance.

'In the cathedral?'

He nodded. 'The chapel attached to it. Every May the fourth, they remove the Shroud from the altar and—'

He stopped. There had been a loud noise below us. I glanced down the ladder and saw Zimotti emerging onto the gallery, holding up his identification wallet and shouting as he made his way through the crowd. The Guard turned to descend, but I grabbed him by the lapel and gestured for Sarah to stay where she was, too.

'Does it have a dome?' I asked. He looked at me uncomprehendingly, and I shook him. 'The chapel housing the Shroud! *Does it have a dome?*'

He nodded, and tried to move a hand towards his rapier. I pushed it aside.

'What time?' I shouted at him. 'What time is the service?'

There was more noise, and I could hear Zimotti's voice below us. The Guard stared back at me blankly.

'They begin at eight o'clock . . .'

The world slowed to silence, and I knew I had made a terrible mistake. I brushed past the Guard and reached for Sarah's hand.

We were in the wrong place – the wrong bloody *city*. The attack wasn't planned for here. It was planned for Turin, in less than nine hours' time.

XXII

Sarah began to climb back down the ladder, and the Swiss Guard and I rapidly followed. I could hear Zimotti making his way through the crowd, and I pushed Sarah the other way, cursing myself for leading us up here. I had foolishly presumed that the next attack would revolve around an individual. But it wasn't Christ's representative on Earth that was the target, but Christ himself – or rather his followers. The documents had mentioned that religious events had an 'easily understood and revered symbolism'. It was hard to think of anything more revered or symbolic than the Turin Shroud: millions of people around the world believed it to be the cloth Christ had been wrapped in after his crucifixion. It was perhaps the greatest icon of the Catholic Church, and an attack on its holy feast day would create headlines around the world. In Italy, the idea that the Communists were prepared to blow up innocent worshippers in a church would scare everyone away at the next election. And if they damaged the Shroud itself . . . but could they really be prepared to do that?

As we moved through the crowd looking for the stairway leading down, I spotted Severn coming round the other way, and froze. I grabbed Sarah by the wrist and ran in the only direction available, pushing through the crush of tourists until I reached the railing. The outside of the dome curved away, and I peered over to see the statues of the Apostles on the courtyard below, and beyond them the crowd in the square undulating like a giant moving carpet.

I turned my attention to the dome itself. A couple of feet down there was a horizontal ring of small windows, like port-holes in a ship. And between the windows, vertical mouldings circled the dome, jutting out from the surface like giant white centipedes. Fixed to the roofs of the windows and running down the centre of the centipedes were dozens of small iron discs, reddish brown with rust. They stirred a dim memory – wasn't the dome illuminated on certain occasions? Perhaps these discs once held the torches. At any rate, they were fastened to the surface with iron spikes. I glanced over at Sarah, and her eyes bulged as she realized what I had in mind. But Severn and Zimotti were jostling through the crowd on either side of us, calling out that it was a public emergency. They would be here any moment. We had no choice.

I took a firm hold of the railing and hoisted myself over, ignoring the screams of a woman behind me. Once on the other side, I jammed my right plimsoll down and under the nearest disc. Would it take my weight? There was only one way to find out. I worked my way down to the bottom of the railing with my hands, flattening the front of my body against the side of the dome as I did. Close up, the surface was covered with threads of black grime and pigeon droppings. I lifted my left leg away for an instant and the disc didn't budge beneath my right foot, so I lowered myself once more and wedged my left shoe into the next disc down.

I took a breath, then looked up, expecting to see Sarah descending the same way. But she was still astride the railing, and she wasn't moving. She had frozen to the spot.

'I can't!' she said, almost sobbing with fear. 'I . . . can't move.'

But she was moving – her legs were shaking. Any moment now and she would lose her balance and fall.

'It's fine,' I said. 'But you have to come *now*.'

As if in answer to this, there was some sort of a commotion to the left, and I looked up and saw Severn leaning over the side of the railing, one hand raised to hold back frightened tourists. There was a pistol in the other, and he was aiming it straight at her.

'Everyone around you ends up dead . . .'

Not this time. Please not this time.

I shouted up to Sarah that she had to move and she shook her head violently, but then something made her realize she had no choice and she brought her legs over and lowered herself down onto the centipede to the left of mine, her shoe reaching the first disc as the shot came, sending a blast of sparks off the railing. This church might not be the target of the operation, but Severn and Zimotti clearly weren't squeamish about damaging it.

I looked up at Sarah, whose face was flushed from the effort.

We had a moment's breathing space, because we were now out of Severn's line of sight and he couldn't shoot around curves. But only a moment: he had probably ordered some of his men to take the staircase and wait for us at the bottom, but the crowds would hold them up and there were several exits. His best chance to catch us now was to follow us over the railings, and I was pretty sure he'd realize it.

I started climbing down the rest of the way, my hands now clutching the spikes that kept the discs in place, which were blisteringly hot after a few hours in the sun. In principle it was easy, like climbing down a step-ladder. But the ladder was curved, and if we made one slip we would fall to our deaths.

We made our way down our separate ladders as quickly as we could and reached the rim of the dome, where there were plinths large enough to stand on. There was a jump of several feet to the next level, but I could see a relief of stone flowers jutting out from the wall between my section and the next plinth along. It looked like a safer bet, so I shimmied over to the next ledge, clutching at a thinner line of centipedes descending from the top, and then crouched and hung my legs over the side. I glanced down and saw that the relief wasn't protruding as much as I'd thought it would, so I let go and tried to angle my body in as I dropped.

My right knee crunched down on the top of the relief, and I let out a cry and threw my hands up to gain a hold before I slipped over the edge. My fingers gripped something, and I looked up to see that they had hooked around the lower lip of the mouth of a fierce-looking stone lion: a relief just above the flowers that hadn't been visible from my vantage point on the ledge. I pulled my other knee up until I was kneeling firmly on the top of the floral relief. Once I was comfortable, I turned around and prepared to lower myself again and jump the final few feet to the ledge beneath.

The pain came from nowhere. My throat felt thick and constricted, and I was being dragged back upward. He had his boots wrapped around my neck and he was trying to crush my windpipe. My eyes rolled upward and I saw a pair of boots and the first few inches of a pair of trouser-legs hanging from the ledge directly above me. The trousers were midnight blue – not Severn, then, but Zimotti. I suddenly felt very cold, and realized that my teeth were chattering.

Zimotti was shaking his legs frantically, trying to swing me out so he could drop me over the ledge and to the ground far below. My fingers started slipping as my breathing began to suffer and I tried to call out to Sarah, who I could hear was still in the next section along, but nothing came from my throat.

Above me, Zimotti was grunting and cursing, but his voice sounded peculiar and I realized that it *wasn't*, in fact, Zimotti but his hawk-faced hatchet man. I hadn't seen him on the gallery earlier. Among his curses, I heard the word 'Fratello' repeated several times and with a shock it hit me that he meant the sniper in St Paul's, who was either literally his brother or a brother in arms, and that he blamed me for his death and wanted vengeance for it. Vengeance for a man who had been given the task of assassinating me, and who had thought nothing of using a defenceless child as a shield.

Fury pulsed through me and I used the strength of it to jerk my head down violently in an effort to dislodge his boots from around my throat. But it didn't make any difference. They were locked there, and squeezing tighter by the moment. As I started to choke and felt my vision beginning to black out, I did the only thing I could think of: I lifted my left hand from the relief for a moment and punched up between the Bird Man's legs, towards his groin.

He screamed, and I quickly reached to grab hold of the relief once again. Stone scratched against my nails and then my fingers gripped tightly, and as they did, the pressure around my neck floated away, and I realized that the Bird Man was starting to fall. I gripped tighter with my hands, and the scream intensified and wind brushed against me and I looked down as his torso cracked against the rim of the ledge beneath and he spun towards the courtyard below, sending a group of tourists screaming.

For a moment I thought it might not have been enough of a fall to kill him, but then the stone beneath him began to turn red and vomit rose in my throat. I winced and gulped it down. My shirt was now soaked in sweat and clinging to my back. And I could hear the sound of someone moving above. It wasn't over. We had to get down before the others came.

My fingers started to slip, and finally I let go. I landed on the ledge and my thighs clenched with the pain, so sharp it took my breath away. But nothing was broken and I was safely in the centre of the ledge. I took a deep breath and looked up to see Sarah preparing to make the same jump a few feet away.

Directly below us – within easy reach – was the white-railinged flight of stairs we had come up, and below that the courtyard with the dead man sprawled across it. We just had to reach that courtyard. After that, we could take the stairs down.

I could sense Sarah hesitating again and decided to lead by example, to show her how close we were. There was a tiled roof a couple of feet from the ledge. I scurried over, then levered myself onto it using the chimney, after which I began creeping down the tiles like a crab.

'See?' I called. 'It's easy.'

There was a thud above me and I looked up, expecting to see Sarah landing on the ledge. But instead I saw Barnes. Christ, they'd brought the lot of them. He was wearing the same fatigues he'd been in at the base in Sardinia, and his pale blue eyes were blazing with hatred. He stood to his full height and his mouth formed a grim smile: he thought he had me. He was grasping something in his hand, and it glittered momentarily in the sun. It had a long, thin blade: a stiletto knife? Severn must have given it to him, because he couldn't have brought it through . . . I stopped. We hadn't come through customs. He could have had it strapped to his leg the whole time.

I looked past him, trying to see where Sarah had gone, but she seemed to have disappeared and the move was a mistake because Barnes saw his chance and leapt forward, pushing me further down the roof and towards the line of railings that enclosed the flight of stairs. As he jerked the knife down, I threw my arms up and grabbed hold of his wrist, managing to stop the blade a few inches from my neck. He grunted, his mouth clamped shut and a hissing noise emanating from his nostrils, and the blade moved closer. I pushed back against him with every sinew and fibre, but I knew that I could only hold out for another second or two at the most. He was older than me, but he was fitter, better trained and, like the Bird Man, he wanted revenge – in his case, justifiably.

There was a blur of movement and his free hand came round in a tight fist, aiming low, and I recognized the old commando move and made to counter it with my forearm. I caught it just in time, but in the meantime the blade continued its descent. I pushed back again. Beads of sweat dripped into my eyes, stinging them, and I tried to blink them away, to no avail. Barnes grunted again, and as the blade dropped another fraction of an inch I prepared myself for it to pierce into me. But then I realized with a flash of intuition what I had to do, and I abruptly relaxed my grip and jerked my head away sharply at the same moment, and the surprise and momentum were too much for him to correct and as his arm came down he lost his balance and the whole upper half of his body tipped over with it, and then I was looking down at the cluster of railing spikes emerging through the top of his head, the tips covered in some dark slimy mixture I didn't want to think about. He moaned one last moan, and then his limbs went into a final spasm and he was still.

I wiped the sweat from my eyes and breathed in deeply to calm myself. Then I called up to Sarah to make the last leap. She did it, making a much better landing than I had done, and then she climbed onto the tiled roof and I helped her over the railings and we walked down the steps into the courtyard. I asked her if she felt she could continue. She nodded, and we left the bodies of Bird Man and Barnes and staggered past the open-mouthed and horrified tourists down the remaining stairs until we reached the square. There was no sign of Severn and Zimotti, but I had no doubt they were coming.

We stumbled through the crowd and into one of the side streets – but where to now? Hiring a car was out of the question, as their next step would be to contact all the rental places, so a description of anything we hired would immediately be sent to every police station in the country. The most anonymous form of travel, and I reckoned our best bet, was the train. A teenager on a bright red Vespa hurtled straight towards us, and I stepped out in front of him, putting my hand out officiously and yelling for him to stop. He slowed fractionally, and as he passed I yanked him by the collar and dragged him off the bike, hoisting myself into his place.

'Get on!' I called to Sarah. She hobbled over and clambered aboard, and I changed gears as the former owner shook his fists at our smoke. Needs must.

XXIII

I parked the Vespa in Piazza dei Cinquecento and we headed into the main hall of Termini railway station, past young people smoking and flirting and generally having the time of their lives. There was a swarm of people surrounding the ticket booth, to the extent that it wasn't clear where one queue ended and the next began. I looked up at the departure board and saw that the next train to Turin was leaving in less than five minutes: the Tirreno, a fast service that stopped at Pisa and a few other places on the way. It was our only chance. We would just have to pay on board, or hope the train was so crowded that the conductor didn't bother to check tickets.

We rushed across to the platform and, to my relief, I saw that it was indeed crowded. Dozens of men were calling to each other as they tried to coordinate an effort to bring all the luggage onto the train. Some were pulling their suitcases tied together with string through the doors, while others were lifting them to their friends and squeezing them through the windows of the compartments.

'What's going on?' I asked Sarah. 'Why are they taking suit-cases to a religious festival?'

She shook her head. 'They're not going to the festival — they're heading north for work. The "economic miracle" has run out of steam down here.'

We made our way through the throng and climbed onto the train, then walked along the corridors looking for seats. We squeezed past students strumming guitars, tourists consulting maps, a monsignor cutting open a garlic sausage, and everywhere these wild-eyed men in their threadbare suits trailing their suitcases behind them. Finally we found a compart-ment with a couple of spare seats, which was otherwise occu-pied by an elderly Mother Superior and a gaggle of young nuns excitedly exchanging gossip and unpacking sandwiches for the journey. A whistle blew and we were off.

As the wheels started gathering pace, the tension within me faded a little. We had lost them. I turned to Sarah. She had circles under her eyes, and cuts and dirt were smeared across her cheeks. She looked much more fragile than when I had first met her in the embassy, but infinitely more beautiful. I leaned across and gently placed my hand against her cheek, and she gave a wan smile in return.

I glanced out of the window and caught sight of a clock in the station. It was coming up to noon, and the departure board had said that we were due to arrive in Turin at quarter past seven. But train timetables didn't mean much in Italy these days, and anything could delay us. Even if we arrived bang on time, we would have only forty-five minutes to get to the cathedral, and I suspected we would have a welcoming committee to evade first – Zimotti would have furnished the local *carabinieri* with detailed descriptions of the two of us. And even if we made it out of the station and to the cathedral, I had no idea what sort of explosive they would use. From what I remembered, the two explosions in Milan had been simple detonators with sticks of dynamite – but my source for that information was the Service's file, and that had also claimed that Arte come Terrore were responsible. And I had a feeling this would be on a much bigger scale than the bombs in Milan. If we did find the bomb in time, the church authorities might listen, but they wouldn't have access to any bomb disposal experts of their own. About all we could hope for was that they would clear the area – but how long would that take at such a massive event?

I wondered if I hadn't just miscalculated horribly. Severn had told me I had got myself into something bigger than I understood, and I was starting to fear he'd been right. Well, we had several hours on this train. I decided to take the opportunity to have another look at the documents, and read them through thoroughly. I didn't expect them to tell me how to defuse the bomb, but they might contain other clues as to what we were up against. I turned to Sarah and told her what I had in mind, and she unbuttoned the pocket of the overalls and handed the bundle across. The cover was torn from our climbing adventure, but the papers inside were untouched.

I took them out and started reading, but after a few minutes the words began to swim in front of my eyes and my temples throbbed with pain. It was too bloody stuffy in the compartment. I asked Sarah to open the window, and it was then that I noticed the Mother Superior peering at me from beneath her wimple. I looked down at the documents and saw the seals exposed on the page. I doubted she could read them, but together with our overalls and bruised faces, her interest had certainly been piqued. I nudged Sarah again. 'Leave that. Let's go and see what they have to eat instead – I'm famished.'

She nodded, and we left the compartment and walked down the corridor, through first class and into the restaurant car. It was shielded from the sunshine by heavy curtains, and was empty: we had only just left the station and it was still too early for lunch. We took a table, and I seated myself facing the glass doors we had come through. A waiter ambled over and I ordered two steaks, a bottle of San Pellegrino mineral water and a pack of cigarettes; he nodded and disappeared.

I took out the bundle and placed it on the table. I decided to start from the other end, at the series of papers that came directly after the strategic document: I hadn't looked at them yet. The first one I picked up was in Italian, and was dated 1 June 1959. A slightly faded letterhead read '*Stato Maggiore della Difesa, Servizio Informazioni delle Forze Armate*' – the old name for military intelligence – and under that was the title '*LE "FORZE SPECIALI" DEL SIFAR E L'OPERAZIONE "GLADIO"*': 'The Special Forces of Military Intelligence and Operation "Gladio"'.

The document was a briefing on the country's stay-behind operation, and I was shocked at how advanced it was. It seemed it had been – and perhaps still was – linked to the Clandestine

Planning Committee, which itself was affiliated to the Supreme Headquarters of the Allied Powers in Europe. The base in Sardinia was mentioned at several points, and appeared to be used primarily as a training centre for the stay-behind army. In June 1959, this had been made up of forty cells: six for intelligence-gathering, ten for sabotage, six for propaganda, six for escape and evasion and twelve for conducting guerrilla warfare against the enemy. The guerrilla cells were described as having hundreds of units each.

I placed the document to one side and turned to the next on the table. This was dated much earlier, from 1948, and seemed to be a formal agreement of cooperation between the Service and the network in the Netherlands. I started looking through the other papers: Germany, France, Spain, Portugal . . . every country in NATO was here, and even a few outside it. The file from Turkey was dated June 1951, and was signed by Templeton, Osborne and a Turkish name I recognized as Cousin Freddie's. All the files related to the establishment of stay-behind networks, sometimes with British and sometimes with American support. I guessed the latter were providing most of the money behind it. The organization didn't seem to have one overarching name: it was simply called Stay Behind in Britain, but was known as Glaive in France, Gladio in Italy, Kontrgerilla in Turkey, and so on.

There were also files on individual Stay Behind officers, including one on Zimotti. It seemed that in the war he had been a member of La Decima, the elite commando frogman unit. After the Italian armistice in 1943, he and about 20,000 other men from the unit had continued to fight in the north of the country on the Axis side, under the command of Valerio Borghese, 'The Black Prince'. They had become infamous for their brutal acts against the partisans, including summary executions, torture and the burning down of villages with a strong partisan presence. In 1945, he was one of the many La Decima members arrested by partisans, but had been one of the lucky few who had been saved from reprisals and taken to safety by the Allies. The Black Prince himself had been rescued by the Americans, but Zimotti owed his life to the British: to William Osborne, in fact, who had been in charge of his case in England before he had eventually returned to Italy.

There was a file on Severn, too. Back in '51, he had felt Osborne was misusing him as a chauffeur, but his trip to Istanbul had merely been his indoctrination into Stay Behind. And just as the Turkish network had been controlled by Templeton, with Cousin Freddie as the local liaison, Severn was now the Service's Stay Behind commander in Italy, working in conjunction with Zimotti. I couldn't see a file for Osborne, but I guessed he was very senior in the whole set-up, if not in charge of it outright.

All of which was very interesting, but there was nothing here I could take to Haggard. Just because Zimotti and others had been fascists during the war did not prove that they had subverted the original networks in any way. The strategy proposal arguing the benefits of false-flag attacks on churches and football stadia was extreme, but it was, after all, merely a proposal. Many such documents were written, but the operations mentioned within them didn't always come to fruition. My throat suddenly felt dry. Had I got completely the wrong end of the stick? Were these simply documents about the original stay-behind networks, kept in the Station safe for perfectly innocent reasons?

The train swayed as it rounded a bend in the track, and I grabbed at the papers to stop them from slipping off the table. My thumb caught hold of one I didn't recognize. I tidied the stack, waited for the train to settle and then picked it up again. It was in English. I read it through, then placed it back in the pile and handed the whole lot back to Sarah, who replaced it in her pocket.

'Anything interesting?' she asked.

I nodded. The last document had been dated 1962, and bore the NATO seal. Its distribution list included senior members of French, German, Italian and British intelligence, including Osborne. And it was nothing short of a manifesto, laying out in detail the justification for resurrecting the original stay-behind networks as an 'anticipatory mechanism' — in short, instead of waiting for Moscow to invade or for the Communists to come to power democratically, to attack the citizens of their own countries and frame Moscow and others as a means of frightening the electorate and imposing strict law and order. It made it clear that national governments had not been informed of the operation — instead, it seemed, one politician in each country, usually a minister of defence, had been indoctrinated into the plan. I hadn't been wrong, after all. The conspiracy was real, and here was the proof.

I quickly explained the situation to Sarah, and she asked me what I planned to do.

'Let's start by getting to Turin and stopping whatever they have planned there,' I said. 'Presuming we manage that, I suggest that the minute it's over you call the Home Secretary, and then take the first flight to London you can.'

The waiter arrived with our meal, and we started eating. I hardly noticed it – the dossier had left a sour taste in my mouth that I couldn't seem to banish and my mind was too preoccupied. I opened the pack of cigarettes and lit one from the book of matches on the table.

'But what will *you* do?' Sarah asked, finally. 'If I go to Whitehall?'

I took a draught of the cigarette – the nicotine pushed deep into my chest and warmed it. 'I don't know,' I said, which was the truth. I hadn't made up my mind if I wanted to enter the lion's den of London again. Back in Sardinia I had been confident that Haggard would be able to deal with Osborne and the rest of his cabal if I could show him proof of what they were up to. Now I knew just how far-reaching the conspiracy was, I wasn't so sure. They had secret *armies* in every NATO country preparing to commit atrocities to stop the Communists. If they couldn't kill me, they would do everything in their power to prove to Haggard and everyone else that I was a Soviet agent. As I was one, they would probably succeed in that – and nobody in London would listen to the allegations of a traitor. Sarah had a much better chance of persuading Haggard without me. 'I might try to head for Switzerland,' I said. 'It all depends—'

I froze. Just visible through the glass doors of the carriage was the blue trouser-leg of a man. The conductor? Or Zimotti? I stubbed out my cigarette in the ashtray. It was Zimotti, and as he stepped inside the carriage I saw Severn standing directly behind him. They must have boarded at the last moment and been combing through the train looking for us. Zimotti's eyes met mine, and then he cried out and they started heading towards us.

I took Sarah by the arm and we started running down the restaurant car, crashing through the doors. To the left was a corridor leading to passenger compartments; straight ahead, the kitchens. On an impulse, I dived ahead. The place was tiny, and thick with steam. White-coated cooks and stewards scattered in alarm as a shot rang out, racing to a door at the far end of the room. I turned to see Severn and Zimotti right behind me. Sarah leapt towards Severn, trying to scratch at his eyes, and as he lifted his gun again I ran forward to help her. But Zimotti had seen what I was planning, and he picked me up and hurled me against one of the workbenches. Behind them I saw a line of steel cauldrons, and he lifted me by my shirt and pushed my head towards one of the vats. It was open, bubbling with boiling water, and I felt a blanket of steam engulfing me and lashed out blindly, trying to reposition myself, but he had a firm grip and the heat was becoming more intense as he pushed my face closer to the surface of the water. I remembered glimpsing saucepans and ladles hanging from the ceiling when I'd come in, and I reached up to try to grab one, but came away empty-handed. I kicked behind me desperately, and one of my legs caught Zimotti in the chest. He reeled back, screaming and cursing me in Italian, and I ducked down as he ran towards me in a rage, grabbing him by the legs and lifting him so he flew over the bench.

There was a dreadful scream as he plunged head first into the boiling cauldron. Without even thinking, I grabbed him by his collar and lifted him out. His entire face was burned, a surface of red sores. I tried to push him back down but he was already reaching out for me, and I lunged for the surface of the workbench. There was a knife there, and I managed to pick it up. As he came towards me, I held the knife firm with both hands as it pushed into his chest. He crumpled to the floor, and his cries of agony sputtered into groans, and then whispers, and then silence.

I made my way through the steam trying to find Sarah and Severn. They were still over by the door, and as I approached them my chest clenched. He was aiming a gun directly at her head.

'Tell me!' he was screaming at her. 'Did you screw the bastard? *Did you screw him?*'

She didn't answer him, and he let out a howl at the realization. He was about to press down the trigger and I leapt towards him with the knife. He saw me and moved to avoid it but he was a fraction too late and the blade glanced across his jaw, and he lost balance and started falling. The gun fell from his hands and Sarah jumped down and grabbed it, then stood again. Her eyes were hard and cold, but her hand was shaking as she brought the gun up and aimed it straight at her husband.

'Don't shoot!' I yelled.

Severn looked up from the floor, the right side of his face soaked in blood and a strange smile on his lips. 'You didn't read it,' he said, and I realized he was talking to me. 'You don't know . . .' He wiped his hand with blood, and cocked his head at Sarah dismissively. 'Enjoy her while she lasts. It won't be long.' His mouth twisted into a grimace, either of hatred or pain, I couldn't tell, and then the shot rang out and there was a small red dot in his forehead. The blood oozed slowly from it and mixed with the blood from the knife wound, and his eyes were like glass.

Sarah had dropped to the floor, and I stepped forward and gently took the gun from her hands. It was a Browning, and it was still hot. I put it on safety and shoved it into my waist-band. She looked up at me dully.

'You understand?' she whispered. 'I couldn't let him . . . I couldn't let him *own* me any more.'

I nodded, and pressed my hand into hers. I didn't blame her: he'd had it coming. What I didn't understand were his parting words. What hadn't I read? The documents, presumably. But I had read them all. Was there another dossier somewhere?

I leaned down and searched through his pockets, turning each of them out to see if he had any papers on him and padding him down in case he had secured them elsewhere. Then I took off his boots to check he hadn't hidden anything in the soles. But there was nothing. Nothing at all.

I turned to Sarah and asked her to pass me the sheaf of documents again. She didn't answer, so I knelt down next to her and repeated it and she nodded and unbuttoned the pocket and passed the packet to me. I flicked through the pages, trying to see if there were any clues as to what Severn had meant, but there was no mention of Turin, no specifics about this attack or its ramifications. Whatever it was I had missed, it would have to wait. We had to get rid of these bodies – the kitchen staff might be back any minute, and the conductor with them.

I jumped over to Zimotti and searched him. He didn't have any papers on him, either, but he did have a wallet containing his identification badge. I took it, then stripped the trousers, shirt and jacket from him and hurriedly put them on over my own. I took off my now-ragged plimsolls and replaced them with his thick-soled boots.

There was a cargo hatch for goods near the door, and I leaned over and slid the cover to one side. Sarah was still dazed, but I persuaded her to stand and we lifted Zimotti's body and heaved it through the hatch. There was a clump as it hit the sides and then it was gone.

We repeated the process with Severn, after which I cleaned up as much of the blood from the floor as I could with a rag. I threw it in the sink, then took Sarah by the hand and we ran back through the restaurant car, to the compartment with the nuns and the Mother Superior. Sarah stepped inside and I was about to follow her when I saw someone walking through the door at the far end of the corridor. It was the conductor.

He was a short, rotund little man with drooping shoulders and a ferrety moustache. I slid the door of the compartment shut and marched towards him. 'Di Angelo,' I said, flashing Zimotti's identification in his face. 'Servizio Informazioni Difesa. Have you seen my colleague? He's with a British agent with fair hair. We're looking for a couple of fugitives.'

He nodded eagerly. 'I saw them heading this way a few minutes ago. I thought I'd better come and investigate myself because half the kitchen staff just barged into my quarters and told me there was trouble at this end of the train.'

I gave him a puzzled look. 'I haven't seen anything. Tell them to get back to their stations. It was a false alarm.'

He hesitated. 'But one of them said he heard a shot.'

I looked at him, and his shoulders drooped a little more under my gaze. 'Do what you are told,' I said sharply. 'This is urgent state business, and I have no time to explain the situation. Do you understand?'

'Yes, officer. Shall I stop the train so you can conduct a search for the fugitives?'

If he stopped the train, it was all over. The *carabinieri* would come on board, and we would be delayed.

I gave him my coldest, most imperious glare. 'If I had wanted you to stop the train, I would have asked you,' I said. 'Did you hear me make such a request?'

'No, officer.'

'Well, then . . .' He looked up at me with ill-concealed resentment, and I pretended to soften. 'I apologize. You are a good man, I know. We all have our jobs to do, and sometimes they're not easy. I appreciate the suggestion, but I don't think we need stop the train just yet – we'll find them soon enough. In the meantime, can you keep your eyes open for me?' He nodded gratefully, and I clapped him on the back. 'Good man. I'll start checking these carriages, and I suggest you go and tell the kitchen staff to return – there may be hungry passengers, and we wouldn't want them to make a complaint, would we? If you see anything suspicious on the way, come and find me at once.'

He nodded and trundled away.

*

As we slowed into Turin's Porta Nuova station, I braced myself for the next hurdle. There was a group of *carabinieri* waiting at the barrier on the platform: no doubt they were armed with our descriptions. I wasn't sure I could bluff them with Zimotti's identification badge – they might look a little more closely at the photograph than the conductor had done, and while there were a few flecks of grey in my hair, it wasn't nearly enough of a likeness. But a bigger problem was Sarah, who had no disguise: her long blonde hair stood out a mile.

The train came to a standstill, and we stepped off and joined the crowd heading for the exit. As I had feared, the *carabinieri* were examining everyone as they came through. I adjusted my collar and took a deep breath. We walked towards the barrier, shuffling through the crush. Any moment now someone would catch sight of Sarah's hair.

I swivelled on my heels to face the person behind me, a hollow-cheeked young man, and flashed my identification at him. Puzzled, he slowed down, and I quickly reached out and grabbed the cap from his head, then threw it to Sarah.

'Put this on!' I told her. 'Try to get through!'

She clamped the cap down over her head, tucking as much of her hair as she could into it, then pushed forward into the crowd.

My victim, in the meantime, had swiftly turned from puzzled to angry and started shouting at me. One of the *carabinieri* at the barrier flicked his head up and began moving towards us. I could see Sarah a few feet ahead, but she had not yet made it through to the other side.

'*Venite subito!*' I shouted. 'Someone has been stabbed here!'

The *carabinieri* froze for a moment, then shouted back at one of his colleagues and the two of them began thrusting their way through the crowd towards the imaginary scene of the crime. It left a gap on one side of the barrier. I pushed past a middle-aged couple and started heading for it. By the time the *carabinieri* had reached the perplexed man, who tried to explain what had happened, I was in the station concourse.

I ran across it and through the colonnaded exit, where Sarah was waiting for me. There was a queue for the taxis, but we didn't have time to wait. We ran to the front, holding up Zimotti's badge to the astonished line of customers. I opened the door of the front taxi and jumped in.

'*Il Duomo*,' I said.

The driver gave a curt nod and put his foot down.

XXIV

The city swept by in a blur, and my eyes fixed on the clock on the dashboard of the taxi. It read a quarter to eight – we had fifteen minutes to find the bomb and stop it. As we came into Piazza San Giovanni, the cathedral rose in front of us, the façade a mass of white marble glinting in the evening sun. And, just visible above it, the tip of the chapel pierced the evening sky.

I paid the driver and we got out and started running towards the square. The crowd was much bigger than I'd hoped, a great crush of people queuing to enter in advance of the service. I waved Zimotti's identification above my head, and people reluctantly let us pass, until we finally reached the doors and entered the cathedral.

Incense hung heavily in the air. A procession of purple-robed priests were walking through the central candle-lit aisle, their chanting echoing around the space. At the far end of the nave there were two massive stairways with signs indicating that they led up to the Chapel of the Holy Shroud. We took the one on the right.

The stairs were steeper than I had expected, and halfway up I was nearly overcome by dizziness. Sarah grabbed my arm, and I shook the feeling away. She gave a taut smile and we carried on climbing, until we were in the chapel. Black and white marble and gilded bronze gleamed, and light shone through the cupola above, striking the ornate altar in the centre like a spotlight. Inside the altar was a magnificent silver chest, and inside that lay the Holy Shroud itself. I looked up at the frescos in the dome above. Barchetti had said 'in the dome', so that was where we had to go.

Sarah pointed to a staircase on the right. As we rushed towards it, I heard a disturbance from below. I looked down and saw one of the priests detaching himself from the procession. He'd seen us. He called out to us to stop, but we ducked into the staircase and started climbing, and then I heard him call out again and the sound of his footsteps echoing on the marble. There had been a tinge of panic in his voice, and I guessed that he was the inside man, the guard to make sure nobody came near the bomb.

There was a gallery directly under the dome, like the Whispering Gallery in London. I looked down and saw that the procession was entering the chapel below, heading for the altar with the Shroud. Ignore them. Concentrate. I looked around frantically. A large enough bomb here would not only destroy the Shroud, but might kill or maim people in the church — perhaps even some of the crowd outside. But where the hell had they put it? As in St Peter's, there was nothing but a bench, which Sarah was now sitting on, catching her breath.

'Stand up!' I told her, and she did so with a guilty start.

'You think it's here?'

'Perhaps.'

I knelt down and took a closer look. Yes, there was a lid to it – it was a chest as well as a bench. Perhaps this was where they usually kept spare parts or cleaning equipment or some such. It had a sliding lid, but I couldn't get it open. I looked for a lock, but there was none. It was simply jammed at one end, and it wasn't budging. I tried to place my nails into the tiny gap between the lid and the rest of the bench to lift it a fraction, but they weren't long or strong enough. Sarah shuffled over and tried with hers, but with no better result. It was useless.

Footsteps were now echoing up the stairs, and they were getting louder by the second. In frustration, I hit the palm of my hand against the lid. It moved. Just a tiny amount, but now there was enough space for me to use my fingers. I formed my hand into a claw and tried again. Slowly, the lid glided open.

I looked down into the chest. There was a bag inside, a faded leather hold-all. Perhaps it had tools in it. Or perhaps a chunk of plastic explosive connected to a timer. I leaned down and unzipped it.

There was nothing there.

I looked again, rummaging my hand around the sides and bottom. It was completely, mystifyingly empty. So where the hell had they planted it? I looked around desperately, at the columns and the pillars and the procession swaying below.

'Any ideas?' I asked Sarah.

She didn't respond, and I glanced up at her. She was sweating, shivering, with a panic-stricken expression on her face. That was understandable, but something about it seemed wrong, like she was terrified of something I wasn't aware of. She placed a finger to her head and said something, but her mouth couldn't seem to form the words, and my skin started to crawl as I realized why. She'd lost her hearing.

'Have you had any muscle pain since you were last here, or sore eyes? . . . Have you had any more bouts of deafness?'

There was no bomb here. Because they weren't using a bomb. They were using *me*.

I looked up. There were three of them, all wearing black robes with masks over the lower half of their faces. The figure nearest to me stepped forward and I saw he had a syringe in his hand. I tried to stand to make a run for it, but I didn't have any strength left and there was nowhere to run anyway, not any more. The other two men held me down, and as the needle plunged into my arm I imagined I felt the liquid pulsing through my bloodstream. They stepped over and I watched as they performed the same task on Sarah, and then my vision started to blur and my eyes closed.

XXV

I was in my dressing gown, waiting. It was night, and we were all assembled in Library, waiting anxiously. Moonlight shone through the window onto the ragged armchairs, and I felt like sneezing from the dust of the books. Thousands of others had made their way through this process over the years – so would I, I told myself. We had been woken and brought down here hours ago. I stared down at the pattern of the carpet, which was brown and red with little flecks of white in it, curlicues, like pieces of gristle in a slice of salami, like sea-horses in an ocean of wine, and I tightened the cord of my dressing gown around my body. It was like a rope, the cord, and I pulled it tight, chafing my skin, already raw from the winter night – there was little heating these days. It was a navy-blue dressing gown, bought by Mother at Harrods before the war, with my label sewn inside the collar. Outside I thought I heard the drone of the planes in the night. Somewhere out there, Father was waiting for me to grow up and become a man . . .

And now the big door opened to reveal Mason, impossibly tall Mason with his great hooded eyes, and he pointed to me.

I stepped forward. He placed the blindfold around my eyes, and I followed him.

I ran through everything in my mind one last time, all the words and facts I had studied obsessively for a fortnight, in the hope that it would soothe my nerves a little.

Mason walked me round the building, took me up one flight of stairs and down another, spun me round, shouted at me from different directions and after a while I stopped trying to figure out where we were going. It didn't matter. Every so often I reacted too slowly to his instructions and felt a swish against my calves and heat rising through the prickles. He had some sort of a whip with him.

I was being lifted into light. There was a moment of release as the cooler air hit my eyes and forehead, the sweat evaporated, and then a terrific blast of heat. Move, look away. Swish.

'Whenever you look away from the light, we will use this,' I heard someone say. He was holding the thing up in front of my face, but everything was a blur.

'We call it the Cat,' said the voice, and I recoiled as it brushed against my face. 'Keep looking at that light.'

Just a lamp, a common or garden lamp. Fix on something else, not on the bulb, or you will damage the retina. Fix just above and to the left and let the light become the background. Then I caught a glimpse of the boy holding the Cat, and realized it was Charles Severn, and I sat up with a jolt, my lungs heaving, sweat pouring off my face.

A nightmare. It had been a nightmare. My Notions test had been fine. I had passed. No bones broken. I was an adult. Severn was dead. A nightmare.

I looked down. A grey blanket and white sheets covered me, but it didn't feel sturdy enough for a bed: a stretcher, then. I moved to step off it, but found that I was strapped down.

As I took my bearings, questions started to flood through my mind, but before I could order them I was pulled up short by the sound of movement very close by. I looked up to see a young man in the uniform of a *carabinieri* standing by the edge of the stretcher. He wasn't wearing a mask, which something told me was a good sign. He was flicking his hand against a catheter tube attached to the stretcher. I followed the line of the tube, and lifted the sheet to see it leading into my wrist.

The man scribbled something down on a board he was holding, and then started walking away from me. I made to call out to him, but then noticed in my peripheral vision that there was something in the place he had been a moment ago. It was another stretcher, and lying on it, her eyes closed peacefully, was Sarah.

'She's fine.'

I looked up, startled, to see a man ducking his head down and entering the room. My stomach tightened.

'Hello, Paul,' he said.

'Hello, Sasha,' I replied.

*

He looked much the same as when I'd last seen him in London – could it really have been only a week ago? – but instead of his usual tweed get-up he was also dressed as a *carabinieri*. I tried to untwist what this meant. They had donned these uniforms in order to get into the cathedral . . . so they could take us out again without arousing any suspicions. But the sheer scale of organizing that meant that they must have been following events very closely for some time. And that they had gone to a lot of effort to rescue us. Why?

Something about the ducking movement he had made suddenly alerted me to the rest of the space I was in. Glancing upward, I saw that the roof was rather low, as grey as the blankets, and metal, and I realized I was in the hold of a plane. There was a porthole in the wall, and I looked out of it with a sense of mounting dread.

But . . . no. There was a stretch of black tarmac. We were still on the ground. We hadn't taken off yet.

Sasha came over to my stretcher and handed me a glass of water, which I gulped down eagerly.

'How fine?' I asked. 'You have to tell me—'

'Better than we hoped,' he said quietly, taking the glass from my hands and placing it on a small trolley at the foot of the stretcher. 'You have both fully recovered and are no longer contagious. It was a fortuitous escape.' He paused for a moment, and something about the pause made my stomach lurch. 'But there are some . . . consequences to your having been infected.'

'What the hell do you mean?'

He ran his tongue around his teeth as he considered how to broach it.

'Sarah has not yet regained her hearing,' he said, finally. 'I am afraid she may never do so.'

I looked across at her, sleeping peacefully in her own world, and felt something break deep inside me.

'But if we had not reached you when we did,' Sasha was saying, 'you would both be dead, as might many others. We were monitoring the Italians' radio communications, and the message about Turin came in very late. But it seems we gave you the antidote just in time. Our doctors tell me that you were within an hour or two of optimal transmission, and that if we had arrived a little later everyone within a few feet of you would have been infected.'

'*Optimal* transmission? What about the people in the church, in the procession? How many feet do they need to have been away?'

He tugged gently at the tuft of beard under his lip. 'We will make discreet inquiries — but, as I say, we feel it was a fortu-itous escape.'

He always sounded so reasonable, that was the problem. If you didn't catch yourself, you could get swept up in it and miss what was really going on.

'Let her go,' I said. 'This isn't about her.'

He paused and looked at me . . . sorrowfully? Can sorrow look reasonable?

'I'm afraid this is not about either of you, Paul,' he said. 'It's about what you know. If we allowed her to go, she would reveal everything – or be forced to reveal it – and the game would be up.' He smiled, pleased at his mastery of idiomatic English. 'The same applies to you. I'm afraid the only option is to put a brave face on it. After all, we have just saved both of your lives. Some would be grateful for that.'

I wasn't sure I was.

'*Why* did you save us?' I asked, making sure to sound resigned to my fate. If I could somehow get down onto the tarmac, perhaps we could reach a border – Switzerland, or Yugoslavia. It depended which airfield they were using. Think of that later. Find a way out of here first.

'Do you remember the tunnel?' Sasha was saying, and I had a flash of the Underground, the sniper's breath against my face as he tried to strangle me.

'In Berlin, I mean.'

I nodded dully, shaking the memory away. Back in 1955, in collaboration with the Americans, the Service had built a secret underground tunnel between West and East Berlin that intercepted the landlines running from the Soviets' military and intelligence headquarters in Karlshorst. As a result, they could listen in to a large portion of the East Germans' communications with the Russians. It was a highly protected operation and I had been far too junior at the time to be indoctrinated into it. But Blake had been given clearance for it and, being the good double he was, had immediately informed Moscow.

'It was a great reverse, of course,' Sasha went on, 'but also an extremely delicate one. It gave us the opportunity to feed disinformation to our adversaries, which would be very useful for furthering other operations. However, if we passed too much disinformation, the British and Americans would soon realize that we knew we were being listened to, and would begin looking for the leak. On the other hand . . .'

'. . . If you carried on as normal, you'd be giving away all your secrets.' I knew the story, and the conclusion to it: they had staged an 'accidental' discovery of the tunnel in '56 and closed it down. The Service had eventually cottoned on to Blake and arrested him, but he'd escaped from prison and defected to Moscow. 'What does the Berlin Tunnel have to do with this?' I asked.

Sasha smiled indulgently. 'I am trying to illustrate how the spirit of compromise can drive an operation, and how other priorities can become factors. With the tunnel, we compromised, continuing to pass important information through it even though we knew we were being listened to. We did this to protect our agent – but we made sure to keep our greatest secrets out of the traffic. Eventually it became too difficult to continue, so we broke it up. There is a similarity with this situation. But I think perhaps this will explain it more easily than I can.'

He leaned over and placed something in my hands. I looked down at it uncomprehendingly. It was a book, titled *The Tide of Victory*. With a start I realized it was the volume of Churchill's memoirs that Barnes had been reading. I remembered Severn's final words: *'You didn't read it. You don't know . . .'* I opened the book. There didn't seem anything unusual about it. I flicked through it, until I reached the end. Taped to the inside of the back cover was a small pouch, and inside it I could see a tightly folded bundle of papers. I shook them onto my lap and picked up the first page. I recognized the handwriting at once: it was Osborne's.

C. – see attached proposal. I initially vetoed but suggest we reconsider in light of this morning's catastrophe. U. taking next flight to S. with medication. See D. gets it.

W.O.

P.S. – Sort out your wife, for all our sakes.

'C.' was Charles Severn. Osborne had inserted this message in Barnes' book and told him to deliver it to Severn on his arrival in Rome. If I understood the postscript, he hadn't wanted to risk sending a message in code to the Station due to Severn's suspicions about Sarah's loyalty, a matter he wanted Severn to sort out – although precisely how wasn't clear. 'D.' was obviously me, and so I turned to the attached document to see exactly how they had planned for me to get it.

It had the same heading as the other dossier – 'STAY BEHIND: STRATEGY AND EXECUTION' – and looked to be in the same typeface. But it had a different date: 29 April 1969, less than a week ago. And it was stamped 'W16', which was the Registry number for Porton Down.

<u>Update on Nigerian virus, as requested.</u>

The virus was isolated from acute-phase sera extracted from the blood of patient HANDSOME

293

in a Red Cross clinic in Awo Omamma, Nigeria
on Friday, March the 28th. Tests subsequently
conducted at that clinic and laboratories here
have confirmed that it is an arenavirus, and
nearly identical to that found in two missionary
nurses in Lassa, near Jos, also in Nigeria,
which we isolated and examined in early March.
There were also marked similarities to samples
taken by the field team in Cameroon in November
1968 (see Annex 1).

This virus, which we have named Lassa Fever,
is both potentially fatal and extremely infec-
tious. It appears to be transmitted to humans
via exposure to rodents, rodent faeces (transmitted via dust in the air), and possibly human-
to-human contact, such as the exchange of bodily
fluids. We believe HANDSOME may have contracted
the virus either via exposure to rodents or
sexual intercourse with ISABELLE DUMONT, who
may have contracted it on her travels through
the country as a war reporter. However, this
cannot be confirmed, as DUMONT was dead before
we arrived at the clinic, and we were instructed
by you not to search for her body.

Jesus. I thought back to my time in Nigeria. I had slept with
Isabelle only once . . . No wonder Severn had been so worried

Sarah might have slept with me — he'd thought I was going to contaminate her with the virus. And I had.

I read on:

Tests on monkeys over a period of several weeks revealed the virus to be very easily trans- mittable via the exchange of saliva or blood: only a few droplets were needed. It is too early to give accurate figures for morbidity or mortality, but we would estimate it to be very high — possibly higher than other arenaviruses. As outlined in my report of March the 3rd, colleagues at the U.S. Biological Warfare Laboratories have already successfully adapted both Yellow Fever and Rift Valley Fever for warfare use. We felt that, on account of its lethality, virulence and lack of known antidote, Lassa Fever was a promising candi- date and we adapted it in a similar manner on April the 23rd.

The adapted strain was so virulent that in some of the cases infection was achieved via the inhalation of respiratory droplets when subjects were over five feet from an infected specimen. Of the nine monkeys we tested, two began exhibiting significant symptoms twenty-four hours after exposure, and died within forty-eight hours. A further two specimens died within the following forty-eight hours. One further specimen began exhibiting symptoms consistent with early stages of the disease on April 27th, and we administered a strong dose of vaccine. The specimen appeared to recover fully within a matter of hours, although it remains to be seen whether or not there will be any long-term effects.

With such a small, non-human sample size, it is impossible to conclude whether this represents an accurate picture of the transmissibility or mortality rate of the adapted strain in the event of humans being exposed to it. However, we cautiously calculate that the incubation period of this strain is twenty-four hours, and that after that time human cases will reach an optimum level of transmissibility.

We believe that this strain could be packaged within a capsule that, on breakage, would distribute particles across a wide area. Although the estimated mortality rate of this virus is lower than in some of the others we have analysed, even with the adapted strain, the shock value of using it would be significant. Some of the symptoms of the virus, such as

```
fever, headaches and chest pain, are similar
to those of pneumonic plague, and we would
expect that diagnosis to be widespread initially.
This would, of course, result in a certain
level of hysteria among the population.
```

That was putting it mildly. I turned away from the text for a moment and looked up at Sasha, who was picking lint off his jacket. I took a breath and forced myself to read the rest of the report.

```
However, such a weapon could take years to
develop, and would involve on-the-ground help
from the Americans, which is undesirable for
many reasons known to you. There is, however,
an alternative method of carrying the virus
that would lead to fewer fatalities than an
aerosol-distributing capsule, but that would
perhaps create a greater impact. This option
could also, we feel, be put into effect within
the next few months and with little cost to
ourselves. HANDSOME has already been exposed
to the original virus, has just woken from
consciousness in our custody in London, and
has been deemed persona non grata. It there-
fore strikes us that, by chance, we may have
the perfect 'live agent' with which to test
the transmissibility of the new strain ...
```

Next to the phrase 'within the next few months', Osborne had scrawled '*Not fast enough. Stick to S.P.*', which I took to be his vetoing of the operation in favour of shooting me in St Paul's. I read the rest of the document in a haze: it consisted of a detailed technical description outlining precisely how they would engineer it so that my body would become the carrier of the strain, complete with dosage recommendations and tables comparing mortality rates.

The thing was signed by Urquhart, of course – 'U.' in Osborne's note. His had been the voice in Sardinia I hadn't recognized as I had emerged from unconsciousness on the operating table: '*He's come to.*' Yes, Dr Urquhart, with his tan under his Father Christmas beard, hadn't been holidaying in Jamaica, soaking up the music – he had been in Nigeria, looking into the disease I had caught and investigating whether or not it could be adapted for use as a biological weapon. The capsules he had foisted on me hadn't been to suppress my symptoms, but placebos.

It seemed they had improvised more than I had thought. When their plan to kill me in St Paul's had gone wrong, they hadn't just let me fly off to Italy. No, they had immediately put into action another operation to kill me – one that would helpfully make me a guinea pig for their future atrocities. Although Osborne had originally vetoed the idea in favour of shooting me at the memorial service, he'd jumped at the chance to put it back on the table. And to make sure I was under a tight leash, he had sent Barnes along as – what? – my warder? Or my nurse? I had a sudden memory of waking in the embassy with him leaning over me. What had he been doing? Checking my pulse?

At any rate, Barnes and Severn had been told to keep an eye on me while Urquhart flew out to the base in Sardinia – 'S.' in Osborne's note – to wait for his guinea pig to arrive. Zimotti had helpfully provided me with a lead to Sardinia. My insistence on going to the meet with Barchetti must have interfered with Severn's plans, but then I had led him to Pyotr and they had flown me off to Sardinia to inject me and begin their little experiment. In the last few days I had suffered muscle pain, hallucinations, headaches, constriction in my chest and many of the other symptoms I had experienced in Nigeria – but I had been so intent on stopping an imagined bomb that I had written them all off as after-effects of a whipping and some loud pop music. Worse, I hadn't noticed that the woman next to me had been developing precisely the same symptoms.

I turned to Sasha. 'How did you get hold of this?' I asked, pointing to the paperback.

He smiled softly. 'The butler did it. Despite some superficial precautions, money still talks, and we have a way into the British embassy. We removed it from Severn's safe just a few minutes before your arrival.' He took the papers from my lap and carefully folded them back into the pouch of the book. 'It will be returned soon enough.'

'After copies have been made, of course.'

'Of course.'

'And how am I alive? The document says there's no anti-dote.'

'No known one. Our scientists have been working on adapting this type of virus for several years, just as the Americans and British have been, and we have developed a range of antidotes. As you were already infected with the disease, it seems they only gave you a tiny dose of the new strain. We think they wanted to see what the effect would be in a controlled environment: to observe how transmissible their new strain might be to other humans before they tried it out on a larger scale at a later date . . .'

My mind jolted back to Sardinia, and my skin crept. They had put me in the same cell as Sarah because they had wanted to see how quickly she would catch the new strain from me. The plan had never been to attack Rome or Turin, but somewhere else entirely. Severn had scribbled '4 May' on the strategy document, but it must have been just a possibility, rather than anything they had yet planned. Once Urquhart was fully satisfied that the new strain could act as effectively as it needed to, they would have injected me anew, then found a football match in Naples or an opera in Venice or whatever suited them, planted me in it and stood back and waited for the crowd to become infected. No doubt they would also have prepared suitable evidence to leak to the press that the carrier of the deadly new plague had been a Soviet agent.

Now I saw why Severn had been so anxious about whether Sarah had slept with me: he had still loved her, and if she had only been near me for a few hours she would have been unlikely to have caught the disease already – the idea was that it took several hours to come into effect. But if we had *slept together*, the chances would have been far greater that she already had it. It was a monstrously warped kind of love, of course – he had still put her in a cell with me to test how fast the disease could spread without us sleeping together.

Only we had escaped before they had had the chance to find out.

The knife Barnes had pulled on the rooftop in the Vatican hadn't been a stiletto blade, but a needle. He had been trying to inject me with the vaccine, because my twenty-four hours were nearly up and I had been about to reach my optimum period of transmissibility, or whatever the scientific term for it was. And that explained Severn's valediction. When he had arrived at the embassy and we were there, he had realized that both the dossier and Barnes' paperback were missing from his safe, and had presumed that Sarah and I had taken both and so discovered the plan to use me as a weapon. But then I had confused him. Instead of trying to leave the country, either to defect to Moscow or head for London, I had inexplicably raced to the Vatican, and then to Turin. At some stage, he had guessed that I was running too fast to have discovered or read the documents in the back of Barnes' book, and was still acting on the basis of the strategy dossier and the various Stay Behind documents.

But those documents were still enough to damn them with – if we had reached Haggard or anyone else who hadn't been involved, the whole thing would have backfired. So they had run after us with needles, in the hope of stopping us before we reached optimal transmission and caused an attack they weren't able to manage, and to retrieve the documents and kill us before we told anyone about their conspiracy. Severn had told me that I didn't know what was happening, not out of any sense of remorse, but because he had realized he had failed to stop me and wanted to taunt me with his knowledge of what lay in store. *'Enjoy her while she lasts. It won't be long.'*

I turned back to Sasha. 'I take it you have known about this for some time,' I said. 'Like the tunnel.'

'The revival of Stay Behind? Since last year. A British agent in Stockholm revealed it inadvertently to one of our assets.'

That drunkard Collins. The Service should have sacked him years ago.

'And you're willing to stand by and let innocent people be killed – and to be blamed for their deaths – just to protect the fact that you know it's going on?' As well as being terrible operational logic, I wondered if it wasn't worse than committing the atrocities in the first place.

'But it is not *we* who will be blamed,' he said. 'Not exactly. It is British anarchists, the Italian Communist party, and similar groups throughout Western Europe. We support these people sometimes, but they are not our real friends. They are like the information we let through the tunnel – not the most important. We do not want to expose NATO's actions at this particular moment. If they kill a great many civilians and blame it on others, then we may do so. In the meantime, the more evidence we have pointing to their involvement, the better.'

They 'may do so' – he didn't seem too bothered.

'How many people count as "a great many"?' I asked.

He gave me another of his patronizing smiles – he seemed to have an endless supply of them. 'I think you have misunderstood the strategy of their operation,' he said. 'In Italy it is called Gladio, and that is an apt codename, I think. It is named after the *gladius*, one of the weapons used by the gladiators: a stabbing sword.' He thrust his fist towards me. 'The wounds it inflicted often looked horrific, but were not that deep – it was an ineffective weapon if you wanted a quick kill, in fact. But, of course, that was not what the organizers of the fights wanted: they wanted slow kills. Do you know why?'

'Yes. Because the longer it took for someone to die, the more entertainment there was for the crowd.'

'Precisely – nobody likes going to a boxing match to see one fighter knocked out in the first ten seconds. And so, too, with Gladio. They are not interested in killing many innocent people – but they want to *terrify* many people, with a superficial but spectacularly bloody wound.'

'That's a pretty poor salve for anyone's conscience,' I said. 'Would you say the same to the families of those who are killed? Or is that why you rescued us? A sudden attack of scruples because the virus would mean more deaths than you could justify?'

'I am sorry to disappoint you once more, but no. We were worried that you would reach London with the documents. That would have been . . . unfortunate. Osborne and the others will, of course, wonder how much you discovered, and what you will tell us. But once we have returned all the documents to the safe, there will be no reason to suppose that you discovered anything at all, and we are confident that the strategy will continue.'

He was actually boasting about prolonging the operation. It appeared that, from Moscow's point of view, the more people who were killed and blamed on proxy groups the better – it would be all the more effective when they held their press conference to reveal that NATO had been behind it. Unlike the Berlin Tunnel, this time they didn't appear keen to call things off and 'accidentally' discover the plot when given the chance.

When Barchetti had told me Arte come Terrore knew about the attack in the dome, he had meant the events in London after all – the 'in' had simply been a slip of the tongue, or because he hadn't known precisely what had happened there. What he had discovered, and what he had been desperate to tell Severn, was that the cell knew that they were going to be blamed for that attack. That meant that they knew about Stay Behind – and so did Moscow. So the whole thing was blown, and Barchetti had needed to warn the Service. When I'd turned up instead of Severn and asked if he thought Arte come Terrore were involved in killing Farraday, he had realized I didn't know about Stay Behind at all, and that something was therefore desperately wrong with my having been sent to meet him. So he'd fled . . . And that was why Pyotr had ordered me to kill him: Moscow not only didn't want the Service to know that they were aware of Stay Behind, but were prepared to kill for it.

A strange sensation ran through me. There hadn't been any

attacks planned for Rome or Turin, but there would still be plans for attacks in Italy and elsewhere. And by killing Barchetti before he got his message to the Service, I had allowed the whole bloody thing to continue, just as London, and Moscow, had wanted.

Unless, of course, I could get out of here.

But how? Something told me they wouldn't take off until Sasha was seated and belted in and had given the go-ahead, so I tried to stall him some more.

'Why didn't you answer my call in London?' I asked.

He smiled tolerantly. 'Has that been bothering you? Let me put your mind at rest there, then. I had no idea about the attack in St Paul's, none at all. My radio man simply had a feeling that the safe house was compromised, and he and his team shut down and moved immediately as a precaution. As soon as I felt we were secure again, I sent Grigori to let you know . . . But you didn't seem especially open to hearing the message.'

So my paranoia had got the better of me. It hadn't been the first time they had moved safe houses – it was good practice to do so every once in a while, in fact. As there had been the risk that they would do so at the same time as I needed to contact them urgently, we had arranged that in such events Sasha would send someone to alert me within twelve hours. And he had done so. But he and his team had happened to move just as someone had taken a pot shot at me, and I had forgotten all about that arrangement and jumped to entirely the wrong conclusion. Perhaps if I had stopped for a moment in that call box in Smithfield and considered that, I might have heeded Toadski's message in Heathrow, and not taken the flight to Rome, and . . . but that way madness lay. Whatever I had done, that bastard Osborne would have tried to kill me. It was a miracle he hadn't succeeded – but at what cost?

I couldn't look Sasha in the face now, but I had one last question to ask him. 'This new strain . . .' I said. 'Is it more effective than the ones developed by your scientists?'

He nodded. There was a moment of silence, and then he understood what I was really asking. 'Yes. The doctors isolated it from you a couple of hours ago.'

I leaned forward to try to hit him, but the strap around my chest held me back.

He stood, and smiled down at me. 'I wish I could make you see how much I admire you, Paul. I've always felt you were a man of high ideals – perhaps too high. Sometimes they must be sacrificed for a greater cause.'

I didn't have any ideals to speak of, but in the land of the blind the one-eyed man is king – if he's not hanged by the mob.

'What greater cause?' I asked. 'Communism – or the Motherland?'

'Both, of course. The second is meaningless without the first. It is true that in this case the interests of the state have perhaps over-ruled strict ideology, because more important things are at stake. But you surprise me – did you really think you and your girlfriend were going to stop this war alone?'

'She's not my—' I stopped myself. It was futile. There was

nothing more important at stake than a perpetual cycle of point-scoring, but he would never be able to understand that.

He gave me a thin smile. 'I think you should sleep now,' he said. 'We'll be leaving soon.'

*

He had left me here, alone with Sarah. Well, why not? We were strapped to our beds in the hold of a plane, about to take off.

But we hadn't taken off *yet*.

I started tearing at the strap, but it was no use: it was fixed tight. Panicking, I began clawing away at it in the hope my nails might break the surface. But I knew that wouldn't help. My eyes raced around the small space desperately looking for something that might help, and trying not to think of how little time I might have. I had to get moving before . . .

That was it. Movement. The stretcher was on caster wheels, albeit with brakes on each one. But if I could create enough energy to lift them . . . At the foot of the bed I could see the glass Sasha had handed me earlier resting on the trolley. But how to move myself towards it?

I placed a hand out of the stretcher and tried to reach down to the floor. I was several inches short. That wouldn't work. So I strained my chest against the belt again, but this time tried to jerk my entire body upwards as I did so. For a moment, the stretcher leapt a fraction of an inch in the air, and as it did I tried to use the momentum by pushing upwards again, and again, until it bounced. Praying that the noise wouldn't bring anyone running, I started jerking from side to side as well as upwards, and gradually the stretcher began to turn. It was infuriatingly difficult to control, but after a couple of minutes I had managed to move myself so that I was almost horizontal to the trolley, and less than a yard away.

I didn't think I was going to manage to get within arm's reach any time soon, so I reached down and removed the catheter from my wrist. Then I reached for the pole containing the intravenous drip bag and tilted it towards me. I quickly unhooked the bag, and then dipped the pole down and took a swipe at the trolley, missing by several inches.

I made it on the fourth attempt, snagging the pole perfectly around one of the trolley's legs. I pulled it towards me carefully and reached out for the glass. Shielding my face with my arm, I cracked the glass firmly against the side of the trolley, sending shards scurrying across the floor. But several shards had remained in the trolley. I picked out the largest and sawed away furiously with it at the base of the strap. Finally it started to fray, and then it broke away.

Gulping for air and soaking in sweat, I stumbled over to Sarah's stretcher and performed the same exercise. She woke while I was freeing her and looked up at me in a daze. I gestured for her to follow me, and she nodded. I knew it could be just moments before they started taxiing across the tarmac, after which we would have no chance. Coming out of the hold I saw that one of the doors was just a few feet away. I ran towards it and pushed the button. It shunted open, and a blast of air entered the plane.

I beckoned Sarah on and she reached the door, and then we

started racing down the metal stairs until we were on the tarmac. Wind whipped across my face, sending a dull ache through my jaw, and the sweat on my back suddenly felt chilled. We must still be in Turin, or nearby. That was good. France and Switzerland were close. I hoped we were nearer Switzerland: we had to get over the border, find a proper doctor . . .

I ran across the airfield, my chest burning and my head pounding with the desire to reach safety. We reached a fence, and beyond it was a road, a motorway of some sort. I glanced back for a moment: Sarah was a few yards behind me, but the plane was still sitting there in the darkness, and there was nobody coming for us. We had made it. We were going to be all right.

It was when we reached the road that I slowed down for a moment, and I felt a tug at my sleeve. I turned to see Sarah pulling at it.

'What is it? Are you hurt?'

I followed the direction of her gaze. In the distance was a line of buildings, shrouded in morning mist. But slowly I realized that many of them were domes.

Onion domes.

It hit me like a kick to the stomach and I knelt down on the tarmac and waited until they came to fetch us.

*

We didn't have to wait long. There were four or five of them: burly men in suits the same shade of grey as the tarmac. Now I saw that a couple of black Chaika limousines were parked on the other side of the plane, and as they walked us towards them I glanced over at Sarah. She gave me a look of sheer panic in return, and I felt numb inside.

Sasha was waiting for us. He stared right through me, then shook hands with the security men and headed into one of the Chaikas. We were led over to the other one, which had a flag pinned to the front grille. The door was opened, and we climbed into the rear. The interior was bright red – Soviet red – with fold-down seats on the side nearest the driver. The leather was cold against the back of my neck. I looked up and saw a man seated opposite us, wearing a uniform: gold glinted on his epaulettes. He was very old, and deeply tanned. He looked alarmingly reptilian, his eyes glinting through a network of wrinkles that spread like tributaries across the landscape of his face, and for a fraction of a moment I had the thought that it was Auden, the great poet revealed as Moscow's puppet-master-in-chief, the final Russian doll in the collection. But it wasn't Auden, of course: the nose was snubbed, and the eyes were tiny sparks in the crumpled papyrus of skin.

'Hello, Yuri,' I said.

'Greetings,' he said, and smiled to show a collection of nicotine-stained teeth. 'But perhaps now you can call me Fedor Fedorovich.' His eyes flicked over Sarah. 'So this is the woman.' The tip of his tongue darted from his mouth and licked at his lips. I shivered inwardly as I remembered his 'daughter' in Burgdorf.

'Are you the maniac behind this idea?' I said. 'This . . .' I struggled to find a word. '. . . game?'

He turned his eyes to me, dipping his head in a mocking bow. 'No,' he said. 'I am not the "maniac" behind the strategy, as you put it, although I have had my input. But I am old now – the new guard do not listen to me as much these days.' He clasped his hands together. 'I know that our objectives have not always been clear to you. As I am sure you understand, we cannot always provide agents such as yourself with the full picture, so you could not know where our priorities lay in this operation. I nevertheless congratulate you for your efforts to save our Italian comrades from being wrongfully blamed for the deaths of innocent civilians, even if—'

'I was more interested in the civilians than your comrades.'

He gazed at me for a moment, then turned his head to look out of the window. 'Take a word of advice from an old man,' he said quietly, and his voice was a little colder now, a little stiff: 'When we arrive, adopt the line I have proposed instead. I think it will help you fit in better.'

He suddenly leaned forward, and I flinched. He smiled at my nerves and lifted a bottle of vodka from a compartment in the door, along with three shot glasses. He thrust a glass each into my and Sarah's hands, then poured out measures for each of us. 'I give you a toast,' he said. 'You must drink it *do dna*: to the bottom.' Then he cried out *'Mir i druzhba!'* – 'Peace and friendship!' – raised his glass and downed the contents, eyeing me carefully over the rim as he did.

I turned and stared out of the window, and saw the domes and spires looming out of the mist ahead. We were approaching Moscow: a new world. It was one I had been heading for since

I had sought this man out in 1945, but my reprieve had finally come to a close – I had reached the end of the road, as another Russian had told me not long ago.

I forced myself to look across at Sarah. Her face was as cool and beautiful as the moment I had met her in the British embassy in Rome. But her mind, I knew, was flooded with confusion and fear. I had brought her to this point. Another life lay ahead of us now, and we would have to draw on all our reserves to survive it – and I must find a way to protect her. She met my gaze and stretched out her hand. I clasped her soft, ringless fingers in mine, then raised the glass in my other.

'*Mir i druzhba,*' I said, and as the liquid burned the back of my throat, Fedor Fedorovich's laughter echoed in my ears.

Among wolves, I thought, howl like a wolf . . .

THE END

BUT PAUL DARK WILL RETURN
IN
FREE WORLD

Author's Note

This book is a work of fiction, but it is set against a background of real events. In the late 1960s, Britain and Italy both witnessed widespread industrial action, the springing up of terrorist groups, and plots against the governments of the day by senior members of their respective intelligence communities. The First of May group did machine-gun the American embassy in London in 1967, and carried out several other attacks and kidnappings until disbanding in the early 1970s, whereupon their mantle was taken up by the Angry Brigade and others. In Italy, several anarchist and Communist groups carried out attacks on civilians at this time, eventually flowering into the Red Brigades and other groups that terrorized the country for much of the '70s and '80s.

As with *Free Agent*, I was inspired by the investigative journalism of Stephen Dorril and Robin Ramsay, particularly a chapter in their book *Smear! Wilson and the Secret State* in which they described attempts to organize a coup in the United Kingdom during this period as part of a longer-term 'strategy of tension' against British Prime Minister Harold Wilson.

Arte come Terrore is fictional, inspired by Germano Celant's essay *Arte Povera: Appunti per una guerriglia*, published in the journal *Flash Art* in 1967, in which he wrote of a revolutionary existence that 'becomes terror' ('*Un esistere rivoluzionario che si fa Terrore*') – I took his metaphor literally and extended it. However, two explosions did take place in Milan in April 1969, and several anarchists were charged in relation to them. Some now believe that those and several subsequent attacks, such as the bombing in Milan's Piazza Fontana in December 1969, which killed 16 people and injured 80, and the bombing of Bologna train station in August 1980, which killed 85 people and injured over 200, may not have been carried out by anarchists or left-wing terrorists, as originally thought, but by right-wing groups with connections to Italy's secret services, NATO, the CIA, MI6 and others.

In 1990, two Italian judges discovered a document written by Italian military intelligence in 1959 that outlined the purpose and structure of a network known as Gladio. In a statement to Italy's parliament on 24 October 1990, Prime Minister Giulio Andreotti confirmed that this had been part of a secret NATO operation, known under different names in other countries, which had been set up shortly after the Second World War as a contingency plan in the event of a Soviet invasion of Western Europe. The plan had involved the creation of 'stay-behind nets': forces that could provide effective resistance to the Soviets, and which had access to hidden caches of arms, supplies and technical equipment in many countries.

The existence of British stay-behind networks and their offshoots had been publicized prior to Andreotti's statement. In 1977, Chapman Pincher wrote in the *Daily Express* of the existence of the 'Resistance and Psychological Operations Committee', which he claimed contained an 'underground resistance organization which could rapidly be expanded in the event of the Russian occupation of any part of NATO, including Britain' and which had links to the Ministry of Defence and the SAS. And in 1983, Anthony Verrier stated in a footnote in his book *Through The Looking Glass* that '*current* NATO planning' (his emphasis) gave the SAS a similar role to that previously held by SOE regarding stay-behind parties. Since 1990, little else has been revealed of Britain's post-war networks, although an exhibition at the Imperial War Museum in London in 1995 noted that junior Royal Marine officers in Austria had been detached from their normal duties in the early '50s in order to prepare supply caches and coordinate with local agents for stay-behind parties.

The CIA established the Turkish arm of the network in 1952, but I have speculated that the British had already done some work along these lines a year earlier. This is based in part on a paragraph in Kim Philby's memoirs in which he stated that SIS's Directorate of War Planning was busy setting up 'centres of resistance' and guerrilla bases in Turkey to counter a possible Soviet invasion while he was stationed there in the late '40s: in other words, a stay-behind network. If Philby were telling the truth, one presumes he informed Moscow at the time, meaning that at least part of the stay-behind operation was compromised from the start. If he was lying, the Soviets nevertheless knew about such plans by 1968, when his memoirs were published.

Following Andreotti's statement in the Italian parliament, many people questioned whether members of Gladio and the other stay-behind networks had turned from their original mission of protecting Western Europe from Soviet invasion to supporting, planning or executing terrorist attacks on civilians – attacks that were then blamed on Communists and others in order to unite public feeling against the Left and bolster the country's security structures. Since 1990, a great deal of information has emerged to support this idea, but despite parliamentary inquiries, arrests, trials, acquittals and retrials in Italy, Turkey and elsewhere, it remains unproven. Until NATO declassifies all its files on these networks, the truth may never be known – and perhaps not even then.

For the purposes of this novel I have presumed that NATO's post-war stay-behind networks were subverted for false-flag terrorist operations, and have used some established facts in the hope of creating plausible fiction. My main sources were Philip Willan's *Puppetmasters: The Political Use of Terrorism in Italy* and

Daniele Ganser's *NATO's Secret Armies*. I am especially grateful to Philip Willan for his comments on an early draft of the novel.

In Chapter XXIII, Paul Dark reads the Italian military intelligence document discovered in 1990, and the figures mentioned there are taken from it. The 'strategy document' he reads earlier is my own invention. Right-wing establishment figures in both Britain and Italy were plotting against their governments during this period and, according to Daniele Ganser, an SIS agent betrayed the stay-behind networks to the KGB in Sweden in 1968. Italian Gladio members were trained by British special forces instructors in England, but their main training facility was a secret military base at Poglina in Sardinia, near Capo Marrargiu. In two separate right-wing coup attempts in Italy, in 1964 and 1970, there were plans to detain left-wing leaders, journalists and activists at this same base. The area between Capo Marrargiu and Alghero is known as The Griffons' Coast, as it is home to the griffon vultures that Paul and Sarah encounter in Chapter XVII. Part of the area is now a reserve for this species.

In Chapter IX, Paul Dark discovers that his handlers in Moscow were initially unsure of the validity of the information he had given them. This is partly based on accounts of Moscow's scepticism towards Kim Philby and other members of the Cambridge Ring during the Second World War. Genrikh Borovik in *The Philby Files* and Nigel West and Oleg Tsarev in *The Crown Jewels* quote declassified Soviet intelligence files expressing these suspicions, including several reports concluding that Philby and the other members of the ring must have been discovered by British intelligence and were unwittingly passing on disinformation. The spies were not fully cleared of suspicion by Moscow until 1944.

The frontispiece quote is taken from a memorandum prepared by George Kennan that set out the case for the United States' use of 'organized political warfare', and is quoted courtesy of the US National Archives and Records Administration (RG 273, Records of the National Security Council, NSC 10/2. Top Secret). The United States' post-war influence on Italy and fear of the Communist party coming to power in that country is widely documented, and it is clear from former CIA chief William Colby's memoirs and other sources that the Americans were instrumental in setting up and running several post-war stay-behind networks, including in Italy.

It is thought that most of the superpowers investigated the use of biological weapons during the Cold War, often developing research carried out in the Second World War. In 1942, British military scientists detonated anthrax bombs on the Scottish island Gruinard: it was not decontaminated until 1990. As far as we know, Britain never 'weaponized' Lassa fever, although the United States and the Soviet Union both suspected the other of trying to do so. In the 1970s, American scientists investigating the disease in Liberia encountered Soviet researchers looking for Lassa antibodies, reagents and samples.

The darkened room in Rome's Galleria Nazionale d'Arte Moderna is inspired by a description of a work in that gallery in Kate Simon's *Rome: Places and Pleasures*, and on the earlier work of Lucio Fontana.

The ball at the top of St Peter's Basilica is no longer open to the public, but it was in 1969, and was large enough to accommodate sixteen stout-hearted tourists. The Chapel of the Shroud in Turin is still under renovation following the fire in 1997. From April 2010, visitors will be able to see it for the first time since its controversial restoration in 2002.

I would also like to thank the Confraternity of the Holy Shroud and the Museo della Sindone in Turin; the staff of the bookshops Ardengo, Tara and Open Door in Rome; Caroline Brick at the London Transport Museum; Isobel Lee, Enrico Morriello, Sandra Cavallo, Francesca Rossi, Isabel de Vasconcellos, Sebastiano Mattei, Craig Arthur, Clare Nicholls, Evelyn Depoortere, Carla Buckley, Grant McKenzie, Helmut Schierer, Sharon and Luke Peppard, Nick Catford, Roger Whiffin, Blaine Bachman, Graham Belton, Ajay Chowdhury, Rob Ward, Phil Anderson, Phil Hatfield, Steven Savile and Tom Pendergrass for their comments, expertise and suggestions; my agent, Antony Topping, for his skilful shepherding of me to this point; my editors, Mike Jones at Simon & Schuster and Kathryn Court at Viking for their faith in Paul Dark; my parents and parents-in-law; my daughters, Astrid and Rebecca; and my wife, Johanna.

Select Bibliography

Christopher Andrew and Vasili Mitrokhin, *The Sword and the Shield: The Mitrokhin Archive and the Secret History of the KGB* (Basic Books, 1999)

Christopher Andrew and Vasili Mitrokhin, *The Mitrokhin Archive II: The KGB and the World* (Allen Lane, 2005)

Charles Arnold-Baker, *For He Is An Englishman: Memoirs of a Prussian Nobleman* (Jeremy Mills Publishing, 2007)

Jeffrey M. Bale, 'Right-wing Terrorists and the Extra-parliamentary Left in Post-World War 2 Europe: Collusion or Manipulation?' (in *Lobster*, issue 18, 1989)

Luca Massimo Barbero (ed.), *Time & Place: Milano-Torino 1958–1968* (Steidl, 2008)

John Barron, *KGB: The Secret Work of Soviet Secret Agents* (Bantam, 1974)

George Blake, *No Other Choice* (Jonathan Cape, 1990)

Genrikh Borovik, ed. Phillip Knightley, *The Philby Files: The Secret Life of the Master-Spy – KGB Archives Revealed* (Little, Brown and Company, 1994)

Tom Bower, *The Perfect English Spy* (Mandarin, 1996)

Andrew Boyle, *The Climate of Treason: Five Who Spied for Russia* (Hutchinson, 1979)

Robert Cecil, *A Divided Life: A Biography of Donald Maclean* (Coronet, 1990)

Germano Celant, 'Arte Povera: Appunti per una guerriglia' (in *Flash Art*, 1967)

William Colby, *Honorable Men: My Life in the CIA* (Simon & Schuster, 1978)

Peter Collins, Ed McDonough, *Alfa Romeo Tipo 33: The Development and Racing History* (Veloce, 2006)

Nicholas Cullina, 'From Vietnam to Fiat-nam: the politics of Arte Povera' (in *October*, issue 124, spring 2008)

Guy Debord, 'The Situationists and the New Forms of Action in Politics and Art' (in *Internationale Situationniste*, No. 8, 1963)

Len Deighton (ed.), *London Dossier* (Penguin, 1967)

Pierre de Villemarest, *GRU: Le plus secret des services soviétiques, 1918–1988* (Stock, 1988)

Stephen Dorril, *MI6: Inside the Covert World of Her Majesty's Secret Intelligence Service* (Touchstone, 2000)

Stephen Dorril and Robin Ramsay, *Smear! Wilson and the Secret State* (Grafton, 1992)

Caroline Elkins, *Britain's Gulag: The Brutal End of Empire in Kenya* (Pimlico, 2005)

Fodor's Guide to Europe (Hodder and Stoughton, 1969)

Fodor's Guide to Italy (Hodder and Stoughton, 1969)

M. R. D. Foot (ed.), *Secret Lives* (Oxford University Press, 2002)

M. R. D. Foot, *SOE: The Special Operations Executive, 1940–1946* (BBC, 1984)

Alec Forshaw and Theo Bergström, *Smithfield Past and Present* (Heinemann, 1980)

Daniele Ganser, *NATO's Secret Armies: Operation Gladio and Terrorism in Western Europe* (Frank Cass, 2005)

Laurie Garrett, *The Coming Plague: Newly Emerging Diseases in a World Out of Balance* (Penguin, 1994)

Roland Gaucher, *The Terrorists: From Tsarist Russia to the OAS* (Secker & Warburg, 1965)

Ian V. Hogg and John Weeks, *Military Small Arms of the Twentieth Century* (DBI Books, 1985)

Harold F. Hutchison, *Visitor's London* (London Transport, 1968)

Alexander Kouzminov, *Biological Espionage* (Greenhill Books, 2005)

Bruce Page, David Leitch and Phillip Knightley, *Philby: The Spy Who Betrayed A Generation* (Sphere, 1977)

Kim Philby, *My Silent War* (Grafton, 1989)

Rufina Philby with Hayden Peake and Mikhail Lyubimov, *The Private Life of Kim Philby: The Moscow Years* (St Ermin's Press, 2003)

George Rosie, 'Integrated scheme for new Heathrow terminal' (in *Design*, June 1969)

W. Ritchie Russell, *Brain Memory Learning: A Neurologist's View* (Oxford University Press, 1959)

Kate Simon, *Italy: The Places In Between* (Harper and Row, 1970)

Kate Simon, *Rome: Places and Pleasures* (Alfred A Knopf, 1972)

Kate Simon, *London: Places and Pleasures* (MacGibbon and Kee, 1969)

Michael Smith, *The Spying Game: The Secret History of British Espionage* (Politico's, 2004)

JEREMY DUNS

David Teacher, *Rogue Agents: The Cercle Pinay Complex, 1951–1991* (Institute for the Study and Globalization and Covert Politics, 2008, online)

Richard Thurlow, *Fascism in Britain* (IB Tauris, 2006)

Anthony Verrier, *Through The Looking Glass: British Foreign Policy in an Age of Illusions* (WW Norton & Company, 1983)

Nigel West, *The Illegals* (Coronet, 1994)

Nigel West and Oleg Tsarev, *The Crown Jewels* (HarperCollins, 1999)

Terry White, *Swords of Lightning: Special Forces and the Changing Faces of Warfare* (BPCC Wheatons, 1992)

Philip Willan, *Puppetmasters: The Political Use of Terrorism in Italy* (Authors Choice Press, 2002)

'Of Dart Guns and Poisons' (in *Time*, 29 September 1975)

A Trip to Italy (Italian State Tourist Department, 1969)

Read on for
an extract from the thrilling
sequel to *Song of Treason*

THE MOSCOW
OPTION

Coming 02 02 12

Published by Simon & Schuster

The extract is an early draft and
may be subject to change

978-1-84737-446-2
£12.99

Late October 1969, Moscow, Soviet Union

I was asleep when they came for me. I was running through a field, palm trees in the distance, when I woke to find a man shaking my shoulders and yelling my name.

I bolted upright, gasping for breath, sweat pouring off me. The man was wearing a cap and looked to be barely out of his teens. Part of my mind was still caught up in the dream – I was sure I'd been in the field before, but couldn't think when or where. I didn't get the chance to consider it further because I was being yanked up from the mattress by my arms. Now I could see that there were two men, both in the same uniform but one without a cap. Neither was part of my usual guard detail.

'Get up, scum!' shouted the one in the cap, leaning in so close that he was just a couple of inches from me. His face was squared off, with a wide jawline and a pug nose, and he was wearing some foul *eau de cologne* that seemed to have been impregnated with the scent of fir trees rolled in diesel. He shoved a pile of clothes into my arms.

'Put these on, old man,' he sneered. 'And make it fast.'

I looked at the bundle. There was a dark suit, crumpled and baggy, a white shirt with sweat stains around the arm-pits, and a pair of slip-on shoes. No belt or tie.

I started to dress, my eyes still half-gummed with sleep. What the hell was going on? I'd been wearing the same grey tunic and trousers since my arrival here, so why the sudden change of clothes? Perhaps they were transferring me to another prison, or to a courtroom – Sasha had often mentioned the possibility of a trial. Or perhaps they were simply dressing me up to take me out to the woods to finally finish me off. I had a sudden memory of a summer's day in 1945, in the British Zone in Germany. The jeep riding through the burnt-out roads with Shashkevich manacled in the back. The clearing. The Luger heavy in my hand as I placed it against his neck. His sweating, shaking. And my finger squeezing down on the trigger . . .

I shivered at the thought, but found to my surprise that I wasn't afraid. There were worse ways to go. I wouldn't feel it, at least. I'd been here six months but it seemed much longer, and the future held nothing for me but the gradual disintegration of my body. I was forty-four, but already felt twice that. Rather a bullet through the head than the prolonged suffering and indignity of old age and disease.

'Faster!' shouted the man in the cap. He must be the senior of the two. I finished buttoning the shirt and, as I leaned down to pick up the trousers, realised for the first time that both men were armed with pistols at the hip.

Judging by the size of the holsters, they were Makarovs.

Despite their resemblance to the Walther PP their combat effectiveness was comparatively poor, and I began gauging the distance between the men, the angles of their bodies and their respective weights, to see if there might be any possibility of catching them by surprise, taking one of their pistols and turning it on the other. But it was just a habit, a tired old spook's reflex. I had no real intention of attempting to escape. There was nowhere to go. Even if I were able to overpower these two, there would be dozens, if not hundreds, more of them.

I adjusted the lapel of the jacket and stood to attention, ready. The suit was a couple of sizes too large for me and stank of stale urine, but it felt almost civilized to be wearing one again. The guards led me through the door of the cell and marched me down a series of corridors, until we reached a large steel door I hadn't seen before. Once unlocked, we walked through it and, for the first time in nearly six months, I found myself outside.

*

We seemed to be on an enormous airfield. I took a deep breath, then exhaled. My breath misted — it was at least a couple of degrees below freezing.

The sky was the colour of slate, and the barbed wire and bare-branched trees formed a strange tracery against it. To my left, I could make out several large buildings, and I recognized their outlines from dossiers I had read and memorized in London years before. I knew, finally, where I had been held all this time. The building we had just left was nicknamed

Steklyashka — 'the sheet of glass' — by its inhabitants, because two of its wings were enclosed in glass. A former army hospital, it now served as the headquarters of the GRU: Soviet military intelligence. It had been my first guess, but it came as a shock nevertheless. I suppose I had made the place another world in my mind, away from the reach of dossiers.

My escorts gripped me by the arms again and we headed across the tarmac, buffeted by the wind. We passed several helicopters and armoured tanks, and I remembered that it was, by my calculations, the last week of October, and guessed they were destined for the annual parade in Red Square.

A car was waiting for us near the perimeter, its engine running. It was a polished black Zil limousine with red flags attached to the mudguards. That was interesting: they were usually reserved for the very top brass. I recalled reading a report that there were only a couple of dozen in the whole country.

The man with the cap opened the rear door and his bareheaded comrade pushed me onto a cold vinyl seat. He climbed in beside me, while his colleague walked around to the other side. Up front, a driver was seated with his hands on the wheel, and next to him was Sasha. There was also someone in the back seat next to me, and as I turned I saw that it was Sarah.

*

Sasha snapped at the driver to head off, and we passed through a barricade and turned onto a broad avenue. I caught the word 'Vladimir', and my heart sank: that was the prison east of Moscow where they had held both Greville Wynne and Gary Powers. But then he said it again and I realized that it was the name of the man with the cap and that he was asking why they had taken so long to fetch me. Vladimir replied that I had been difficult, and Sasha grunted disapprovingly. They were in an almighty hurry, clearly, but there was something else to it. An edge of panic? I decided not to think about what it might mean: I'd find out soon enough.

I looked towards Sarah. She sensed my gaze and turned to me. As our eyes met, a thousand thoughts went by unspoken. She was wearing a shapeless grey dress, but although she seemed thinner and her blonde hair was cut brutally short, she otherwise looked much the same as when I had last seen her, in the back seat of a limousine like this one about six months ago. I felt a hollowness in my stomach as I remembered it. We had come to a stop on a barricaded street, and I had watched helplessly as she had been swiftly bundled into another car and driven away. I had vowed to myself that I would protect her come what may, but when the moment had arrived I'd offered no protest. But she had *survived*. I had long given up hope of that. I had felt that they wouldn't risk giving her any freedom, for fear she might reach the British embassy and tell them everything we had learned in Italy. As a junior member of the Service, she had very little information to give them. Once they had extracted it, I had reasoned, they would have seen little point in keeping her alive.

But they had. I tried not to think what they had put her through instead, but an image of the girl Yuri had kept in his rooms in the camp in Germany, and of the way he had flicked his tongue over his lips at his first sight of Sarah, flashed into my mind nevertheless. Repulsion and rage coursed through me.

It had soon become clear to me that Yuri, or Colonel Fedor Fedorovich Proshin, as I now knew his real name to be, had been the mastermind behind my career as a Soviet agent, from my recruitment at the age of twenty onwards. He had greeted me in Moscow, but it was no hero's welcome. I was one of several British double agents who had ended up here: Kim Philby, Donald Maclean, Guy Burgess and George Blake. But unlike them, I was no longer a Communist, and had been brought here against my will, whereas they had all defected by choice. After I had been put through a comprehensive – and extremely unpleasant – medical examination, Yuri had proceeded to interrogate me about every aspect of the twenty-four years since I had sought him out in a displaced persons camp in the British Zone of Germany. He hadn't presented it as an inter-rogation at first, even installing me in fairly comfortable quarters, but the armed guards had never left any doubt about the truth of the situation.

He had started every morning the same way: once I was seated, he would open up my dossier and read directly from the reports my handlers had sent to Moscow at whichever point in my career we had reached. After that, the questions would begin.

'Why did you cut off all contact for eighteen months after this meeting?'

'Why did you not mention that Burgess and Maclean had come under suspicion?'

'Why didn't you tell us about Penkovsky?'

And so on, *ad infinitum*. Part of me had been expecting it – the documents I'd discovered in Rome had revealed that for several years they had suspected me of being a plant by the Service, feeding them carefully selected secrets along with a healthy dose of disinformation; in effect, a triple agent.

That theory had eventually been discredited in '51 and I had been cleared as "highly valuable", but now Yuri revived it. The material I had taken so many risks to give them meant nothing to him. It was only the information I had *neglected* to hand over that he found telling. But while it was true that the higher I had risen in the Service the greater my access to classified material had been, my seniority had often made it harder for me to hand material over, because so few others had such access. If it had ever come to light that the Soviets had this kind of information I would have immediately come under suspicion. Yuri had dismissed this argument with a wave of his hand. While my actions would have had me strung up in England, from his perspective I was an erratic agent with perplexing gaps in his story, who for good measure had betrayed several Soviet agents and even killed two of them. It didn't help that I made no attempt to conceal that I was disgusted with myself for falling into their arms, and with him for the way in which he had recruited me.

He had finally lost patience with me in June, and it was then that I had been moved into Steklyashka, where one day I had been marched into a briefing room and been confronted by Sasha, who I hadn't seen since we had arrived in Moscow. He had been my handler since the early Fifties, but any hope that he might prove to be any more understanding as a result was rapidly dispelled. He had barely acknowledged our past relationship, and was even more hostile than Yuri had been. I'd always known that his friendliness towards me was contrived, of course, as real as the intimacy a prostitute shows a wealthy and potentially long-term client, but it had still come as a shock when it was switched off so swiftly, and so absolutely. The familiar 'My dear Paul' had no longer issued from his lips, and his benign condescension had been replaced by a cold and sometimes frightening implacability.

At first I had thought his behaviour had been a pose, a way to get me to talk more through making me want to recapture the old bonhomie, but I had soon realized that there was nothing forced about it, and that this was in fact his real self – or, at least, his Soviet self.

I looked at him now, partly obscured by the back of his seat, staring at the road ahead of us. He was wearing a uniform and *ushanka*, neither of which I had ever seen him wear before, and he didn't look right, somehow. I knew every inch of his face, from the lines around the eyes to the bristles of his pointed beard, but I found it increasingly hard to associate him with the cheery fellow in the tweed coat and polka-dot tie, who I had met in an assortment of pubs, cinemas and dives in London, a book of postage stamps under his arm. English Sasha had always seemed podgy and harmless, but Soviet Sasha was a burly bear of a man with an air of barely repressed violence emanating from him. Over the years he had often told me that he loved London, and I wondered if that had simply been a lie to get me on his side, or if his recall to Moscow had hardened him, and he had forgotten his appreciation of the good life he had once led in the West.

Perhaps he was simply scared. My failures as an agent reflected badly on him, and possibly even placed him under suspicion of disloyalty. After Stalin's death, Khrushchev had been, relatively speaking, benign, but Brezhnev had started pushing things back in the other direction: arresting dissidents and sending them to labour camps or into "internal exile". Perhaps that was where we were all going now, to some *gulag* in Siberia where we would freeze our arses off until we died.

Whatever the reason, when Sasha had taken over my case any remaining pretence that I was simply an agent undergoing a debriefing had vanished. I was unequivocally a prisoner, placed in a small concrete cell and entitled to one bowl of thin soup and three cigarettes a day. Every morning and afternoon I had been made to write an account of my career, operation by operation, month by month. After that, I would be summoned into a small office, where he would question me at length on everything I'd written. We had reached June 1961.

The car took a sudden turn, throwing my shoulders against the door. The windows were covered by grey curtains, but there was a small gap near the edge and I peered through it at the streets speeding by. Giant portraits of Lenin lined the roads, but I saw very few other cars. It must still be quite early in the morning. Domes shone faintly in the distance, and there was a glint of copper in the sky, a refraction, I imagined, from the giant stars of the Kremlin. But then we took a turn — we didn't seem to be going that way.

The car slowed to a halt in front of a nondescript building painted a faded orange, and I was dragged out by one of the men. The other stayed in the car with Sarah, and I wondered fleetingly if it would be the last time I would see her.

It had started to snow now and the wind was sharper, biting into my cheeks and stinging my eyelids. Sasha led the way to a sentry box manned by two lieutenants in light blue greatcoats, both armed with finely polished semi-automatic rifles. A pigeon pecking at the ground nearby suddenly came to a stand-still and turned in the same direction, its chest puffed out, and for a moment it looked like it was imitating the sentries. All it needed was a few brass buttons and a minitature *ushanka* to complete the picture, but a moment later it returned to its pecking, and the illusion was broken.

Sasha handed some papers to one of the men, who looked through them, then turned and spoke into a small grate in the wall. There was a loud hissing noise, and I saw that the whole section of wall was in fact an air-locked door. With some effort, the sentry pulled it open and stepped inside. After a moment's hesitation, Sasha motioned to me, and we followed him in.

We were in a dimly lit space, smaller than the size of my cell. I could see the sentry just ahead, wrestling with the lock of another, much larger, door. Once the door was open, we walked into a room with concrete walls and a large blanket of green netting in the middle. The sentry knelt down and pulled this to one side, revealing a small wire cage recessed several feet into the floor. He climbed down into it and Sasha and I followed suit. The sentry pulled a lever in a box on the side of the cage, and with a loud cranking noise we started descending.

It was then that I recognized the mood I hadn't been able to identify in the car. It wasn't panic. It was fear. They were all terrified out of their wits, and I couldn't blame them. Those had been bomb-blast doors we had just come through.

We were entering a nuclear bunker.

SIMON &
SCHUSTER

Go back to where it all started . . .

Jeremy Duns

Free Agent

**MARCH 1969. JOHN AND YOKO ARE IN BED
HAROLD WILSON IS IN NUMBER TEN
AND PAUL DARK IS ON THE RUN**

British agent Paul Dark has had a stellar career – until now. A Soviet
defector has credible information that there is a double agent within MI6,
and Dark finds himself in the frame. Arrest could be only moments away.
Worse, he has discovered that everything he has believed in for the last
twenty-four years – the very purpose that drives him – has been
built on a lie.

Now he wants answers, no matter what he has to do to get them.

Free Agent is an intense and twisting spy thriller set during the height of
the Cold War – and it keeps the surprises coming until the final page.

'Excellent' *Guardian*

'A cross between James Bond and Jason Bourne' *Literary Review*

'As spare of prose as it is cleverly convoluted of plot' *Daily Telegraph*

ISBN 978-1-84739-451-4

SIMON &
SCHUSTER

Free Agent is available from your local bookshop or can be
ordered direct from the publisher.

978-1-84739-451-4   **Free Agent**   £7.99